Tanya heard a low ██████████████
She had no idea wh ███████████████
half open.

It came flooding ████ ██ ███. ███ ███ █████ ██ ███
altar in the middle of the underground Satanic temple.
The sound she was hearing came from the Satanists
themselves, as they stood in a circle around her.

Tanya became aware of a weight on her body and
glanced down to see that it was the sword she had
noticed when she had first been brought into this cavern.
The pommel was toward her, the crosshilt just below her
breasts, and the blade extended down and across her
pubic area.

With a start, she heard a voice above her. She recog-
nized it as that of the Satanic Cardinal Ganganelli.

"Prepare to meet our Lord," he said. Then he picked
up the sword and held it high.

"Mighty Belial," he cried, in stentorian tones. "Here
lies that which we promised Thee. All we ask in return is
that You send out Your fury to destroy the land that calls
itself the United States of America …."

When a hellish Cardinal unleashes demonic forces on
America, the U.S. government is forced to roll out its
most secret and lethal weapon: the Committee. Join
these five psychic defenders as they struggle to over-
come an ancient entity so evil that the Forces of Light
themselves may not be enough to prevail against it ….

Other Books by Raymond Buckland

Anatomy of the Occult (Weiser, 1977)
Buckland's Complete Book of Witchcraft (Llewellyn, 1975
   1977, 1987)
Buckland's Gypsy Fortunetelling Deck (Llewellyn, 1989)
The Tree: Complete Book of Saxon Witchcraft (Weiser, 1974)
Doors to Other Worlds (Llewellyn, 1993)
Here Is the Occult (House of Collectibles, 1974)
The Magick of Chant-O-Matics (Parker, 1978)
A Pocket Guide to the Supernatural (Ace, 1969)
Practical Candleburning Rituals (Llewellyn, 1970, 1976, 1982)
Practical Color Magick (Llewellyn, 1983)
Scottish Witchcraft (Llewellyn, 1991)
Secrets of Gypsy Dream Reading (Llewellyn, 1990)
Secrets of Gypsy Fortunetelling (Llewellyn, 1988)
Secrets of Gypsy Love Magick (Llewellyn, 1990)
Witchcraft Ancient and Modern (HC, 1970)
Witchcraft from the Inside (Llewellyn, 1971, 1975, 1995)
Witchcraft…the Religion (Buckland Museum, 1966)
Truth About Spirit Communication (Llewellyn, 1995)
Ray Buckland's Magic Cauldron (Galde Press, 1995)
Advanced Candle Magick

With Hereward Carrington
Amazing Secrets of the Psychic World (Parker, 1975)

With Kathleen Binger
The Book of African Divination (Inner Traditions, 1992)

Under the pseudonym "Tony Earll"
Mu Revealed (Warner Paperback Library, 1970)

Fiction
The Committee (Llewellyn, 1993)

Video
Witchcraft Yesterday and Today (Llewellyn, 1990)

Cardinal's Sin

Psychic Defenders Uncover Evil in the Vatican

Raymond Buckland

1996
Llewellyn Publications
St. Paul, Minnesota, 55164-0383

Cover art: Aaron Hicks
Cover design: Tom Grewe

Cataloging-in-Publication Data
Buckland, Raymond.
Cardinal's sin : psychic defenders uncover evil in the Vatican / Raymond Buckland.
    p.   cm.
    ISBN 1-56718-102-3
    1. Psychics—United States—Fiction. 2. Witchcraft—United States—Fiction. 3. Cardinals—Vatican City—Fiction. I. Title.
    PS3552.U3378C37   1995
    813'.54—dc20   95-4811
                                                    CIP

Llewellyn Publications
A Division of Llewellyn Worldwide, Ltd.
P.O. Box 64383, St. Paul, MN 55164-0383

For
TARA

my wife, lover, soul-mate,
best friend, invaluable critic
and ardent enthusiast

Acknowledgements

My thanks to Nancy J. Mostad for the spark of an idea, to Christine Star Mountain and Marlene Skilkin for valuable astrological help, to David Jones ("Three Feathers") for Shawnee ritual details, and to Paul Hoffman for details of Vatican life.

1

There had been no low-pressure areas anywhere in the Caribbean for weeks. The Straits of Florida were calm. No hurricanes in the making; not even a small tropical storm. Ed Francis, retired New York mail man and amateur meteorologist, tapped his barometer, noted that it was steady with a normal pressure of 30 inches, nodded appreciatively, and turned away. Had he remained with his eyes focused on the instrument he would have been amazed to see it come alive. The mercury suddenly started to drop, falling rapidly to 29 inches. It was to drop even further—down to an incredibly low 26.15.

But as Ed stepped out of his house for an early morning walk along the beach, he did become aware of the sudden wind. A great gust blew him back against the side of the house, rolling him along the siding like a cloth doll. The wind began to howl and its pitch rose higher and higher. People already on the beach cried out in pain and tried desperately to run for shelter as the sand was whipped up to become a veritable sand-blasting machine, streaking their faces and the exposed parts of their bodies with blood.

Huge waves came crashing in. Rain started to fall in torrents as the skies grew black.

Ed struggled to his feet and tried to get back to his house but was blown across the front lawn, only to be battered against the side of his car. Frantically he tried to open the door, but fell and was swept underneath the vehicle, clawing at the exhaust pipe to stop himself. He managed to cling on and slowly swing himself up on the leeward side, away from the wind, grimly hanging onto the door handle. The car's front window was open and he pushed his head and shoulders inside, struggling and wriggling to get all the way in. He finally fell onto the front seat and quickly rolled up the window. As he sat, gasping for breath, the vehicle started to move, sliding sideways across the road to come up against the curb opposite his house. Slowly it tilted, then fell over and over, rolling across the grass. Finally it crashed against a group of solid palm trees, right-side-up with its hood stuck between two firm trunks. Bruised and battered, Ed peered up over the edge of the window, praying that the glass would not blow in under the force of the wind.

He saw the tiles start to blow off the roof of his house, like a giant deck of cards scattering to the winds. Then the roof itself lifted up and disappeared. From the beach he heard, over the cry of the wind, the screams of people being sandblasted to death, their clothes and skin being scoured away.

Suddenly a crumpled pick-up truck, battered and rolled almost into a ball, came bowling along heading straight for Ed's haven. It smacked into the side of the car, crushing the door and steering wheel against Ed's body and driving the car deep in between the trunks of the trees. Ed screamed in pain. The wind roared through the broken windows. Tree trunks, house debris, chunks of metal, tops of palm trees; all came smashing into the clump of trees encasing Ed.

Wind speed rose dramatically, reaching a never-before-recorded 160 miles per hour and then gusting to well over 200 miles per hour. Waves crested at over twenty feet high before crashing onto the shore. A Category 5 hurricane had been unleashed on the tip of Florida with no warning whatsoever. Everyone was caught unprepared. Palm trees bent to touch the ground, house roofs flew through the air, and walls crumbled and fell. The pressure fell so low that windows burst, refrigerator doors popped open, glass jars exploded.

A giant wave came surging in across the land, adding to the devastation and drowning the many caught in its path. Even faster than it had come in it rushed back through the area, causing further death and destruction. There was a brief lull as the eye of the storm passed overhead. Then it all started up again.

In less than twenty-four hours it was over. The storm turned to the northeast and headed back out to sea, rapidly diminishing in strength.

Wreckage lay heaped around a small clump of trees—twisted metal, savagely torn pieces of buildings, part of a roof, a section of wall, a garage door. Smaller trees and a broken telephone pole were entwined in the still-standing palm trees. Somewhere in the pile lay a battered Cadillac half-filled with water. Lying on the front seat, partially crushed, was the body of Ed Francis.

1993 had been a bad year for floods. By early July, Illinois, Iowa, Minnesota, Missouri, Nebraska, South Dakota, and Wisconsin had suffered terribly. The Williamsons remembered it well. They could never forget it. Their farm was north of St. Louis, not far from West Alton. They had seen the Missouri River rise steadily that year; by July 6 it had spread two miles out of its bed and the entire town of West Alton had had to be evacuated as surging waters threatened the levees. Rain continued to fall; the swollen river continued its attack.

The river flow rate reached 975,000 cubic feet per second, normal being 160,000. The Williamsons had watched their land, their livestock, and all their worldly possessions disappear beneath the muddy waters. By the end of the month the Missouri crested at 48.8 feet. Flood stage was 32 feet. The federal government approved disaster aid in the amounts of $1.15 billion in crop disaster payments, $45.3 million for temporary jobs in flood clean-up, $120 million to the Army Corps of Engineers to repair locks, dams, and levees, and $700 million more for the Coast Guard, highway and bridge repair, SBA loans, restoration of wildlife refuges and federal parks, disaster-related community development, and so on. An immense bill to pay for an unexpected freak of nature.

The Williamsons had debated long and hard about whether or not they should return to the land which had been in their family for over a hundred years. They finally decided in favor of it. After all, how often could such a flood manifest?

Old Sam Williamson, the family patriarch, came awake in the early hours of the morning. It was still dark outside and he didn't have to be up for another two hours at least. But something had awakened him. He lay there for a long time listening. It was raining.

For two years, ever since the '93 floods, he had grown restless whenever it rained—an occurrence he had previously enjoyed. His two sons, Robert and Will, had taken to teasing him for it.

"Come on, Dad! It's only a shower. I don't think it's going to sweep us away again, not yet anyway."

He would relax and laugh with them; they were good boys. Yes, he thought, he was getting fearful in his old age. What was the word they used, these days? Paranoid? Yes, he was a bit paranoid and didn't mind admitting it.

So he lay there listening to the rain. But why had he woken? Something pricked at him; some strange inner feeling that told him that this wasn't paranoia.

He quietly got out of bed—no point in waking Martha—and padded across to the window. It was a dark night with what moon there was buried behind the heavy clouds; he couldn't see much. He went through to the bathroom, not to disturb anyone, and opened the window. The rain blew in on him, startling him and bringing him wide awake. Feet padded on the linoleum and he turned to find Duke, the big black labrador, standing contemplating him. Duke never woke up at night. Old Man Williamson listened. In the distance he could hear it: the roar of fast-moving water.

There was no way that the river could have risen any great amount in the short time since the previous evening; no way! Even if the many small and large rivers feeding in upstream should swell and carry unusual amounts of water down, there was no way they could come to face the nightmare of 1993 so quickly again. Or was there?

Lena Somerset rolled over and tried to get back to sleep. She thought she'd got over the period of insomnia after John had died; he'd been gone eight months and three weeks now. At first she'd found it impossible to sleep in the big bed all by herself. She'd even taken prescribed sleeping pills to get some rest. But she thought all that was behind her. She'd been sleeping well for almost a month, so why was she suddenly awake?

Then she felt it. The slightest tremor that gently rocked the bed. She heard something fall off a shelf in the bathroom. So that was it, she thought; just another earthquake.

There were pluses and minuses to living in southern California, Lena thought. The clear blue skies and wonderful weather; the incredibly beautiful Pacific Ocean below the cliffs where she lived; the open-mindedness of the people—all these far outweighed the earthquake tremors and occasional periods of drought. Besides, in the nearly thirty years that she had lived in San Diego she'd never known anyone to be seriously injured because of an earthquake.

Then it hit. She screamed as the house seemed to be ripped off its foundations and flung down the hillside. The roof was twisted off and the walls fell away. A huge gilt mirror from the opposite side of the room was flung across to smash down on Lena's head, crushing her skull like a rotten pumpkin. The gas pipes were wrenched apart and sparks from the sputtering electrical system ignited the gas. The whole house exploded in a billowing mushroom of flame and smoke, only to be extinguished when the house fell into the blue waters of the Pacific.

The tornado seemed to materialize without warning. One moment the sky was clear and the next there was the awesome, terrifying, black funnel that could spell death.

Didi Howell was in her boyfriend's 1940 Chevrolet pick-up truck trying, half-heartedly, to make him keep his hands to himself. He'd given her a ride home from school and seemed to think that that entitled him to free range over her body. She'd known this would be the case ahead of time, and it was part of the reason she'd accepted the ride. Jason Gardiner was the school's star quarterback, and any girl would have given her right arm to be in Didi's place. They were parked at the trailer park, just short of Didi's parents' trailer.

"No, Jason. I've got to get in. My mom's waiting for me."

"Aw! Come on, Didi. Just a quick kiss."

He leaned across and their lips met. She felt his hand slide under her short skirt and took her time stopping it. She finally pulled back.

"Jason! I've got to get out."

"So how about I pick you up later? We could take in a movie ... or something."

He had a wicked smile, she thought. She paused a minisecond then nodded.

"Okay. Seven-thirty?"

As she got out of the truck she realized that the sky, which had been so clear, was suddenly dark. She slammed the truck door and stepped back. As she did so she heard what sounded like a hundred 747 jetliners swooping down on her. She screamed as the truck was picked up, dashed against the trailer and, together with the next-door trailer, sent spinning away in the midst of a swirling, blinding wind-maelstrom of dirt and debris. Didi was sent flying backwards, striking another trailer that sat rocking on its foundations. Hysterically she watched the tornado cut a wide swath down the middle of the trailer park, picking up and tossing mobile-homes like a giant destroying a child's toys.

2

Luigi Cardinal Guiordano, prefect of the Congregation for the Propagation of the Faith, hurried down the corridor toward the Borgia Room of the Vatican, almost breaking into a run as he went. His fat, round face was red and perspiring from the unaccustomed exertion of moving at anything faster than a slow walk. Dino Cardinal Scimonelli, cardinal secretary of state of the Holy Office, met him at the door to the room.

"Is the Holy Father here yet?" Guiordano gasped, mopping his brow with a silk handkerchief.

"Not yet," the taller, olive-skinned man replied sourly. "Luckily for you! It would never do for you to be late for a consistory."

The two made their way into the room and took their places with the other cardinals of the curia, for the ritual meeting of the pope with his senate. They were settled only moments before the arrival of the pontiff himself.

The pope was old, thin, and frail of body—but strong of mind and purpose. His election, on the death of Pope John Paul II, had surprised many, for he was almost eighty, the curial retirement age set by Pope Paul VI's 1970 decree. It was rumored that clamor in the curia for a return to an Italian pontiff had been his strongest qualification.

All of the resident cardinals, plus some half dozen or more who were visiting the Vatican, had been called together for this meeting. The *plenum,* or maximum number of cardinals, is one hundred twenty. These are scattered around the globe with only forty or so living permanently in Rome; eight of them in apartments in the Apostolic Palace.

The pontiff's great beak of a nose swung from side to side as he looked over his council before making the Sign of the Cross. Then, the invocation to the Holy Ghost over, he led straight into the business for which he had summoned his cardinals. It was to discuss the increasing number of reports, received from around the world, concerning the involvement of Roman Catholic priests with young children: a situation strongly denied as a problem to those outside the church.

At the back of the room a short, plump, cherubic-faced cardinal wearing gold-rimmed glasses glanced, and nodded almost imperceptibly, toward his neighbor, a tall gaunt man with prominent cheekbones. The taller cardinal's lips briefly tightened in acknowledgement before he returned his attention to the pontiff.

Patrizio Ganganelli, the plump cardinal, was sixty-five. He had an almost-bald head framed by silver-grey hair. Beneath black eyebrows his dark brown eyes peered out through his spectacles, moving constantly from side to side as though he was afraid of missing something. His short, stubby fingers tugged at his lower lip whenever he was agitated—as he was now.

The consistory dragged on for over three hours with much discussion but little or no progress. Throughout the meeting Cardinal Ganganelli kept peering surreptitiously at his watch, through his gold-framed spectacles, and uttering long, irritable sighs.

Finally, with no agreement reached on how to control the situation other than to gather more details of alleged incidents, the pope drew the meeting to a close by uttering the time-honored phrase, "How does it seem to you?"

He didn't wait for an answer to the traditional, rhetorical question but got up and swept out of the room. The red caps were removed as the cardinals bowed their heads in submission.

"Come!" muttered Ganganelli to the gaunt-faced cardinal. "I want to speak to you before you disappear anywhere."

As the two men moved toward the exit the other cardinals broke apart to let them pass, turning away to avoid eye-contact. Ganganelli did happen to catch the eye of the cardinal secretary of state of the Holy Office but that individual stonily turned away to start a conversation with a dark-skinned cardinal from Calcutta. All noticeably avoided the pair as the crowd of red-clad figures moved out of the great Borgia Room. Patrizio Ganganelli seemed not to notice any aloofness from his peers and, gripping the arm of the taller man, strode purposefully away from the meeting room and down the corridor to the left.

Born into a farming family in Sicily, Ganganelli had run away from home and travelled to Rome. There he eventually entered the clergy, for the sense of power it gave him. Fifteen years ago he had received the nominal title of Archbishop, and was named to a long defunct bishopric in North Africa, a not-uncommon practice to reward those who had shuffled papers in the Vatican for twenty years or so. Subsequently he had received the red hat from Pope John Paul II.

His companion, Gualtiero Cardinal della Rovere, was five years older. He had graduated from the Ecclesiastical Academy, the training school for Vatican diplomats. A titular archbishop at forty-five, he had been given a foreign assignment to become *nuncio,* a papal ambassador, in Tripoli, Libya. He had received his red hat at the end of his tour of duty.

Despite his age, the tall della Rovere still stood straight. He had black hair, with no trace of grey, which he kept well-oiled and brushed straight back. Above his prominent cheekbones his almost black, beady eyes stared out at the world in defiance. His mouth was small, thin, and cruel. No one had ever seen it smile.

The two were a strange contrast in looks but akin in outlook. Ganganelli's deceptively cherubic features were a perfect mask for the dark malevolence that sometimes flashed from the never-resting eyes.

"What's the matter?" della Rovere asked.

"Nothing's the matter," Ganganelli snapped. "I wanted to know if you'd heard anything yet about a date for our friend to visit?"

The angular cardinal glanced about him before shaking his head. "Not a word. I did as you said and sent a fax to him but he hasn't replied yet."

Ganganelli snorted. "What's the point of the Vatican moving into the age of computers and faxes if everyone ignores them? Send him another!"

He turned and stomped away, leaving the other red-clad figure standing looking after him, a long, hard, unfathomable look on his emaciated face.

3

Patrizio Ganganelli descended the stairs and stomped along a lower corridor. He was annoyed. He wasn't used to being ignored.

He made his way across to the Vatican Library. From the very beginning of the Christian era, popes had collected documents. Nicholas V had founded the library in the mid-fourteenth century, and it had been enlarged and elaborately decorated later by Melozzo da Forlì and the Ghirlandaios. Today the library houses over 700,000 printed volumes, 60,000 codices and 7,000 incunabula, plus sixteenth-century astronomical instruments, priceless frescoes, and rare and precious manuscripts. The Sacred Museum of the Library contains a collection of bronze, gold, enamel, ivory, and ceramic objects, plus papyri discovered in the catacombs.

All of this, however, was immaterial to the portly cardinal as he strode purposefully through the main room of the library, between glass display cases and priceless wall hangings to the double doors at the back. His black thoughts were with the imagined machinations of modern communication systems as he pushed through the doors.

"Your Eminence!" The ingratiating voice of the librarian interrupted his thoughts. "What a pleasure to see you again today. May we be of assistance to you?" A shabby little man appeared, hurrying out of his cubicle, his white hair tousled. He smiled obsequiously at the cardinal.

Ganganelli waved a flabby hand and peered around the ill-lit room that housed the many thousands of dusty volumes that comprised the inner sanctum of the library.

"Just let me into the Rare Books Division, Father Peretti," he said. "You know my needs."

The elderly cleric hesitated. He was not supposed to allow anyone into the Archives without specific permission from the pontiff himself. Anything prior to 1903 was off-limits without that permission. The librarian had tried to point out this fact many times previously to the arrogant and aggressive cardinal but had got nowhere. Thousands of reports from nunciatures since the sixteenth century and earlier were kept in the Vatican Secret Archives. They included intimate details of the illicit love affairs of kings and emperors and the cabals of courtiers and churchmen. He blinked his eyes rapidly and nervously and avoided the other man's gaze.

"Your Eminence … "

"Oh, let's not go through all that again, Peretti. I've told you to go to the Holy Father himself if you want to. I'm sure he'll be happy to confirm that I can have access to whatever I need. Now, let's get on with it, shall we?"

Unhappily, the meager librarian turned and led the way back to the door into the rare book department. He fumbled finding the key while the cardinal tut-tutted behind him. With his hands shaking, he finally found what he was looking for and unlocked the door.

"Good. Now get back to work," Patrizio snapped as he pushed the stoop-shouldered little man out of his way and hurried into the room. "I'll call you when I need help finding something. Make sure you're within earshot."

Father Peretti turned slowly away and went back to his catalogs. It wasn't Christian to hate, he knew, but he certainly found his patience sorely tried by this particular cardinal. His Eminence knew perfectly well that there was no way he, a mere "book-shuffler," could approach anywhere near the Holy Father even if he had the audacity to try to checkup on the cardinal. No, the pope was well guarded by many tiers of officious, fiercely jealous, "pontifical courtiers": the *Roman Curia*. They were all trying to outdo one another, and were invariably over-ambiguous, evasive, and secretive. Monsignors maneuvered cardinals who were used by archbishops. Key departments were controlled by tight little groups of mid-level officials with their own networks of connections in other branches of pontifical bureaucracy. One has many colleagues but few friends in the halls of the Vatican, the librarian reflected.

"Father Peretti!"

He sighed. Already Cardinal Ganganelli needed something. Taking a deep breath, he returned to the Rare Books Division.

"Peretti, I need the collections of Leo III, Sylvester II, Honorius III, and Urban V."

"Yes, Your Eminence. Let's start with Pope Leo III, shall we? There are, as we know, a number of works in that collection. Anything in particular we're looking for?"

"Just give me the register for that collection and I'll let you know which volumes to pull. You know how I work."

"Yes, Your Eminence."

Father Peretti was an old man, but he had spent almost his whole life in the Vatican Library. There was no way he could remember every single manuscript in it, but he had a very good idea of the generalities of the various collections. As he climbed wearily up the spiral stairway to the mezzanine he went over in his mind the interests of the four popes the cardinal had named and what they had in common. Why should His Eminence have such an interest in them? It wasn't the first time that he'd asked for these particular collections. In fact, come to think of it, Patrizio Cardinal Ganganelli had delved into the works of these four popes more than anyone he'd ever known.

The old man pulled out the register for Leo III, the late eighth/early ninth-century pope, and blew off the dust. Not that there was much dust; Cardinal Ganganelli had been using it on a regular basis. He started back down the iron stairway and then it hit him. He almost lost his footing and grabbed the railing as he stumbled.

"Don't go committing suicide while I'm here," the red-clad figure called, his eyes gleaming from behind the gold rims of his spectacles as he looked up at the old man. "Just get that register down safely."

"Yes, Your Eminence. Right away."

Father Peretti had realized what the four popes had in common ... they all had been practitioners of ceremonial magic.

4

It was good to be back in Washington, D.C., thought Duncan Webster as he drove the rental car out of the airport. Too long a time in the town could become wearing, but he always enjoyed brief visits. As a writer, he found the Smithsonian Institution's various museums, together with the Library of Congress, to be the main attractions. And, of course, it was always nice to have a friendly visit with his old friend and mentor, Senator Bill Highland. He rolled down the window and let the warm summer air blow through his blond hair.

It was Bill Highland who had been responsible for bringing Dunk—as he was known to his friends—to the nation's capital. At thirty years old, an author and expert on many aspects of metaphysics, Dunk had been talked into forming a committee of like-minded experts in order to battle a group of United States' enemies which had set out to undermine the nation's defenses a short while back. After that first exciting, if disquieting, occult battle it had been decided that the Committee should continue to meet on a semi-annual basis, just to keep an eye on the metaphysical state of the union.

The Committee consisted of Dunk and his old friend Earl Stratford, a slightly older parapsychologist and psychic investigator who lived in New York and taught classes at the New School for Social Research; Elizabeth Martin, who lived in Ohio, and was probably the country's best psychic, having achieved outstanding ESP scores time and again when tested as part of a program at Duke University; Rudolf Küstermeyer, an elderly German occultist, archivist at the University of Hamburg, well versed in astral projection and all aspects of magic, both high and low; and lastly, Guillemette Flaubert, a Voudoun priestess, native of Haiti but living temporarily in the Bahamas. The senator had arranged to pick up the tab for bringing the friends together twice a year, an arrangement that made the reunions non-stressful and even—they all readily admitted—enjoyable.

Dunk checked into what was becoming his "usual" suite at the Jefferson Hotel, on 16th Street NW, and after unpacking called the front desk to find out who else had arrived.

"Dr. Stratford has checked in, sir, as has Ms. Martin," he was informed. "Professor Küstermeyer advised that his flight would not be in until early evening, and Ms. Flaubert is expected at any moment."

He thanked the clerk and hung up. Leaving the suite, Duncan hurried along the corridor and tapped gently on the door of Beth Martin's room.

"Dunk! Oh, but it's good to see you."

The beautiful redhead threw herself into his arms and hugged him passionately. Dunk laughed as he kissed her and returned the hug.

"Hey! Let's get into the room at least, Beth."

Laughing, she released him and let him come in far enough that she could close the door. Then she hugged him again.

"It hasn't been that long since we were together," Dunk said, slipping an arm around her and walking her back into the room. "Less than a month since you visited me on the West Coast, if I'm not mistaken."

"I know, I know," she said, her eyes on his face. "But I still miss you whenever we're apart, even for a few days."

They sat on a Georgian loveseat by the window and gazed out at the hazy sky above the capital. Duncan slipped his arm around her shoulders.

"Who else is here?" Beth continued.

"So far just you, me, and Earl. I only just got here myself. Needless to say, you were the first person I checked on."

"Well, let's give Earl time to unpack before we go checking on him," she said, a mischievous sparkle in her eyes as she snuggled against his chest and peered up at him.

The phone rang.

"Damn!" Beth reluctantly got up and moved across to answer it. "Hello?"

"Hi, Beth. Tell Dunk that Guillemette is with me and we're waiting for you both down in the bar." There was a click followed by the telephone tone. Beth hung up.

Dunk raised an inquiring eyebrow.

"Earl," she said. "He and Guillemette are waiting for us down in the bar. I guess we have to go and join them."

Earl Stratford looked the professor he was, in his navy blue business suit and maroon bow tie, his spectacles firmly on the bridge of his nose. As always, his dark moustache and beard were neatly trimmed, his hair brushed straight back. He raised his glass, sipped his drink, and smiled around at the other three.

"Time flies," he said. "Here it is the summer solstice and we're back together again. Seems like only yesterday it was Yule and we were right here. At this very table, unless I'm mistaken."

"And you were drinking the same disgusting concoction, my man," Guillemette said. In her late thirties, her cheekbones high and prominent, her hair long and brushed to a glistening ebony, she was an attractive Haitian woman who caused many heads to turn wherever she went. She raised her rum and Coke. "Why can't you drink a real drink, Earl?" Her brown eyes flashed and her white teeth sparkled in a friendly smile.

He gazed down at the olive floating in his martini and pursed his lips. "Do not be fooled by the innocuous looks of this beast," he said. "It has powers of which you are not even aware."

They all laughed.

"Well, I have to stick to non-alcoholic drinks," Beth said, "whether I like it or not. Happily, I like it."

"It's too bad alcohol interferes with your ESP powers," Duncan sympathized.

"Oh! And here's a small sample of those powers," Beth said. She got up, a slightly puzzled look on her face, and turned around to face the entrance to the hotel bar.

"What is it?" Guillemette asked. They all turned to look.

Suddenly the familiar, tall but stooped, figure of Rudolf Küstermeyer appeared in the doorway and stood looking around. Beth waved to him. "I somehow knew Rudy was nearby," she said.

The next morning, after breakfast, they all met in Dunk's room.

"Looks like a great day," Earl said, gazing out the window. "Let's do our usual bit so that we can get on out and enjoy this city."

"If it's anything like the last couple of times, there won't be anything to pick up," Beth said, settling into a large armchair. "I still think it's ridiculously expensive to bring us all here to do this."

It was their custom to start their psychic scanning of the country as soon as possible after arriving in Washington. Since the original psychic battle that had brought them together they had subsequently found all to be quiet and peaceful.

"That's what you said last time," Dunk said, smiling. "Remember what the senator's response was? 'I'll be delighted if we never do have to use your unusual talents, but keep at it.'"

Senator Bill Highland had gone on to say, "We— the whole country—could be in deep trouble if we had another episode like the last one with those Russian and Cuban psychics. Imagine if some other group started working against the United States, using paranormal means, and we hadn't even bothered to check on the possibility. No, it's well worth any expense. I'm happy to keep bringing you all to Washington."

The five friends of the Committee settled into their routine of psychically scanning the nation's capital, through meditation, skrying, and astral projection. They would also check out the more obvious trouble spots around the globe using this expertise, and try to ascertain that no one was planning any supernatural warfare on the United States. There was no guarantee that they'd cover everyone and everything, they knew, but they did the best they could.

"All seems calm and clear from where I'm sitting," Earl said, returning from an astral excursion to the Middle East.

"And I'm not picking up anything negative at all." Guillemette sat in a corner of the room, at a small table, holding a crystal pendulum over a map of the world. "I'd go so far as to say it's unusually quiet," she said.

"I agree," Beth said.

"But I am concerned."

They all looked at Rudolf. His penetrating black eyes stared out at them from under his bushy eyebrows; his brow furrowed. The frown deepened and his troubled eyes settled on Duncan.

"What do you mean, Rudy?" Dunk asked. "What did you pick up?"

The elderly German shook his head slowly. *"Nein.* It is not that I 'picked up' anything, *mein jung Freund.* It is an inner feeling; a … premonition."

"You think there's someone out there, plotting against us?" Beth said.

Again he shook his head. "As I say, I cannot put my finger on it. But, as you all know, these feelings are not casual. There is always a cause."

"You know," Duncan suggested, "we always do these scans both in the early morning and again in the late evening. Let's really give it all we've got this evening. Let's have an early dinner and then really check and double-check one another. We've certainly learned to respect Rudy's—and everybody's— hunches. I think this bears further investigation."

They all nodded.

5

The long, black limousine, with State of Vatican City (SVC) plates, glided around the Colosseum and turned right near the Arch of Constantine, past the Baths of Caracalla. It travelled down a narrow road lined with private villas hidden behind high walls, and exited the city through the battlemented towers of the Gate of St. Sebastian.

Inside the vehicle the two figures riding in the rear, each wrapped in black, spoke not a word.

As the car hit the uneven paving stones of the Via Appia Antica, the chauffeur slowed and cruised along to the third milestone, headlights stabbing the darkness. Finally the vehicle came to a halt at the fourth century church of San Sebastiano. The two passengers got out and the limousine pulled away. The shorter of the two figures led the way through the deserted basilica to the entrance of the Catacombe di San Sebastiano, closed to the public at this late hour.

The catacombs were a pagan burial ground long before becoming a Christian cemetery. They consist of three super-imposed levels that extend for a total of seven miles below the ground, meandering through soft volcanic rock.

The two cloaked figures entered and descended the main steps to the second level, turning along a narrow passageway. They passed two or three other stairways, descending and ascending, and moved along passages lined with tombs, carved out of the soft, red tufa. Their dark shadows swept across the walls, first ahead of them and then behind, as they moved past the bare electric bulbs spaced along the rough, rock roof. Other passages crossed the one they followed. Small and not-so-small chambers opened out as chapels and temples, at unexpected points.

Passing through a deserted chapel, the two proceeded to a small stairway reached through a narrow vault behind the chapel. Here the electric lighting ended, and the cloaked figures took a battery-charged electric lantern from a hook in the wall to light their way as they descended. As the taller figure stepped down, his outer cloak caught momentarily on the rough rock wall, giving a brief glimpse of red silk beneath the black before he disappeared toward the lower level.

At the lowest level it was a quarter of a mile walk through narrow, meandering corridors, past many still-sealed tombs, to a small but heavy oak door set into the rock at the end. The ancient, darkened wood of the door was strengthened with black bands of iron and studded with heavy bolts of metal. Strap hinges reached almost all the way across to the great iron keyhole.

As the leader of the pair swung open the door, soft sounds of chanting reached out from the semi-darkness beyond. The leader grunted in satisfaction. Fifty yards on the passageway turned sharply to the left and opened up into a low-roofed chamber. A dozen figures were gathered there, their shadows dancing wildly on the walls in the flickering light of a hundred candles.

The newcomers threw off their cloaks and the Mass of St. Sécaire began.

6

By the end of dinner, the skies had darkened and rain was falling heavily. Lightning stabbed through the low-lying clouds and thunder rumbled about the capital city.

Earl Stratford stood in Duncan's suite, looking out at the storm, his hands thrust deeply into his pockets. Behind him the others of the Committee settled themselves into their chairs and prepared for a long evening's work.

"Come on, Earl," Dunk called. "Looking at it won't stop the rain."

"Can you believe this?" Earl said, as he turned away from the window. "That cute little weather girl on the television said we were due to have sunshine for at least the next ten days. She never mentioned a word about a storm coming."

Guillemette laughed. "You were too busy studying her cuteness to take in all she was saying about the weather, my man."

"No, seriously. I mean, I know these forecasters are nowhere near as accurate as they'd like us to believe, but after all … "

"Do not worry about it, *mein Freund*," Rudolf said. "It will all be clear by tomorrow and you will be able to do your sightseeing."

"Come on, now," Duncan said. "Let's settle down. I suggest we start out with some concentrated probing, but let's first erect a really good psychic barrier."

There was some throat-clearing and shuffling, as they each closed their eyes and relaxed. Guillemette had taken off her shoes and slipped down to sit cross-legged on the floor. The others, on chairs, made sure their legs were uncrossed and settled their feet flat on the carpet. Beth rested her hands, palms up, on her knees, as did Duncan; the other two held their hands in their laps.

There was silence but for the deep breathing coming from the five, as they cleared their minds of thoughts and allowed the light of purity and protection to come in and fill their bodies. Once satisfied that they had been cleansed, they extended the light, seeing it expanding into a large ball, to enclose all of them and most of the room.

"Are we ready?" Duncan asked quietly.

With eyes still closed, each murmured assent.

"Then I'd like you all to go out for a few moments and try to feel the general vibes; test the waters, as it were. No rush. Take as long as you need."

It was difficult without specifics to check, Duncan thought as he allowed his astral body to slide out of his physical body. Since their last adventures they had all become quite adept at this process.

The physical body has an invisible double, known as the astral body or etheric double. This is the part of

one which departs at sleep—or any time of unconsciousness—and has experiences which may or may
not be consciously directed. It is memories of astral
journeys which are the true substance of most dreams.

Dunk saw Beth emerging from her sleeping shell
and went to her side. Taking hands, they rose up
together through the various floors of the hotel to
emerge in the night sky above. There they found Earl
once again studying the brilliant light display that
seemed to envelop the whole city. They were quickly
joined by Rudolf and Guillemette.

"Let's all take a different direction," Dunk
'thought' at his friends. He sensed their agreement and,
letting go of Beth's hand, zoomed across the sky to the
west of Washington, toward Virginia. He was momentarily startled when a great flash of lightning exploded
beside him, but quickly reminded himself that it was
powerless to do any harm to his astral being. All the
same, he rose above the thick storm clouds and was
relieved to come out into the brilliance of the sunshine
for a few moments, as it lit the tops of the clouds in the
last few moments of the day.

He felt that if there was anything to be found it
would be down nearer the city so, reluctantly, Duncan
slid once more below the roiling, black clouds and
swept out over the thousands of buildings, now all lit
by streetlights as night descended upon them.

There was no sense of evil that he could feel, and
he was even starting to enjoy the magnificence of the
storm, when a tremendous crash and flash led to a
whole section of the city below him being plunged into
darkness. It was closely followed by a second, neigh-

boring, section going black, and then a third. The electrical grid must have got a hold then, he thought, for no other areas went black.

Duncan swept back and forth across the sky, over lit and unlit neighborhoods, before finally deciding to go back to the hotel. As soon as the thought came to him, he found himself right there, hovering over the Hotel Jefferson. With a last glance around, he returned to his body, once again entering it with the speed of thought.

"That was truly exciting, in the storm," Beth said, her green eyes wide and flashing.

"You could feel the energy, even on the astral," Rudy agreed.

"It always scares the bejeepers out of me," Earl said ruefully. "I know it can't hurt me—I'm on the astral plane and the storm's on the physical—but I still get palpitations. I'm not too good with storms at any time," he added, taking off his glasses and vigorously polishing them.

"Well, anyone have anything to report?" Dunk asked, looking around at them.

"There are a lot of bad vibes in some sections of this city," Guillemette said, her face serious. "But I guess that's true of any big city these days."

"Unfortunately, yes." Earl nodded.

"But you got nothing intrinsically evil; of the type we're on the lookout for?" Dunk persisted.

The woman shook her head.

"And what about you, Rudy? Did you pick up on anything? Any more to your hunch?"

The elderly German pulled his old, curved, briar pipe out of his pocket, studied it for a moment and then, deciding against a smoke, put it back.

"Nein, mein Freund. I do not know what it was before—it was just … something. I cannot explain."

"That's all right," Guillemette said. "That's what we're all about—feelings; emotions; intuition. I believe you felt something."

The others murmured in agreement.

"But you're all agreed there was nothing out there right now?" Duncan persisted.

"No."

"Nothing."

"Zilch!"

"How about your ESP, Beth? Anything there?"

The petite redhead blushed slightly as all eyes focused on her. She shook her head. "N-no, Dunk. No, I don't pick up anything … except … "

"Yes?" several of them asked at once.

"I don't know. It's silly. I think it must just be the storm. Yes! That's it—it's the storm."

"Why do you not let us be the judge of that, Elizabeth?" Rudolf asked, leaning forward and patting her hand with his.

"Yes. What exactly is it, Beth?" Dunk asked.

She tried to focus her mind. It wasn't easy when she wasn't sure exactly where she was trying to focus it. She closed her eyes and the others fell silent. Her mind reached out and probed in all directions. With a gasp she opened her eyes wide.

"What? What was it?"

"It *was* the storm—but a hundred times more powerful than it should have been," she said. "It's difficult to explain. It's almost as though nature itself was crying out to me. I picked up agony, confusion, and anger."

They were all silent for a long moment.

"You know something?" Earl said, finally breaking the silence. "There's been a hell of a lot of bad weather lately. Anyone noticed that?"

One by one each nodded.

"A lot of earthquakes on the West Coast," Duncan said. "Much more than usual, it seems. And we all read about, and saw on television, those terrible floods in the Midwest."

"Don't forget the tremendous cold last winter," Beth added. "Everyone said it was unseasonably cold. I know in my part of Ohio it got down to minus thirty degrees. Minus thirty! It's never, ever, done that before."

"Europe was much as always," Rudolf said. "But I did hear about your crazy American weather." He chuckled. "You do not always have the best of everything, it seems."

"It's almost as though the weather was on some sort of schedule," Earl said, tugging at his beard. "I'd swear we've been having disasters here and there on an almost regular basis."

"Turn on the television, Beth," Duncan said.

"What?"

"Right behind you. Turn it on, would you?"

She did and they all concentrated on the screen. A domestic comedy of predictable humor was playing.

Earl looked at Duncan. "You afraid of missing this episode or something, Dunk?"

"Sssh! No. Wait a minute ... "

Even as he spoke the program was interrupted with a notice saying SPECIAL REPORT. Then the national news anchor was there.

"Good evening. Reports are coming in from all across the country of fierce weather patterns. Several minor earthquakes have hit the San Francisco Bay Area, the largest measuring 5.2 on the Richter scale. Another, measuring 5.5, did extensive damage in southern California. Meanwhile, two separate tornadoes have touched down in parts of Texas, damaging a farm outside Houston and destroying a mobile home park in Amarillo. Fierce storms are lashing the East Coast, with many areas losing electricity. The whole of southern New Jersey is without power, as are parts of Washington D.C. and Maryland. Three people are known to have died after being struck by lightning in Conway, New Hampshire. The National Weather Bureau has posted storm warnings for all coastal waters. We'll keep you updated as reports come in. We now return you to your normal progra … "

The screen went blank then filled with static snow. Beth turned it off.

"Son of a bitch!" Earl was always the expressive one.

7

"Look Joe, get off my back, will ya? I'm good for the money, you know that. Christ! I've been in to you for more than this before! I tell ya, I'm expecting a check in the mail any day now. What's your beef?"

Arnie Summers clenched the telephone savagely and struggled to keep his normally loud voice on a low and even keel.

"Anyway, Joe, I told you not to call me at the office anymore. The boss is getting real uptight about personal calls ... All right, all right! So I'm difficult to reach. A top reporter has to move around a hell of a lot, y'know ... What? ... Oh, up yours!"

He slammed down the phone and angrily swung back to his keyboard. What the hell was the matter with Joe anyway, he thought? He was always happy enough to take the bets, why did he suddenly have this concern that he wouldn't collect? Glaring through a red anger Arnie's eyes gradually focused on a yellow stick-on note attached to the screen of his terminal. Someone must have stuck it there while he'd been on the phone.

"See me!" it said in scraggly handwriting. It wasn't signed, of course. MacKay's notes never were. But there was no mistaking the untidy scrawl of the newspaper's senior editor. In his nine years with *American People's News* Arnie had never known the boss to write anything more on a note than "See me!" The bastard should get them printed up, he thought as he lit up a Camel cigarette. Taking a long, hard drag, he pushed himself up out of his chair and sauntered off towards the editor's office.

In his mid-forties, Arnie Summers was not a happy man. He was unhappy at work, he was unhappy with his wife, unhappy with his girlfriend, unhappy with his bookie, and now—he somehow knew—he was about to become unhappy with his boss. Running his nicotine-stained fingers through his short and thinning brown hair, he swore to himself and pushed open the door to MacKay's office.

"Where the devil d'ye think ye've been?" demanded the fat, bald figure at the desk, not looking up while he shuffled papers. "I sent for ye six and one half minutes ago. Time is money, y'know, Summers!"

Wearily, Arnie closed the door behind him and advanced on his boss. He glanced down. As usual the desk looked as though it had weathered a ticker-tape parade. Arnie seriously doubted that there really was a desk underneath the reams of paper, news-clippings, artwork, layouts, and memos that covered the surface. Yet MacKay always knew exactly where everything was; give him credit for that. He was a mean slave-driver, but he really knew his job.

"What's the meaning of this?"

MacKay punched out a hand to the terminal on his right and swung it around so that Arnie could read the screen. There was his own story, just as he'd readied it for that week-end's edition, with his brilliant 60-point headline: THE END OF THE WORLD IS AT HAND!

"What's the matter? You don't like it, boss?" Arnie asked, looking for somewhere to deposit his cigarette ash. Seeing nothing, he surreptitiously flicked it onto the floor.

"Apart from the triteness of your head, I think the whole thing is in very poor taste—even for readers of *American People's News*, and that's saying something!"

Arnie was surprised. The newspaper was one of the country's top tabloids, available at supermarket check-out counters across the nation. It was right up there with the *National Enquirer, Star,* and the rest of them. What was MacKay's bitch?

"D'ye not think that the tone of your article will promote panic amongst the good citizenry of these United States?" MacKay's beady little eyes bored into his star reporter. "And if they panic, will ye not tell me who is going to be around to buy our newspaper?"

Arnie studied his writing on the screen and couldn't help thinking that he'd done a damn fine job. Just the way he'd been told to do it. And if you really thought about it, the ongoing, escalating bad weather—from rainstorms to hurricanes to earthquakes and tornadoes—was enough to make you want to panic.

"You're not going to change it, are you?" he asked, suddenly worried.

The tubby Scotsman sat back, sadly shaking his head.

"I dinna like it, not one bit, Summers. But I've always said I'd go with what you wrote. No, I'll not change it this time. But I've been noticing this is beginning to be a trend in what ye're reporting. And I have to say, I dinna like it. I dinna like it one wee bit! You understand me?"

Arnie nodded and, behind the wall of paper, dropped the cigarette end on the floor. He felt a strange pleasure in grinding it into the carpet.

"Is that all?"

"Aye! Get out o' my sight!"

Arnie turned and left. Hell, he thought, I need that promised check to get Joe off my back.

8

"It's been a hell of a couple of days or so," Bill Highland said, sinking his teeth into a thick slice of pizza, overloaded with six different toppings. "You wouldn't believe the damage that's been done."

"I think I would," Duncan said, sipping his beer. "I know firsthand how destructive earthquakes can be and I've sure seen enough TV footage of other types of natural disasters."

The senator dabbed at the corner of his mouth with a paper napkin. "Disaster is the operative word here," he said and took another bite.

The two sat on stools at the bar of the Saucy Statesman, on 16th Street. It was Bill Highland's favorite pizza bar, second only to Flying Dutch's at the corner of Rhode Island and 17th as a lunchtime eatery.

"But putting aside the weather—if only we could—what have your committee members got to report on the safety of our nation, Dunk?"

The blond Californian swallowed a bite of pizza and shook his head. "Nothing, really, Bill. We've been doing our regular scans—a little astral projection, some dowsing and mind-reaching, skrying … "

Highland held up his free hand. "Spare me the details, Dunk. I swear I'll never understand all this mysterious stuff you do. I'm just thankful, though, that you're able to do it. You know I'll always be thankful to you for what you guys did last year."

"Forget it," Duncan nodded. "But, as I say, right now we can't seem to pick up anything being directed this way. All seems to be clear."

"Seems to be?" The older man fixed his one-time student with a questioning stare. He knew Dunk well enough to be able to recognize some hesitation in the younger man's responses.

Duncan thoughtfully chewed another slice of pizza and washed it down with a mouthful of beer before replying.

"I don't know, Bill. We've pretty much decided that it has something to do with the weather. It may be interfering with our processes in some way. As you know, the weather's been really unusual lately. So it's probably just some sort of atmospherics that are making us feel uncertain."

"How uncertain?"

Duncan shrugged. "Only a little. It's like peering through a telescope and being virtually certain that you can see everything there is to be seen. But then there's this little fuzzy blur down at the bottom edge and you're not sure if it's a fingerprint on the lens or something material. You just aren't able to pull it into focus. Know what I mean?"

"I think so. Damn! That was good pizza. I could almost go for another."

Duncan laughed. "Same old Bill! I swear I don't know where you put it all."

They drained their beers and the senator called for another round, while Duncan finished off his food.

"So what's the final verdict?" Highland asked.

"Before I give you one I'd like you to get me some information, if you would, Bill."

The senator nodded as he reached for his fresh beer. "That's what I'm here for. What do you need?"

"It has to do with weather patterns. Can you check with the U.S. Weather Bureau—or the National Weather Service, whichever it is—and get me a profile of the weather over North America for the past nine or ten months? Exact dates of weather happenings; concentrations of occurrences; see if there are any patterns of any sort?"

"Uhuh. No problem. When do you want them?"

"As soon as you can. We've all got pretty flexible schedules; no one's got to dash off home for anything. We're willing to stick around for a while and see if we can't wait till the weather calms down and we can do a better job of sweeping the country."

"Well, all reports are that things are calming down again. Though, of course, we don't seem to have had much warning previously before a flare-up." He looked hard at the two slices of pizza remaining on Duncan's plate. "You're not going to finish those?"

Smiling, Dunk pushed them his way.

"Thanks. Tell me, what exactly are you looking for in these weather patterns? I'd have thought it'd be more profitable to look forward, to what might be in store for us, rather than to look back at what's been."

Duncan shook his head. "Not necessarily. Earl's got an idea that there's been a very real pattern to the events we've been through. Something like a recurring schedule for disasters, if you like."

"A regular timetable?"

"Yes. These are natural phenomena but, if Earl's right, they seem to have been following a most unnatural pattern. We're just going on memory but it sure seems that way. We'd like an official print-out, report, or whatever, that will show exact dates."

The senator nodded. "Anything to help the Committee follow up on its hunches," he said between bites.

9

"There's a Henry Struthers waiting for you, Senator."

"Struthers? Struthers? Doesn't ring a bell. Who is he?"

"He's with the National Wildlife Federation." Connie Beach, Bill Highland's personal assistant, met him at the door and walked with him across to the door to his office, pressing a small pile of papers into his hands as they went. "He didn't have an appointment but he was very upset and very insistent, so I squeezed him in. Don't forget you've got a Health Care Committee meeting in ten minutes."

"Thanks, Connie. Okay. Oh, and by the way — get me some statistics on U.S. weather over the past twelve months. Right across the country. I want details of every storm, tornado, hurricane, earthquake ... everything. And I want to know just where it occurred and the exact date and time. As well as the National Weather Service, get onto the National Oceanic and Atmospheric Administration; they operate the National Severe Storms Forecast Center in Kansas City. You might also check with the National Hurricane Center in Miami and the Eastern Pacific Hurricane Center in San Francisco."

"Yes, Bill." Connie scribbled in her memo pad.

The senator went into his office to find a small, nervous man sitting on the edge of the chair in front of his desk. He was dressed in a rumpled grey suit and wore a tie emblazoned with a picture of a spotted owl. His vivid blue eyes peered out through the thick lenses of his spectacles. He tugged nervously at a scraggly moustache. When the senator entered the room, he jumped to his feet like a frightened schoolboy.

"Sit down, sit down, Mr., er, Struthers, isn't it?"

"Yes. Yes, thank you, Senator. Thank you for seeing me on such short notice."

Bill settled behind his desk and, throwing down the pile of papers his assistant had given him, flipped open his appointment calendar to glance quickly down at the crowded agenda for the afternoon. He sighed. "What exactly can I do for you, Mr. Struthers? I'm sorry to say I don't have a lot of time."

"Oh, that's all right, Senator. It won't take but a moment. You see, it's the behavior patterns."

"I beg your pardon?"

"The behavior patterns, Senator."

Bill hazarded a guess. "Are we talking about the spotted owl?"

Struthers looked startled, then relaxed a little and smiled. "No, Senator. At least, not specifically the spotted owl. It's everything really."

"Everything? Can we be a bit more specific?" He sneaked a glance at his watch.

"Of course. I'm sorry, Senator. It's everything— birds and animals. All creatures across the continent.

Their behavior patterns have suddenly changed. We think it's the weather."

"We do?"

The little man nodded vigorously. "There has been so much bad weather, all across the country. Sweeping in and out with incredible changes of temperatures. It must be driving the creatures crazy. It's really upsetting their behavior patterns."

Bill Highland sighed. He leaned forward and pressed the button on the intercom.

"Connie? Tell Senator O'Cork I may be a little late for that meeting, would you?"

10

As Duncan entered the lobby of the hotel he met Earl, hurrying through with a pile of newspapers under each arm.

"What've you got there, Earl?"

"I've picked up the nationals and a number of out-of-town papers. I wanted to get full reports on all the weather problems of the last couple of days."

"Good. Bill is getting us a breakdown on abnormal weather right across the country, over the past twelve months. He's getting the official printouts from the weather office for us. We'll then have a spread of a year to see if there's any real pattern to what's happening."

"Well, I hope there *is* a pattern, or something. There's got to be some explanation for this bizarre weather."

They went up in the elevator to Duncan's suite and found the others waiting for them.

"What did the senator have to say?" asked Guillemette.

"I gave him the report on how things went last night," Dunk replied. "And I asked him for those weather reports. He'll get them to us as soon as possible."

"I have a strong feeling we are on the brink of something, *meine liebe Gefährten.*" Rudolf filled his pipe and tamped down the tobacco.

"You mean something to do with enemies of the United States?" Beth asked. "But how on earth could that be? I mean, what has that got to do with bad weather?"

"Right now we can't answer that," Dunk said, walking over to the window and gazing out. He ran his hands through his hair. "Weather is a natural phenomenon. It's not like an attack with missiles or even something underhanded like the astral spying we found last time." He turned back to look at his friends. "But I think I agree with Rudy; I think there's something sinister going on here. Hopefully we'll soon find out what and how."

"How are we set with regard to how long we can stay here?" Guillemette asked. "I'm free myself. I don't have anything pressing to get back to the islands for."

"How about the rest of you?" Dunk asked. "I'm okay too. I'm working on a book, of course, but I don't have a deadline fast approaching. Beth, how about your real estate stuff?"

"I do have to be back for a house closing on the thirtieth. That's the only thing that's important in the immediate future. I guess, if necessary, I could fly back for that and then return here. Do you think this is going to become a long, drawn-out thing, Dunk?"

"I just don't know at this stage, Beth. Rudy, how are you fixed?"

The tall German waved away the cloud of blue smoke puffed up from his pipe and shrugged his bony shoulders. "As you know, I am semi-retired. As archivist of the university library of Hamburg I am not overwhelmed with work in the middle of the summer. *Nein,* it will be no problem. I can stay for awhile if need be."

"And I'm likewise affected by the summer break at school," Earl said. "Nothing pressing for me either."

"Good. Then that's settled. We should know within a couple of days whether or not this is really a developing problem or if it's just a coincidence that the weather's messing up our psychic senses."

Earl had spread out some of the newspapers so that they could all see the various front pages and their headlines.

"My God! Look at what's been going on!" Guillemette muttered. "I didn't realize there'd been so much devastation over so many different areas."

"Hailstones in Virginia!" Beth cried. "And ice storms in North Carolina? In late June? That's ridiculous!"

"And there were a lot more than just those two tornadoes in Texas they talked about on television," Earl remarked. "See? Five altogether in the Dallas-Fort Worth area, six in South Dakota, two in Alabama and nearly a dozen that did a lot of damage in Kentucky."

"Yet Europe is as usual," Rudolf said, picking up the New York Times and studying it. "London, Paris, Hamburg—all as usual. Most strange."

"If the cold war was still on, I'm sure a lot of people would be blaming the Russians," Beth chuckled. "Actually, I've heard that weather patterns haven't been the same since Chernoble." Her face grew serious as she gazed at Duncan, a question in her eyes.

He smiled at her. "I don't think we can attribute all this to Chernoble, Beth. That was some years back now, anyway. So why would this happen now; and with such incredibly severe, and unseasonable, weather? No, there's got to be some other explanation."

"The bottom line," Earl said, his brow furrowed, "is that weather is a natural phenomenon. How could anything—or anyone—change it, and change it to be so destructive?"

11

 Arnie Summers stood beside the whirring web press and looked, with satisfaction, at the headline screaming across the page of the newspaper he had pulled from the conveyor belt.

"No shit the end of the world is at hand!" he muttered. "Or the end of my world'll be at hand if I don't get that fucking money!"

He dragged his eyes away from his own byline, glanced briefly at the promise of details on British royal family indiscretions, on the lower half of the page, and threw down the newspaper. He stalked out of the noisy press room and made for the coin phone located at the turn in the corridor.

He punched in a long string of numbers, followed by his telephone credit card number, and waited.

"Let me speak to him," he said, when someone finally came on the line. "What? ... No, it's just coming off the press right now. It'll be hitting the streets later today."

He hooked the receiver against his shoulder and dug into his pockets, looking for a cigarette.

"Look, what about this money you promised me? ... No, you said when I faxed you the copy ... What?" He lit the Camel and spat a tiny bit of tobacco off his tongue. He got a good grip on the receiver again. "Look, I faxed you the copy, you okayed it, and now the fucking story is coming off the press! What more d'you want? ... You promised me the money and I need it!"

He quickly looked around to see if anyone was coming, then lowered his voice and spoke through clenched teeth into the mouthpiece.

"Now see here, we had a deal ... Yeh, well I've been doing just that these past three times and you said you were pleased with it ... Look, this latest one's a doosey! You're gonna love it ... Yeh, trust me!"

He took a long drag on the cigarette as he listened.

"All right. You wire that money to me today, you hear, and I'm your man ... Yeh, right! 'Bye."

He hung up the telephone and stood for a long moment drawing on the cigarette and thinking, his brows knit together.

"Hey, what's up, Arnie?"

A short, roly-poly, totally bald man came down the corridor and passed Arnie. He paused before entering the press room.

"Get lost. I'm thinking," Arnie responded.

"Ah! So that's why you look so pained!" The fat man laughed loudly at his own joke, opened the door to the clatter of the presses and disappeared inside. Arnie uttered a profanity and went the other way.

Five minutes later Arnie Summers left the building, crossed the parking lot and got into his green, 1968 Mercury Cougar. It took three slams of the door before it would stay closed and several minutes of whirring the starter and pumping the gas pedal to get the engine to fire. Finally, the car's exhaust pipe blowing black smoke, Arnie drove out of the lot and headed downtown.

"Wonder if I can get these bastards to spring for a new car?" he thought to himself. "They damn well owe me. But who can tell with fuckin' Italians?"

He turned onto the parkway and watched the speedometer needle slowly claw its way up to sixty. A slick new sportscar swung across into the lane in front of him. Arnie leaned on the horn till he saw the driver look in the rear-view mirror, then gave him the finger.

"He's going to get his," he muttered. "They all are. You'll see!"

Twenty minutes later he went into a Western Union office and came out with a smile on his face and a fatter wallet.

12

Patrizio Cardinal Ganganelli lived in a modern Vatican-owned apartment house in the Piazza della Città Leonina, just north of St. Peter's Square, and across the street from one of the main entrances to the papal enclave. The cardinals heading the curia's departments of bishops, of education, and of orthodoxy, not to mention the cardinal *camerlengo*, also lived there.

Despite the convenience of the tenancy, Cardinal Ganganelli's apartment was not one of the better ones. In fact, it looked out on the crowded bus terminal and entrances to the underground public toilets—facilities that always seemed to prove inadequate for the huge crowds that frequently gathered at St. Peter's Square. But Ganganelli would not change his small apartment for a more elegant one in the Apostolic Palace itself—supposing that one of the few should become available—for it gave him some measure of independence; he did not have to have his visitors cleared by the Swiss Guard and pontifical security officers at the Vatican's gates.

Gualtiero Cardinal della Rovere, Ganganelli's portentous cohort, lived outside Vatican City. With another fifteen or so cardinals he resided in a massive structure built by Pius XI, in the teeming, earthy Trastevere district on the right bank of the Tiber, downstream from the Vatican.

In exchange for saying the occasional mass and attending a few other ceremonies at a nearby religious order for which he acted as "protector," Cardinal Ganganelli enjoyed having two or three nuns as his personal staff. They cooked his food and cleaned his apartment for him. Cardinal della Rovere was not so lucky. He had one nun who would look in occasionally to do some light housework, but she had no culinary skill whatsoever.

The two cardinals, Ganganelli and della Rovere, came out of Ganganelli's building and strolled toward St. Peter's Square. To anyone passing by they appeared to be discussing church business. Both men had frowns on their faces.

At the edge of the square they paused and the shorter, heavier cardinal said, "Now this has to be done immediately. Can I count on you?"

Della Rovere nodded curtly, turned on his heels and strode away through the many tourists who seemed to be there at all times of the year.

Ganganelli stood for a moment watching the red-clad figure go. Then he too turned and made his way towards the Apostolic Palace.

"I really don't think he can see you today, Your Eminence."

"Have you asked him?" Ganganelli snapped.

The young priest hesitated. As an ecclesiastical assistant he was used to speaking for his cardinal, but he was not used to other cardinals pressuring him.

"N-no, Your Eminence. But he told me ... "

"Go and ask him!"

The secretary went unwillingly away. Ganganelli paced up and down. Despite his corpulence, the cardinal was an active man. He hated to sit still unless there was a need for it. When the secretary returned, he growled at him.

"Well?"

"His Eminence says he can spare you just five minutes, Your Eminence." The priest kept his eyes lowered and refused to meet Ganganelli's eyes.

"Hmm! Good."

As cardinal dean of the sacred college, Cirillo Cardinal Todeschini was indeed a busy man, and begrudged speaking with anyone he didn't have to. He barely glanced up at Ganganelli when the other entered his office. He kept on, signing the bottoms of a number of papers piled on his desk.

"So good of you to see me, Your Eminence," Ganganelli said.

The hint of sarcasm was lost on Todeschini. "What do you want?" he asked, still not looking up.

"It's about my request for the use of the catacombs of Praetextatus."

The dean cardinal paused and glanced up at his visitor momentarily before returning to his paperwork.

"Ah, yes. I remember. An interesting request. For some time in November I believe it was, wasn't it?"

"October thirty-first, Your Eminence."

"A significant date."

Ganganelli said nothing.

"The old pagan festival of Samhain, is it not?" Todeschini looked up and then sat back in his chair, putting down his pen and bringing his fingertips together in a steeple. "Why do you want to use those old tombs, Eminence?"

Ganganelli shrugged. "Those, or some others. It is immaterial—though those are the ones I have requested."

"The catacombs were old pagan burial sites before they became Christian, is that not so, Eminence?"

Ganganelli locked his eyes on those of the other man and stared at him until the dean cardinal looked away.

"So we have been led to believe," Ganganelli said quietly.

"Mm. Well, I have not yet spoken to the Holy Father about this."

"Surely there is no need to bother His Holiness on such a slight matter?"

Todeschini shrugged. "It is at my discretion. But we are barely out of the month of June. What is your hurry, Eminence?"

Ganganelli allowed himself a small laugh. "The wheels of the Vatican turn exceedingly slowly. I am merely assuring myself that I will not be overlooked or forgotten, Your Eminence."

"Hrmph! There is no fear of that, I feel. This is the third time you have followed up your initial request, if

I am not mistaken." The dean cardinal shuffled some of his papers. "May I suggest that you leave this with me, undisturbed? I must presume that you have in mind some special program for the Feast of All Saints?"

Once more Ganganelli said nothing.

Todeschini waved a hand at him, not looking up again. "You may go, Eminence."

13

It was the end of June before the Committee had gathered together all the information it needed. Despite Bill Highland's putting pressure on the various departments, the emergencies declared in many areas worked against him. There was no way of getting information in a hurry. Finally, Beth flew back to Ohio, to her fledgling real estate business, and did what she had to before returning to Washington, D.C.

Eventually all were gathered once again in Duncan's suite at the elegant Hotel Jefferson, on 16th Street NW.

"Here's the information Bill managed to get for us," Dunk said, setting up a large fold-back sketch pad on an easel he had borrowed from the hotel. "I've arranged it in a way that I think will bring home some significance to you. I may have been reading too much into it but, well, we'll see what you get out of it. I've actually separated what might be termed 'unusual weather' from what is normal for the area and time of year. If you want to see the complete weather report, I've got it here—but, as I say, I've just listed the out-of-the-ordinary on this chart."

He flipped back his blond hair with a toss of his head, turned back the cover sheet, and showed the first page. It was detailed:

DATE	AREA	WEATHER
NOV 2	North-Central	Heavy, unpredicted snowfalls throughout area, with Kansas, Illinois, and Missouri experiencing up to 2 to 3 feet of snow; unseasonably cold temperatures dropping to well below freezing.
	Southeast	Heavy, unpredicted snowfalls, with depths of 4 feet recorded in Alabama, South Carolina, and Georgia. Unusually cold temperatures throughout area, from South Carolina down to the tip of Florida. Ice storm causing power outages in Mississippi and Louisiana.

	West	Ice storms in northern California, Utah, and Arizona.

Duncan gave them a moment and then turned the page.

DEC 23	Midwest	Heavy, unpredicted snowfalls across entire area; blizzard conditions in many parts; all five Great Lakes completely frozen. Wisconsin, Michigan, Ohio, Indiana, and Illinois experienced numerous power outages of unusual proportions.
	East	Heavy, unpredicted snowfalls and ice storms from Maine down to Florida; unseasonably cold temperatures, well below freezing, from New Jersey down to South Carolina.
	South	Severe cold in Deep South,

		Florida, Georgia, Alabama, Mississippi, Louisiana, and parts of Texas, with temperatures dropping to -25°F.

He turned the page again.

FEB 3	Across USA	Below-freezing temperatures across entire nation.
	North	Unpredicted severe snowstorms—blizzard conditions—in Connecticut, Pennsylvania, and Wisconsin.
	East	Temperatures to -50°F, with exceptionally deep snow (5 to 6 feet) in all areas.
	South	Unseasonal cold; unpredicted ice storms bringing down power lines in Mississippi, Arkansas, Alabama, Tennessee, Kentucky, and on up to Maine.

West	Sudden, unpredicted, torrential rainstorms bringing mudslides in central and southern California.

"Wait a minute!" Earl cried. "I already see one thing that sticks out. The word 'unpredicted'."

Everyone murmured agreement.

"'Unpredicted snowfall'; 'unpredicted ice storms'," Guillemette said. "What is this, my man? Does this mean the Weather Bureau isn't up to its job?"

"I believe it is much more than that," Rudolf said. "But let us continue. Let us see what else is happening up until this past week."

Duncan turned the pages. The next date was March 22, then May 1, and finally, the most recent, June 22. They all absorbed the information—snow and sub-freezing conditions virtually across the country, followed by severe flooding and mudslides. There had been earthquakes, thunderstorms, hurricanes, and tornadoes. Everything imaginable and unimaginable in the way of bad weather was there. And all listed by date.

"Wait a minute! Wait a minute!" Beth cried. "I've got it!"

Duncan looked pleased. "I knew someone would soon. Anyone else?" He looked around at the puzzled faces.

Then Rudolf let out an exclamation. *"Mein Gott!* Of course! How could I not see that at once? The dates!"

"What?" Earl sounded perplexed. "What about the dates?"

"Yes! Of course!" Guillemette let out a squeal.

"Disregard all the weather information, Earl," Dunk said. "Just jot down the dates on a piece of paper. You'll see."

Earl took up a pad and started copying from the big sheets. It didn't take him long to catch on.

"Of course! The Wheel of the Year!"

"I just listed the major, most unusual weather happenings," Dunk said. "And the dates, as you see, are approximately six weeks apart, all the way through."

"And not just any old six weeks apart," Guillemette said, her dark eyes aglow.

"No. The dates are those of the Wheel of the Year, as Earl said. The major sabbat dates of the pagan year, with the cross quarter days."

"I see the dates," Beth said, tentatively, "but I have to admit I'm not too clear on their significance."

Rudolf stood up and walked over to the pad. He took up a felt-tip pen that Duncan had used to set up the sheets. Turning to a fresh page he drew a large circle.

"This represents the year, *meine reizend* Elizabeth, and here ... " he drew a line across bisecting the circle, "it is divided into two. This was the old division of the year, at Samhain and at Beltane, or November Eve and May Eve. In the early days humankind would be able to grow food to eat in the one half of the year but have to hunt animals for food in the other half, the winter months."

He drew another line across, dividing the circle into quarters.

"Now we add the cross quarter days: Imbolc, or February Eve, and Lughnasadh, or August Eve, tying in with the breeding of animals and with the harvest."

"Lughnasadh the Corn Maiden and Imbolc the Crone," Guillemette murmured.

The old German nodded. "The old wheel of the agricultural world," he said. "And superimposed upon it, the wheel of the seasons, marked by the passage of the sun."

He drew two more lines bisecting the others.

"Here we have the two opposites: Yule, December 21, and Midsummer, June 21; the winter and summer solstices. And here March 21, the spring equinox, and September 21, the autumnal equinox."

"But this doesn't make any sense," Earl cried. "How could these severe weather happenings occur exactly on these dates?"

"But wait a minute." It was Beth again. "I don't know if I'm being especially dense, but these dates aren't exactly the same as those you've just put up, Rudy. Look, you've got December 21 and March 21 and April 30, for example, but those weather dates are December 23, March 22 and May 1. They're the same distances apart, more or less, but not quite the same dates."

"You're right, Beth," Dunk said. "But I think our observation's still valid. See, there was a three day difference back in November—November 2 rather than October 31—but by the most recent ones, May 1 and June 22, there is only a one-day delay. It's as though they couldn't quite get it right to start with, but they gradually fine-tuned it."

"They?" Earl looked at each of the others. "Who's 'they'? I mean, are these natural phenomena that, for whatever strange reason, are falling on these dates, or are we talking about someone actually causing all this?"

"And if it really is a 'they'," Guillemette said, "then how, in the names of the gods, are they doing it? And why are they doing it?"

"Meine Freunde," Rudolf said, "these are the questions we have to answer. For if there is, as you say, a 'they' causing these terrible things, they must have great power, incredible power — I shudder to contemplate it — and we are the ones who must fight them!"

14

The limousine with the SVC plates pulled away from the arrivals building at Leonardo da Vinci International Airport and started its twenty-mile drive back to the city. Inside, Cardinal Ganganelli studied his fellow passenger, openly staring at him through his spectacles.

Archbishop Majeed Borzorg-Alavi, though Persian by birth, was presently nuncio, or papal ambassador, to Tripoli. A thin-lipped ascetic, who physically reminded Ganganelli of his friend della Rovere, he was on an official visit to the Vatican. It was more than coincidence that the visit was at a time when Cardinal Ganganelli needed to confer with him. He clutched a bulging briefcase to himself and looked slightly uncomfortable under Ganganelli's gaze.

"We shall talk at my apartment," Ganganelli said.

Majeed looked at the cardinal.

"Not at the Vatican, Your Eminence?"

Ganganelli laughed. "The place is dead after one o'clock. It's siesta time. Nobody—and I mean nobody—does anything much in the afternoon. The

Polish pope tried to change things and get everyone moving right after lunch but even he had to give up and join the general lethargy."

"But then surely this would be a good time for us to talk?"

Ganganelli shook his head. "Siesta or not, there are ears everywhere in Città del Vaticano. And tongues that wag and wag. No. We will be far safer at my apartment."

At the Leonina building, Ganganelli dismissed the limousine and then led the way up to his apartment, where he chased out the two nuns who were cleaning it.

"Sit down, Your Excellency," he said, indicating a leather-covered armchair in the living room. "Would you care for a drink? Punt a Mes, Sambucca, Cinzano?"

"Er, just a small Cinzano, if I may."

Ganganelli poured the archbishop's drink and treated himself to a hefty measure of Sambucca with the obligatory three coffee beans. He lowered himself into an overstuffed chair and took a long gulp.

"I have a lot to accomplish while I am here, Eminence," began the archbishop. "I trust I will have an audience with the Most Holy Father ... "

"I wouldn't count on it," Ganganelli interrupted. "If you do, it'll be in a collective audience for no more than fifteen minutes, I guarantee."

Majeed thought about that for a moment. "No matter. It's only a matter of form anyway. I have to attend one of the weekly meetings of the Sacred Congregation of the Sacraments and Divine Worship while I'm here, and there's a financial matter I have to sort out with the Administrator of the Patrimony of the Apostolic See."

"I can show you where to find them. But we've got more important things to discuss, and that involves finances also."

The ascetic nodded. "Indeed, Your Eminence. I have all the papers here." He pulled his briefcase onto his lap and unlocked it.

"You passed along my memo to the man in charge?" Ganganelli leaned forward slightly.

Majeed nodded. "Muammar Qadhafi was very pleased with all that you had to say."

Ganganelli sat back and looked quickly around, as though to be sure that no one was there to hear the name of the Libyan leader.

"He accepted the proof that you gave him, of what you are able to accomplish, and he has said that he will guarantee the amount specified," continued Majeed.

"I want more than a guarantee," Ganganelli said quietly. "I asked for a downpayment. A very substantial downpayment, if you recall. Do you have that?"

The archbishop looked slightly ill at ease.

"It's not easy—even in my diplomatic position—to bring such a large amount of money with me. I ... "

"I didn't ask you to bring it with you, you fool!" snarled the cardinal, all the veneer of the good host stripped away. "I spelled out that it should be placed in the numbered Swiss account which I gave. Are you saying this has not been done?"

"I—well, Your Eminence, I ... "

"'Eminence' shit!" Ganganelli said, coming to his feet. "Let's stop fucking about, Majeed! Let's get over to the Vatican right away and you can make good use of these goddamned modern fax machines they've got there. I want you to tell that bastard Qadhafi that I can just as easily turn my powers on him as I can on the United States of America! Do you get my meaning, Your *Excellency?*

15

Duncan slowed the rental car and turned right onto Atlantic Avenue. "Not far now," he said.

Beth turned to smile at him, her lightly-freckled face aglow, her green eyes sparkling. "I've really enjoyed the drive, Dunk. But then I always enjoy being out with you."

He smiled back at her, taking in her red hair blowing in the slight breeze from the partially lowered window. She was truly beautiful, he thought. He reluctantly returned his attention to the road. "The A.R.E. has what's probably the best metaphysical library in the country," he said. "I've come here many times to do research."

"A.R.E.—that's what? Something ending in 'Edgar', for Edgar Cayce?"

He laughed. "No! It's the Association for Research and Enlightenment. Part of the Edgar Cayce Foundation. It's a big, modern building right next door to the original old building that used to be the hospital where Cayce worked. Right across the road from the ocean."

They had rented a car and driven to Virginia Beach, home of Edgar Cayce, the "Sleeping Prophet."

The other three members of the Committee had gone to New York. All were on research expeditions relating to the weather phenomena. Dunk pulled into the large parking lot and they got out of the car, stretching themselves.

They went into the large, white building housing the library and climbed up, past the modern sculptures, to the second floor.

"I love libraries," Dunk said. "There's so much knowledge available, just sitting there on the shelves waiting for you to find it."

"I know what you mean, Dunk. I've always loved books, too. Wow! This is big, considering it's all metaphysical."

Duncan led the way over to where the books on Witchcraft were shelved. "There's something here I want to show you."

He ran his fingers along the shelf and then pulled a weighty tome from its place. Quickly flicking through the pages, he finally stopped and handed it to Beth. She found herself looking at an old woodcut showing a woman in medieval dress and a tall, pointed hat, handing what looked like a length of knotted rope to a man, obviously a sailor. In the background a sailing ship sat at anchor.

"What's this?"

"Back in the Middle Ages it was believed that Witches could conjure up the wind and that they could then, magically, bind the wind into a knot in a rope. They would sell these knotted ropes to sailors."

"What on earth for?"

Duncan chuckled. "If a sailor found himself becalmed, he could undo one of the knots and get himself a wind."

Beth laughed.

"Don't forget, we're talking Middle Ages," Dunk said. He pointed at the page. "Now see here, there are three knots in the rope. If the sailor just undid one knot he would release a gentle wind. Two knots and he got a big wind. All three knots and he had a gale on his hands."

"Convenience packaging," Beth chuckled. "But they couldn't really do that, could they, Dunk?"

"I wouldn't be too quick to say no," he said seriously. He put back the book and then pulled out another one. "You know what they say? 'Where there's smoke, there's fire'. There must have been a lot of this wind-selling going on for someone to trouble to comment on it in the form of a woodcut illustration. And if it didn't work, I'm sure sailors wouldn't have kept buying the knotted ropes. You know there's been a lot said, over the centuries, about certain people being able to control the weather. Enough said that one might suspect there's something to it. Here!" He handed her the other book. "Look in here at the report on the witches of Berwick, in Scotland, in the year 1590. I'm going to be digging about a bit, but you can read this and let me know what you think."

He went off along the stacks and Beth found a nearby table to sit at and read. And what she read made her think. It seemed that the Berwick witches had been recruited by Francis, Earl of Bothwell, who was an heir to the royal throne. He wanted the witches' help in getting rid of the king so that he could inherit the throne. King James VI, of Scotland, was about to marry young fifteen-year-old Anne, of Denmark, and embarked across the North Sea to fetch her and bring her home. In the later trial of the Witches, when Bothwell's plot was revealed, it was shown that the Berwick Witches had caused a great storm to come up; one which almost sank James's ship and caused him to lose a large amount of treasure overboard. As proof of the Witches' powers their leader, Agnes Sampson, told the king the exact words that he had spoken to his bride on their wedding night, in Oslo. Since no one but himself and his bride could have known the conversation, this was proof enough for James that they had supernatural power. Indeed it was mainly because of this encounter with the Witches that, when he later became King James I of England, he caused his new translation of the Bible to be so heavily slanted and biased against the Old Religion.

"Well? What d'you think?"

Duncan slipped into a chair beside Beth and peered over her shoulder at the book.

"It's scary," she said. "From all of this, yes, I believe they had tremendous powers."

"Just remember that things only seem scary when you don't understand them," he said. "Once you start to learn how things work, they stop being scary."

She wrinkled her nose. "I know. Poor choice of words. But I guess what I mean is that it's frightening to think that someone really could bring about a storm." She looked intently into his eyes and took his hand in hers. "Do you really believe that there's someone so powerful that they could affect the weather patterns of the entire United States?"

He squeezed her hand.

"All I can do right now is try to keep an open mind. We have to face the fact that it's a possibility. And there I agree with you—it's scary!"

16

Room 315, the General Research Division of the New York Public Library, was unusually quiet, Earl thought. Usually when he was there it was crowded. But then this was early July and most of the students who usually helped fill the halls were already out of harness and heading for the beaches of Long Island and New Jersey.

Rudy had gone along the corridor to the Rare Book Division, to do some research there. Guillemette had left them outside the library and gone off to visit friends downtown.

Earl sat down at one of the computer terminals and punched up SUBJECT. He typed in the word MAGIC. A long list of titles and authors appeared on the screen and he started reading through them, making an occasional note in his notebook. Then he started filling out call slips to give to the young woman at the desk.

Guillemette ducked into the subway entrance outside the library and took a train down to 19th Street. She got off and hurried around a corner and down a couple of blocks. At the intersection she paused for a moment and looked up at the old building on the opposite corner. Like several buildings in this part of the city it had been decorated, above the lower floor windows, with carved representations of the old pagan God of Hunting: the Horned God. The heads bore the horns of the animals who had been hunted by early mankind, while the faces were made up of the leaves of the forest, leading to the appellation "foliate mask" for that form of carving. She smiled to herself, wondering if the architect had realized the origins of the figures he'd used.

"He probably just thought it was a nice, decorative motif," she murmured to herself. She crossed the street and went through a small door at the corner of the building, next to a used bookstore. She climbed the stairs to the third floor and tapped on the door.

There was no reply. She tapped again, this time a series of sharp raps in a pattern. The door opened and a tall, fine-boned, black woman stood there smiling.

"Guillemette! I don't believe it!"

They fell into each other's arms and hugged. Then the taller woman led Guillemette into the apartment and closed the door.

"Girl, what are you doin' in New York?"

"It's just a flying visit, *Mamaloi.* I didn't even know I'd be here till we left this morning."

"You left the Bahamas this morning, child?"

"No. I've been in Washington, D.C. It's a long story. Oh, it's good to see you again!"

Mirari Jauregi sat her visitor down in a large arm-chair and then busied herself making herbal tea. Guillemette looked around the small, dark, one-room apartment with pleasure. She always loved coming there. There was such a warm feeling of belonging; a vibration of love and positive energy. Banners, in a variety of rich, vibrant colors, hung in each corner; incense burned on a small altar against one wall; wooden carvings of the Voudoun loa were scattered throughout; and bunches of herbs hung from a rack over the kitchen area. The room was lit by candles of every size and color—sitting on bookshelves, on top of dressers and tables, even stuck into the tops of bottles standing on the floor.

"It's just as I remembered," Guillemette said. "I love this place."

Mirari laughed. "You always say that, every time you come here, girl. You been sayin' it since you was six years old."

"Has it been that long?"

Mirari was probably not related, but Guillemette had always looked upon her as an aunt. She was certainly a very close friend of Guillemette's mother. All three women were Voudoun priestesses in their own rights. Guillemette and her mother had been initiated and "learned the secret of the asson" in Haiti; Mirari had been a spiritual leader first in New Orleans and then, for as long as Guillemette could remember, in New York.

They sat and sipped their tea, content to just enjoy one another's company. Mirari never seemed to age, Guillemette thought. She looked at the older woman's high cheekbones, slim figure, narrow waist, and firm, full breasts. She had to be in her late sixties and was still exceptionally beautiful. "I hope I look that good at her age," Guillemette thought.

"You will, girl!" Mirari answered her thoughts, as she so often did. "You always did take after me. Your mama say that if she hadn't been there at the birth she'd aswore you was my daughter." She threw back her head and laughed. Guillemette couldn't help joining in, even though she'd heard the story a hundred times.

"Now, girl. What you come for? Not just to visit your old aunt, I'm sure." Her black eyes sparkled in the low, flickering candlelight.

Guillemette put down her tea cup and leaned forward.

"You're right, of course, *Mamaloi*. Not that I wouldn't come to see you just for the sake of seeing you anyway."

Mirari waved a hand, dismissing the obvious.

"No. I've come to talk to you about the weather."

For the first time the older woman looked surprised.

"The weather, girl? What you say?"

17

Patrizio Ganganelli was in an unusually pleasant mood. It was a beautiful day and he hummed to himself as he strolled about the Vatican Gardens. Fifty-eight acres of lush, well-tended gardens formed a barrier from the outside world on the north and west of the Vatican. Winding paths flanked by multicolored jonquils, begonias, dahlias, and gladioli, groves of massive oak trees, ancient fountains and pools made the area a much-sought-after escape from the hurry and scurry of the offices of the Apostolic Palace.

Ganganelli turned off onto a secondary path as he saw a large crowd of tourists approaching, led by a tour guide. "That's what spoils these gardens," Ganganelli thought. "They shouldn't allow these peasants onto the grounds; this should be for the use of the papal court only."

"Hey, Father!"

A voice broke the quiet of the gardens. Someone was yelling. Frowning, Ganganelli turned to see who it was. He was surprised by a tall man in an American serviceman's uniform, waving at him and running across the grass in his direction. The soldier was followed by a young blonde in shorts and a halter top.

"She'll never be allowed inside the Papal Palace," Ganganelli muttered to himself.

The American ran up to the cardinal, and waved to the blonde to hurry up.

"Say, Father," he said. "I was wondering … "

"I am a cardinal," Ganganelli said, icily.

"Yeh? Say, we have them back in Virginia. Pretty little red birds they are." He laughed at his own joke. "Sorry, Father … "

"Eminence!" Ganganelli hissed. "You will refer to me as 'Your Eminence'."

"That's right, Harlan!" The blonde had arrived, puffing and panting. She attempted a curtsey to the cardinal. "I was brought up Catholic—when I was a little kid, that is. This here's a cardinal all right."

"Would you kindly not stand in the flowerbeds?" Ganganelli said.

"Oops! Sorry." The blonde stepped out from among the jonquils. "Did you ask him, Harlan?"

"I was just going to. Father Your Eminence, we were wondering if I could take a picture of my intended, here, standing beside you? P'raps with the old palace in the background? What d'you think?"

Ganganelli could feel his blood beginning to boil. He took off his gold-rimmed spectacles and, pulling out a silk handkerchief, commenced furiously polishing them.

"This is not your ridiculous Disneyland! We are not here for the benefit of the tourists; not to be photographed for some inane family snapshot album! If you want to see these gardens I suggest you get back with your group of - of - other banal picture-takers and concentrate on the statuary. I want nothing to do with you!"

His face bright red, the portly cardinal turned on his heel and stormed off, leaving the young couple open-mouthed and speechless. As he swung around by a fountain and headed for the sixteenth-century summer house of Pius IV, in the middle of the Gardens, he heard a small cry from the blonde.

"Sorry, Your Eminence! We sure didn't mean anything … "

Ganganelli clenched his teeth and swore under his breath. Three sari-clad nuns from Calcutta, closely followed by two black bishops from Tanzania, came out of the summer house. Ganganelli stood firm in the center of the walkway, growling, and they all had to walk around him. He then went into the dark building and sat down. As he took several deep breaths, the red haze in front of his eyes slowly started to fade.

It was the American uniform that had triggered it. Patrizio Ganganelli sat with his eyes closed and was eight years old again. He was in the back bedroom with his six brothers and sisters, all of whom were asleep. But Patrizio wasn't asleep. He was gripping the worn curtain that served as a door to their room and peeping around it at the commotion in the living room.

His mother had come home less than an hour before, pushed into the house by three American soldiers. All three were drunk, and had brought half a dozen bottles along. The big, burly leader of the Americans — a sergeant — had thrown off his jacket and then ripped off Patrizio's mother's blouse. He could still see the military stripes on the jacket where it had landed on the floor close to the curtained doorway. He had locked his eyes onto it as he listened to his mother's screams. One by one all three of the men had raped her. Then they had left, the last to go throwing a twenty-dollar bill down on his mother's body, where she lay sobbing on the floor.

Patrizio hated Americans. He hated America. He would do anything to make the whole country pay for what its soldiers had done to his mother.

"Are you all right, Your Eminence?"

"Huh?" Ganganelli shook himself and opened his eyes. A worried-looking priest stood before him, hands clasped together, a look of concern on his face.

"Are you all right, Your Eminence? You don't look well."

The cardinal struggled to his feet and took two good gulps of air. He waved his hand at the priest.

"No, no, Father. I'm fine. Just leave me alone. I'm fine."

He went out of the summerhouse and headed for his apartment.

18

From the A.R.E. library, Duncan and Beth took the little elevator up to the Meditation Room. The Association for Research and Enlightenment was enthused about meditation, recommending it be practiced by virtually everyone. The results could certainly be extraordinarily beneficial. Duncan and Beth both meditated on a regular basis, though they did not follow the Cayce method but a variation on it, devised by Duncan.

The room was decorated in pale shades of pink and lavender, with gossamery curtains in those colors hanging ceiling to floor. One was immediately put into the right mood for introspection.

"Why, this is beautiful!" Beth exclaimed as they entered. She spoke in an appropriately hushed voice, for others were there in the seats, eyes closed.

"Shall we sit down?" Dunk whispered, ushering her into the back row of comfortable-looking chairs.

They stayed there meditating for a long time and Dunk was vaguely aware of other people coming and going. Eventually he came out of it, slowly grounded himself, and opened his eyes.

The room was now empty except for the two of them. He glanced at Beth. She still seemed to be in a deep meditation. He couldn't help taking the opportunity to stare at her and take in her beauty.

They had developed strong feelings for one another—Dunk would even call it love—and over the past year had spent a lot of time together, either in Ohio or California. They had even talked, vaguely, of moving in together, but hadn't finalized any plans. After her divorce, Beth had not wanted to get too involved right away, and so had stayed in Ohio and started a small real estate business. Duncan, in his apartment overlooking the beach in San Diego's La Jolla, wrote his books and bided his time.

He quietly got to his feet and moved across to the windows. The room, high above the main building, looked out at the ocean, where the Chesapeake Bay opens into the Atlantic. It was a sunny day and the view magnificent. Dunk suddenly started as a man's voice spoke behind him.

"Dunk, *mi pral!* How be ye?"

He turned to see who it was who knew him, and why they were speaking aloud when it was obvious that Beth was still meditating. He was surprised to find no one there.

"Dunk!"

The voice came again. It took Duncan a moment to realize that the sound was coming from Beth's mouth. The voice, so deep and masculine, and sounding vaguely familiar, called him again.

"Dunk?"

He moved across and sat down next to the redhead.

"Yes," he said quietly. "Yes, I'm here. Who is this?"

He realized that Beth must have gone into a spontaneous trance and was channeling, as a spiritualist medium might. It was probably someone who was dead wanting to speak to him, he thought. After years of sitting in séances he'd had many such encounters, and was familiar with the phenomenon. But even so, he still found it a little unnerving to carry on a conversation with a disembodied voice.

"Who are you?" he repeated.

"Dunk! *Mi pral*, it's me! Don't you *jin* me?"

Suddenly he recognized the voice, and understood the words.

Excitedly he said, "Reg? Is that you?"

From Beth's throat came a deep, hearty chuckle. The voice was that of Reg Lee, an English Romany, or Gypsy, who had been a friend of Dunk's for many years. The voice and the Romany words confirmed it — *mi pral* meant "my brother" and *jin* meant "know." The only thing that surpised Dunk was that Reg was — so far as he knew — still very much alive and well, and living in a little village in the south of England.

"It *is* you, isn't it Reg?" he asked.

"Indeed it is, *mi pral*. Indeed it is."

"But — are you … I mean, are you … well, still alive? Still on this plane?"

Again came the throaty chuckle.

"As ever, *Lavengro*. They can't get rid of me, y'know. Eighty-five years old and still going strong."

Lavengro meant "writer," and was Reg's usual form of addressing Dunk.

"Reg. Do you know how you're speaking to me? I mean, do you know you're coming to me through another person, a medium?"

"O' course I do, Dunk, *mi pral.* And a beautiful gal she is too! But I mustn't waste time. This isn't easy. *Lavengro,* there's danger building around you. It's *waffe-dopen* —evil; danger! I see it. Danger on a grand scale. I had to warn you."

"Danger? Reg, what d'you mean? What sort of danger?"

"Danger is danger, *Lavengro.* It's coming. *Waffe-dopen.* Evil. Be ready for it."

"How do you know this, Reg?"

"I was told. I was warned in *dukkerin';* as I was for-tunetelling. Now I'm warning you. I tell you, I'm afraid for you, *Lavengro.* Take care. I have to go. *Kushti bok, mi pral.* Good luck!"

Beth gave a snort, almost like a snore, and woke herself up. She was disoriented for a few moments, then looked at Duncan, her green eyes blinking.

"What happened? I mean, where … ?" She looked around as though getting her bearings. "Whew! That was some strange meditation, Dunk. I must have gone really deep. I tell you, I don't remember anything of what I was doing."

Duncan took her hands in his and looked into her eyes.

"Are you okay, Beth?" He looked and sounded concerned.

Beth wrinkled her brow. "Yes, Dunk. Yes, I'm fine. It was just for a moment … I was—I don't know! Probably I just fell asleep instead of meditating. I woke up with a start, that's all." She smiled at him and squeezed his hands. "I'm fine, Dunk. Really I am."

19

Burian Volynskji, Ukranian bishop, walked along the glass-enclosed, frescoed *loggia* in the Apostolic Palace toward the conference room. When he got there he found more than twenty other people already waiting, scattered around the big conference table, on what turned out to be incredibly uncomfortable chairs. No one was speaking to anyone else. Burian noted both priests and nuns. Of the former, the three closest to where he decided to sit were from Third World countries. He also noticed another, who later turned out to be a Greek.

After some ten minutes of silence — but for the constant repositioning of the bodies on the chairs — the door at the end of the room opened and a short, stocky cardinal entered, carrying a bulging briefcase. He closed the door behind and advanced to the only upholstered chair, at the head of the conference table.

"I am Patrizio, Cardinal Ganganelli," he said after he had settled. He peered into his briefcase and pulled out some manila-bound files, which he placed on the table in front of himself. He quickly glanced around, looking hard at each of the silent figures, his bright eyes unblinking through his spectacles.

"You're all here, I see. Good! Sister Joseph, of …" he glanced at a folder, "… Flatbush, New York—what a strange name!—you will close those doors for me."

The nun jumped up, quickly moved across and closed the big double doors out to the corridor. She scurried back to her seat.

"Now," Ganganelli continued. "I have been given to understand that you are all ready and more than willing to assist in our undertaking."

It wasn't a question, but he glanced up and let his eyes briefly meet with each of theirs. He seemed satisfied and continued.

"It has taken us a long time to find you all, believe me. So many in our—what shall I say?—religious environment have lost all feelings and passions and opted to settle into a life of dullness and mediocrity; they have lost all sense of retribution. But not you … not from what I see in your records here!" He tapped the files.

"Now, some of you are living in the United States already. You others will be going there for the first time. That's all right. We need a wide variety of backgrounds and talents. We already have a large battalion of people over there working for us. You will help swell the numbers. You are all going to major cities there."

"Your Eminence?" It was a young priest with a strong Brooklyn accent. He had been showing an interest in the nun who'd closed the doors, after hearing she was from Flatbush.

"What is it?" Ganganelli's voice made it clear he didn't like to be interrupted.

"I … I'm sorry, Your Eminence. I just wondered—is our work tied in with the Vatican, here? I mean, does His Holiness … ?"

Ganganelli flipped open one of the folders and studied it as he spoke.

"So far as you are concerned, Father Casale, you are under my jurisdiction. You are answerable to me and me alone. And, should it ever become necessary, I will see to it that you are protected. Do you understand?"

The young priest nodded.

"You report only to me!" He looked around at everyone. "Do you all understand that?"

There were murmurs of assent.

"Given the nature of our undertaking, I would think it extremely obvious whether or not the Most Holy Father … " (he said the words as though they left a bad taste in his mouth) " … was involved in what we are trying to accomplish." He looked hard at the young priest. "You have a young brother, Michael, and a sister who is very ill, I see."

"She has cancer," the priest said quietly.

The cardinal nodded. "It would be well to give them a passing thought should you decide to speak to anyone other than me about your assignment."

The priest paled, but said nothing.

"Now! You should all have your instructions memorized. I want you to send reports back to me, at each instance, advising how the people in your area are coping with the problems they will be experiencing. And it's part of your job—perhaps the most important part—to move among the people. Preach to them, if that's your job; spread the word that the government cannot cope. There are always nay-sayers. You will back them! The people will be on the brink of panic; it's your job to push them over. You will feed the fervor!

"When the time comes—and you all know the date—you're on your own when it comes to getting out. You've got escape routes mapped out, and it's up to each of you, as individuals, to take that route. With any luck, you'll all make it!"

Burian Volynskji glanced around the table. He saw the eyes of fanatics and he saw the eyes of defeated men, such as the young priest from Brooklyn. He snorted to himself in disgust. Bishop Volynskji was a fanatic.

20

Ganganelli felt pleased with himself. The new group looked promising. God knew, it wasn't easy to find the sort of people he needed in the Roman Catholic clergy. It had been a worldwide search, involving checking the records of novices, seasoned clerics, and even bishops, and examining the backgrounds of all, but especially those who had run afoul of the system in one way or another—a minor slip, a momentary indiscretion, a temporary lapse of propriety. He had to acknowledge Gualtiero della Rovere's part in that. The man had worked diligently to track down anyone who might also be of their frame of mind. The Vatican computer had been a boon. Thank God for progress!

There had also been many who were not attached to the Church. Quite a few who had been excommunicated and those who had, at some time, been indiscreet enough to speak out against Mother Church. The Church was no stranger to scandal, and Ganganelli had not been reluctant to make contact with those disavowed and to bring them into his personal fold.

The cardinal entered the Vatican Library and made his way to the rear. He sat and waited for Father

Peretti to bring him the book he had demanded—from the reign of Pope Gelasius III—one of the so-called "banned" books. He'd had to resort to blackmail to get it out of the weak little librarian. Ah yes, he thought, it was good to have knowledge, especially knowledge of others' indiscretions. When he had first learned of Father Peretti's impropriety with a young acolyte from nearby St. Gioacchino, he'd filed the information away in his head, knowing it would one day come in useful. Today it had.

His mind returned to the group he had just left. That weak priest from Brooklyn would have to be watched. As would a couple of others. But compensating for them, there was such wonderful new blood as Ukranian Bishop Volynskji and one or two others. Yes, he felt pleased. Things were progressing well.

"Your Eminence."

The librarian, eyes cast down, placed a dusty volume in front of the cardinal and then quickly melted away. Ganganelli grunted. He blew the dust off the book and opened it.

Yes, the plan was proceeding exceedingly well. Working with "the Brothers," he had very ably demonstrated the powers at his command. And now, in addition to destroying the country he hated, he would be wealthy beyond his dreams. Not bad for a fat little bastard from the slums of Via Ardeatina!

Ganganelli looked down at the book. It was difficult to read the elaborate handwriting of the thirteenth century pontiff. Born Bernado Masci, as Pope Gelasius III he had ruled a scant two years, from June 12, 1292, until May 2, 1294. But in those two years he had made tremendous strides in the occult sciences, proving beyond the shadow of a doubt that personal power of incredible proportions was available to the one who had the courage to take it. And now he, Patrizio Cardinal Ganganelli, had access to those journals and workbooks, and would ensure that the knowledge gained was not lost and locked away from the world. He, Patrizio Cardinal Ganganelli, would take that power and use it, supplementing the power he already had and intensifying it a thousandfold! If … no, not if but when … he became pope, he might consider taking the name Gelasius. But—time enough to think about that.

He adjusted the gold-rimmed glasses and started to study.

21

"Tonight's the night, if our suspicions are correct."

Duncan stood and looked at his friends. They were once again gathered in his suite at the Jefferson Hotel. The hotel was rated one of the finest in the world, according to Bill Highland. It was certainly opulent. Each of its 104 rooms was uniquely decorated. Duncan's had an antique four-poster bed with a plump, eyelet-trimmed comforter and pillow shams. There was a Napoleonic cherrywood *bibliothèque* filled with rare books against one wall and a French Empire Louis XVI bureau at another. Beautifully framed original oil paintings decorated the walls, and Persian rugs covered the hardwood floors. An Italian crystal chandelier hung from a carved-plaster rosette-motif Adams ceiling.

Rudolf sat straight-backed on a chair he had pulled out from the escritoire by the window. Earl and Guillemette sat close together on a rose-and-gold silk-covered Chippendale sofa. Beth was sunk into a comfortable armchair. Dunk walked up and down, restlessly, occasionally stopping to lean on the back of another straight-backed chair.

"August Eve," Earl said. "Yes. If we're right, we should have an onslaught of abnormally bad weather tonight, or tomorrow."

"It may not be here in Washington, however," Rudolf said, his dark eyes peering out from under his shaggy eyebrows. "The records showed that only certain areas of the United States were hit at any particular time. I do not think that our mysterious enemies have the power to affect the whole country at one time."

"Let's hope not!" Guillemette said, with feeling. "I'd hate to think of anyone having that much power."

"It feels so frustrating, Dunk," Beth said. "Just sitting here waiting."

He nodded. "I know. But at this stage of the game there's nothing else we can do. We don't know who they are. We don't know where they are. We don't know why they're doing what they're doing."

"Or even how they're doing it," Earl added.

Dunk grunted agreement. "But at least this will confirm that we're right," he said. "If there's unusually bad weather tonight or tomorrow—let's say within a thirty-six-hour period—something really unprecedented for the time and place, then we can be certain it's not natural and that someone or something is behind it."

"Some*thing?*" Earl raised his eyebrows.

"We cannot rule out anything, no matter how improbable it may seem at first sight," Rudolf said.

"I suppose you're right. Just so long as it's not little green men from a flying saucer!"

Everyone laughed.

"Did anyone watch the weather forecast?" Dunk asked.

"Yes, I did," Beth replied. "It couldn't have been better. Sunshine for the next several days and seasonably warm. No hint of anything dire for any part of the country."

"Hmm. Well, we'll see."

"What did you two find down at the Cayce place?" Guillemette asked.

"It was fascinating," Beth said. She reached down for a large brown envelope at her feet and, placing it on the nearby coffeetable, began pulling papers from it. "Dunk made photocopies of all sorts of stuff. See for yourselves." She handed around the sheets to the others.

"Basically, I ran down a surprisingly large number of examples, from history, of people controlling the weather," Dunk said. "I discounted hearsay and superstition, but I think you'll be amazed at how many actual cases there've been, and well-documented ones, at that."

"Anything on the scale of this present problem?" Earl asked, peering over Guillemette's shoulder as she pored over the papers from the envelope.

Dunk shook his head.

"No. I have to admit there isn't. But there have been cases where groups of people—usually labelled 'Witches', of course—supposedly worked together to create storms."

"If they could create small storms, why not large ones? There is no reason why it could not be done on a larger scale." Rudolf pulled his ever-present pipe from his pocket and started charging it with tobacco.

"Apparently there was one example of that," Dunk said, nodding. "Not well documented I'm afraid, but nonetheless worth considering. Way back in the sixteenth century, when the Spanish Armada was threatening to invade England, it's said that the leaders of the Witches of England gathered together a large number of their covens. Working together, they conjured up a monstrous storm that completely destroyed the entire fleet of ships."

"Ah, yes!"

"Of course! I'd forgotten that," Earl said. "I've heard that story many times, now that I think about it. Didn't the same thing happen in World War Two, with the threat of invasion by Hitler?"

Dunk nodded. "Yes. A similar scenario but without the conjuring of a storm. A group of covens got together and sent out strong thoughts that Hitler could not come over to England, that it would be useless to try to invade."

"And he didn't!" Earl said, with glee. "Though I guess you'd have a hard time proving that the Witches were really responsible for that."

"I'm sure you would," Beth said. She turned to Rudolf. "How did you do in New York?" she asked.

"The investigations of both myself and our good friend Earl, here, went equally well in New York," the German replied, puffing clouds of blue-grey smoke into the air. "We concentrated on the magical aspects, the mechanics of conjuring entities or directing forces. Some of the old grimoires were useful there—*Le Dragon Rouge, Le Véritable Dragon Noire, Le Petit Albert, The Pansophy Of Rudolph the Magus, The Arbatel, The Heptameron, The Key Of Solomon* ... you know them all."

"Well, we know *of* them," Earl said. "I wouldn't say we're exactly familiar with them, though. Leastways, not me. Even though I just spent a day or two digging into them. How about you, Dunk?"

Duncan shook his head.

"Bits and pieces from here and there, that's all," he said. "But I guess you really *are* familiar with them all, Rudy, aren't you?"

The thin-faced German puffed on his pipe and slowly nodded his head. "*Ja.* I have a good working knowledge of most of them, I would say." He looked thoughtful for a moment. "It is a shame we cannot get into the Vatican Library in Rome," he said.

"Oh?"

"*Ja.* They have the largest and finest collection of occult books in the world. *Ach,* such a waste! What I would not give to be able to get into there!"

"The Vatican has occult books?" Guillemette sounded incredulous.

"Oh, yes," Dunk said. "They've been collecting them for centuries. Probably to see what they're up against."

"*Nein.* Not just that," Rudy said, waving his pipe at the blond-headed young man. "There were many bishops and archbishops who had a leaning toward high magic. Do not forget that the main things necessary to study the subject are time, money, and education — knowledge of Latin and Greek, etc."

"Ah, yes! And it was the Church that had all of those, especially the time and the finances," Beth said.

"You say there were bishops and archbishops into this stuff?" Guillemette sounded surprised.

"Cardinal Cusa; Cardinal Cajetan; Bernard de Mirandole, Bishop of Caserta; Udalric de Fronsperg, Bishop of Trent; Nicephorus, Patriarch of Constantinople," Rudolf ticked them off on his fingers. "And not only them, even some of the popes. Pope Leo III, Sylvester II, Honorius III, Urban IV, to mention just a few."

"I'm amazed!" Earl looked around at the others, his eyes wide.

Guillemette chuckled. "I guess I shouldn't really be surprised. I've had my doubts about what goes on in the Vatican for a very long time!"

Earl chuckled too. "Well, there's little chance of you getting into their library, Rudy. Unless you become a priest!"

Beth let out a great sigh. "So, let's get this clear," she said. "If there's unusual weather activity this time—really unusual ... and destructive—then this being the next 'Spoke', as it were, in the Wheel of the Year, our suspicions will be confirmed and we'll know that someone really *is* causing it?"

"Right!"

"And knowing that, what we then need to do is to locate them and stop them."

"A bit more than that," Earl added. "We need to discover their motive. They've been causing billions of dollars worth of damage across the country. Billions! If this keeps on, it'll soon be trillions! Why, for God's sake? What have they got against all the people who've suffered, and the hundreds who've died, in the floods and quakes?"

"Bill Highland says all this money it's costing the government could be better spent on the homeless, health care, fighting drugs and crime ... you name it. But there are also side issues developing," Dunk said.

"Side issues?"

He nodded. "Apparently the severe weather—the storms, snow, floods, etc.—has been adversely affecting wildlife. Not just endangered species, though that's bad in itself, but all sorts and varieties of animals, including huge herds of wild moose and elk. From golden eagles and bluebirds to cardinals and hummingbirds, many seem completely disoriented, and all sorts are actually migrating out of season. Thousands of creatures have suddenly changed their behavior patterns through confusion with the weather. It's becoming a very real problem. Thousands of head of meat and dairy cattle are affected also, which in turn affects the economy."

They sat quietly absorbing all this news, until Earl finally broke the silence.

"A professor at the University of Illinois has suggested that the eruption of Mount Pinatubo, in the Philippines in 1991, is to blame for the weather," he said.

"It is true that such an eruption can create radiation variations in the atmosphere which will trigger severe climate anomalies for many years," Rudy said. "But that does not address the question of dates; the too-neat six-week intervals between catastrophes."

"I hear a bunch of religious fanatics have gathered on Mount Shasta, in northern California," Beth added. "They say the end of the world is at hand."

"Funny!" Guillemette laughed, "That's the exact headline I saw on one of those terrible tabloid newspapers in the Seven-Eleven down the street."

"*Ja*, well, that is the sort of thing that can promote panic, not just among religious fanatics," Rudy said, his face serious. "People can take just so much in the way of disasters, but when they keep on, and on, and on … well, there are bound to be people who crack."

22

The four men left the clubhouse and reached the first green early in the morning. What had started out the previous week as a friendly game of golf had developed into a hard-fought, bitter competition between the two pairs. Nothing would satisfy the losers but a return match the following week. Now they stood silently on the green as the first man teed off.

They had all eschewed caddies and rode two electric golfcarts, piloting them with grim-faced determination from green to green as the game progressed.

By the time they reached the fifth green, the sky had clouded over. It happened suddenly, without their noticing. What had started as a bright, sunny summer's morning suddenly became a cold, dark, and windy day. Thunder rumbled in the distance.

"Damn weather's against us," said one of the men.

"Forget it!" said another, concentrating on his putt. "Nothing's going to stop me today."

"Me neither," agreed another.

Their actions suited their words as rain started to fall. Ignoring the downpour, they carried on with their game.

By the seventh green they could hardly see fifteen feet, for the pouring rain.

"Goddamn it! We'll have to sit it out!"

The men climbed into their respective golf carts and sat, silently and miserably waiting for the storm to pass.

With a tremendous crash that left an acrid smell in the air, a gigantic bolt of lightning hurtled down and split the leading golfcart in half. Its shock tossed the second cart aside like a child's toy. The four men— brother golfers—were scattered about, their dead bodies at grotesque angles amidst a welter of golf clubs, bags, and shards from the carts.

Lake Winnepesaukee, in the middle of the Lakes region of New Hampshire, was calm and placid as a father backed his pick-up truck to the slipway. His son was out of the cab, at the side, waving him back.

"Okay, Dad! Hold it!"

The son climbed up on the trailer arm and flipped the catch releasing the winch. The sixteen-foot boat slid down and into the water. Within ten minutes the truck and trailer were parked off to one side and father and son were safely ensconced in the fishing boat.

"Stow the beer cooler where we can grab it easily, and tuck the food cooler up for'ard."

"Aye, aye, dad!" The fair-haired boy in the cut-off denims did as he was told. "You got the bait?"

His father grunted and busied himself setting out the fishing poles.

"Okay, son. Fire up that Evinrude and let's get on with it. Time's a-wastin'."

The boat left a small wake on the clear surface of the water as it slid out from the dock at Weirs Beach and headed for the middle of the seventy-two-acre lake.

"Just keep it at half throttle," the father said. "We'll enjoy the ride out."

They waved to the few other vessels out so early and both contemplated the day's enjoyment that lay ahead.

"Forecast was good," the boy said, breaking a long silence.

"Uhuh!"

It took nearly half an hour to reach their favorite spot. There they cut the engine and dropped a sea-anchor. The lake was deep.

It was over an hour later that they noticed the sudden choppiness of the water. Glancing up, they were surprised to see that the sky had become overcast. The boat tugged at its lines as the wind increased.

"Weatherman never said anything 'bout this," said the boy, looking uneasily at his father.

The man studied the water and then the sky.

"Best pull in the anchor," he said. "Them waves are getting up. Best play it safe and head in a spell."

But before they could even get up the anchor the waves had increased to three or four feet in height. The father was worried. He lunged forward and cut the line, freeing the boat so that it spun around in the churning water.

"Get that engine goin', son," he shouted over the sound of the wind. "Let's kick butt and get the hell out of here!"

The old Evinrude started immediately and the son tried to turn the boat for shore. A line of waves hit the side and the boat almost tipped, taking on water.

"Head her into the wind!" screamed the father. "We'll make for one of the islands if we can."

But they couldn't. The waves were increasing in size by the second. One huge wave hit the bow of the boat just as it dipped. It was too powerful, and the boat couldn't pull up again. Suddenly it was full of water.

"Grab your life-vest!" shouted the father, mentally cursing himself for not having insisted on wearing them from the start.

Another great wave hit the boat and it turned turtle; flipping completely over. Two figures bobbed in the water for a short period, then disappeared.

■

23

"A tornado touched down at Goreham, in southwestern Illinois," Bill Highland said. "On the banks of the Mississippi. Winds were estimated in the region of 350 miles an hour. The tornado charged into Indiana across more than two hundred miles. It completely destroyed a school full of children, an old folk's home, three trailer parks, two whole towns, and a hospital. Early estimates are of 1300 killed and 800 injured."

"My God!" Beth's face was white.

The Committee members sat in the senator's office, getting the official report on the storm which had hit in the early hours of that morning.

"We had the disaster dates and general details of the weather before," Earl said, equally pale, "but we didn't have the death and injured figures. This really brings it home as to what's going on and how bad it is."

"You've heard nothing yet," Bill said, his face drawn.

"Give it to us, Bill," Dunk said. "We do need to have this detailed."

The others nodded.

"Most tornadoes hit between noon and sunset," Bill continued. "These didn't. They hit in the early morning. Another group of tornadoes—about twenty of them—hit Virginia and North Carolina at about the same time as the one I just mentioned. These ripped across about 180 miles of country, killing at least 1200 people and leaving thousands homeless. Another group of about thirty tornadoes hit from Louisiana to Georgia, killing over 600 people—120 in one town alone."

"I didn't know tornadoes went in bunches," Guillemette said.

"Oh, yes. Back in the 1880s there was the 'Great Southern Outbreak', starting in Mississippi, with a batch of sixty tornadoes, and as recently as 1965 there was a batch of fifty-one of them in eastern Iowa and extending over six states."

"What is the force of these things?" Rudolf asked. "How do you measure them? Strictly by miles per hour of the winds?"

"We have what we call the Fujita scale," Bill replied. "It was dreamed up in the sixties by a Japanese physics professor. It puts the tornadoes into six categories, from F0 to F5. You might call the F0 very weak, with wind speeds of forty to seventy-two miles an hour. The F5 is deemed 'incredible'. Its wind speeds are anything from 261 to 318 miles an hour. That's the one that will blow a piece of straw through a tree trunk!"

"But didn't you just say that this morning's Illinois one was 350 miles an hour?" Duncan asked.

"Uhuh!" The senator nodded. "What comes above 'incredible', I wonder?"

"Anything else to report?" Earl asked.

"Oh, yes. We've only begun," Highland said. "Lightning strikes, with deaths—a honeymoon couple in Ohio and four golfers down south who were blasted out of their golf-carts; massive floods along the Missouri and Mississippi rivers; drownings—including three in Lake Michigan and a father and son out fishing in New England; blizzards, snowstorms even ... you name it, we had it! Total deaths estimated at close to five thousand, property damage in the multi-billions of dollars—again! Lightning started a fire in Chicago that almost rivalled the old Great Chicago Fire of 1871. I tell you, Mrs. O'Leary's cow had nothing on this one! A series of lightning strikes stretched the fire departments past their limits. This time it was in the northwest, away from the lake, but the winds fanned the flames till whole city blocks were raging. It's estimated nine thousand buildings were destroyed and about twelve thousand badly damaged. Cost? Again in the billions, if not trillions!"

"I've got a feeling you're saving the worst for last," Duncan said, running his hands repeatedly through his hair. "Let's have it, Bill."

The senator pushed aside the piles of papers and computer print-outs that he'd been referring to and picked up a sheet of paper that they could all see was boldly labeled TOP SECRET.

"In terms of lives lost this is minor," he said. "But in terms of importance to our nation, well—it's kind of up there, believe me."

They all listened intently.

"Are you familiar with Cheyenne Mountain?" Bill asked.

All but Earl looked blank. "Isn't that the one in Colorado?" he asked.

"Right! Outside Colorado Springs."

"It's some sort of humungous facility carved right into the mountain itself, isn't it?" Earl said. "I don't know the details, but it's something to do with space defense or something?"

"It's the United States Space Command Head-quarters, Space Defence Operations Center." Bill nod-ded. "Yes, it's what might be termed one of the seven wonders of the modern world. It took three years of continuous blasting to hollow out the granite innards of Cheyenne Mountain, and then another two years to build the compound. There's a four-and-a-half acre complex of underground buildings and passageways with an exterior forest of antennas pulling in signals from all around the globe. There's SPACECOM there. That includes NORAD."

"NORAD?" Guillemette looked puzzled.

"North American Aerospace Defense Command," Earl said.

"Oh!"

"There's the most massive array of computing power in the free world contained inside that moun-tain," Bill said. "All vital to our space defense."

"And … ?" Dunk's face was tense.

"And an incredible lightning storm has virtually wiped out the entire field of antennas, has caused the twenty-five ton steel doors to malfunction, sealing everyone inside and, relevant to that, has destroyed the life-support system. There are people inside the moun-tain—hundreds of them—who are suffocating!"

24

Except for the greater width and excellent maintenance of its surface, the road up to Cheyenne Mountain looked much like any other mountain road in the area. The mountain itself was unexceptional—until one got close.

"My God!"

Earl spoke for all three of them as the Jeep Wagoneer turned a corner and finally gave them a view of the upper slope. It looked as though a giant hand had sliced off a section of the mountain's surface from the southern face and replaced it with gargantuan doors painted to resemble the granite of the mountain itself. These doors now stood slightly apart, the gap between them marking a black, straight-line crack down the side of the mound.

They stopped at the doors to show their IDs, provided by the senator before they left Washington. They were then permitted to drive into the cavernous interior and follow the signs to the underground parking facility.

"This place was designed to ride out any nuclear explosion," Bill Highland said, shifting gears. "The whole humungous thing—the entire laticework of fif-teen underground buildings—is floating on a sprung bed of 1300 heavy steel springs, to absorb impact. They've got enough food, water, and power to keep everyone alive for a month, locked in here, should they have to."

"So what happened?" Duncan asked. He was sit-ting in front with the senator. Earl was in the back of the vehicle.

"First report was that the whole life-support sys-tem was down," Bill replied. "It's ridiculous that some-thing designed to withstand a nuclear attack could be put out of commission by a lightning storm. But that's what happened. Thank God the technicians were able to bring the system back on-line in a very short time. Now I want to find out why it happened, and if it can happen again." He glanced sideways at Duncan. "I must say I'm still not sure exactly why it's necessary for you two to be here, though."

Dunk pointed ahead to a parking space and turned to the senator.

"It's the same reason for a psychic wanting to hold a piece of clothing, or something which belonged to a missing person."

"It's a contact," Earl said.

"Right!" Dunk nodded. "By coming here we make contact with something that's been dramatically affected by the storms. Whether it will actually help us hone in on the perpetrators or not, I don't know. But it's worth a try."

They got out of the vehicle and were checked into the facility by a stern-faced marine sergeant, who detailed two men as an armed escort for them.

Heavy steel doors slowly moved apart to allow them into an elevator. They descended what seemed like several floors and then transferred to a moving walkway that took them into what turned out to be the nerve center of the mountain.

"Where, exactly, are we headed?" Earl asked.

"I've been here a couple of times before—though not recently," Bill replied. "We're on our way to what's known as the 'Crow's Nest'. It's the room overlooking the huge SPACECOM computer room. In the Crow's Nest, the Commander-in-Chief has all information at his fingertips: all the information on the technicians' monitors, and that on the large projection screens that you'll see dominating SPADOC."

"Who's the Commander-in-Chief?" Duncan asked.

The senator turned to one of the escorts.

"Marine?"

"General Briggs Packard, sir," he said. "With Major General Prestwood as Chief of Staff."

"General Packard's a four-star general, if I'm not mistaken?" Bill said.

"Correct, sir. And General Prestwood's a two-star."

"Impressive," Earl murmured.

They arrived at the end of the moving walkway and turned down a corridor to the right. Their two-man escort each slid a card into the slot at the side of the first door they came to and pressed buttons on the console. With a click and an almost imperceptible whir, the metal door slid to one side and they entered an outer chamber. Again the marines activated a security clearance, and again a door slid to one side. The senator led them into a large, busy room, with one huge wall of glass slanted outward to give an uninterrupted view down into the cavernous main computer complex.

The rear wall of the room they had entered was covered with a bank of computer monitors, and other monitors were dotted about, with personnel sitting at desks in front of them.

"Welcome to Cheyenne Mountain, Senator."

A large African-American man in the uniform of a four-star general, with six rows of medal ribbons on his chest, advanced on the party and saluted Bill.

"Thank you, General Packard," Bill said, and introduced his friends. The marine detail saluted the general, turned, and left.

"Would you be kind enough to give a quick overview of what goes on here, General, to bring the Committee up to date?" Bill asked.

"Of course." General Packard led them forward so that they could see down into the main room. "This is probably as formidable a concentration of computers and computer power as you are likely to find anywhere in the world. Maybe not quite as up-to-the-minute as the National Security Agency's, but far outweighing them in terms of sheer size and bulk."

"What is this information, and where is it coming from, sir?" Duncan asked.

"Everywhere!" The general chuckled. "Or so it seems. We're linked into satellites that are gleaning information from U.S. nuclear subs tracking Russian subs—they can transmit underwater by way of ultralow-frequency radios. And we receive directly, by over-the-horizon radar, from Ballistic Missile Early Warning Systems, aimed at Russia, on the Arctic tundra. Teal Sapphire, an infrared launch detection satellite 23,000 feet above the earth, is keeping watch on missile pads around the world, including the Middle East. We keep track of over fifteen thousand pieces of man-made hardware orbitting the globe. Should any single piece make an unplanned move, change course, do anything strange in the way of maneuvers, then we're right on top of it and can alert the appropriate people."

"And should this all get closed down somehow, then we've got zilch in the way of defense information," Earl muttered darkly.

"And how is this information received, sir?" Duncan asked.

"That's where we've been badly hit by this damn storm," the general replied. "Just off on one side of the mountain we have antennas by the thousand. They bring in the signals from all over the world, coming in by landline, microwave, and satellite. The complex there is heavily guarded and secured. But, of course, we weren't expecting this sort of an 'attack'." He shook his head grimly. "Three of my people —all good men— were killed in that lightning storm."

"I'm sorry to hear that, General," Bill said.

"How are the antennas connected to this inner complex?" Earl asked.

"Fiber-optic cables into the basement." The general shook his head in bewilderment. "As I've said, we're supposed to be able to withstand nuclear attack ... but those damn fiber-optic cables were melted by this lightning blast!"

⚡

The senator and members of the Committee were shown the workings of the Crow's Nest and then the general passed them on to an army major, who took them on a tour of the facility. Three hours later, they finally emerged outside at the parking area.

"But, goddamn it, I've got Press credentials!"

An angry, raised voice greeted them as they emerged from the elevator. They saw a small, wiry man with a red face under thin brown hair waving his wallet at the stoic marine guard and trying vainly to intimidate him. Since the marine sergeant was twice the other man's size, it wasn't working.

"I'm sorry, sir. Press credentials or not, you're not allowed inside these facilities without express permission from SPACECOM."

"Shit, man! We're no longer at war with the Soviet Union, y'know!"

"I must ask you to vacate these premises, sir, or I'll have to have you removed."

The two men stood toe-to-toe for a long moment, until the rumpled little man backed down and turned away, mumbling to himself as he fumbled for a cigarette.

"What about the First Amendment, then? How about Freedom of Information? Shit! I'm paying your fucking wages! I'm a tax-payer ... more or less."

He spotted the trio as they moved across to the Jeep Wagoneer.

"Hey! Yo! What gives? What's going on in there?"
He ran across to the three of them and stood leaning on

the hood of their vehicle, puffing on a Camel. "Can you help me? I'm a journalist, and that goddamn marine punk sees fit to keep me from getting into this fucking mountain and finding out what's going on."

"What do you mean, 'what's going on'?" Bill Highland got into the car with the others and buckled up his seatbelt. He moved to close the door but the newspaperman was too fast, moving forward to hold onto the door and stare at the senator.

"Wait a minute! You're Senator Highland, aren't you? Say, what's going on to bring you here, Senator? What can you tell me?"

"Absolutely nothing," Bill responded. "Now, would you please let go of that door and let me get about my business?"

"Name's Arnie Summers, Senator." He stuck out his hand, which Bill ignored. "You've probably seen my byline on any number of lead stories over the years."

"With which newspaper, Mr. Summers?"

The man grinned. "Contributing journalist to *American People's News*," he said, glossing quickly over the name. "I had a lead that there'd been some severe damage done to this defense facility, Senator. I've flown all the way out here from the East Coast. What can you tell me about it?"

"I've told you … nothing. Now step aside, please."

Arnie kept hold of the door.

"Heard it reported that some people died and that part of the mountain had caved in. That right?"

"No, it's not. Sergeant!" Bill shouted to the marine, who immediately started running in the senator's direction.

The newspaperman quickly let go of the door and stepped back.

"Now there's no need for that, Senator. I'm only doing my job, y'know. So which bit's not true—the people being killed or the mountain falling in?"

Bill slammed the door and started the engine. He let out the clutch and made Arnie Summers jump out of the way as he drove forward and swung off toward the exit.

"The nerve of that guy," Earl said. "Is he typical of the press, Bill?"

"Of the yellow press, pretty much so, yes," the senator replied. "They try to scrape a story wherever they can. And what information they can't get legitimately they're not opposed to making up. Many of them, that is."

"Can't wait to see how he quotes you in next weekend's issue," Duncan said, grinning. Everyone laughed, except the senator.

25

The five Committee members sat on one of the benches alongside the long, narrow reflecting pool between the Lincoln Memorial and the Washington Monument. The sun shone down brightly, warming them. Dunk and Earl had just finished telling the others the details of the Cheyenne Mountain facility.

"I can't even imagine a place like that," Beth said. "It sounds like something out of a Spielberg movie!"

"Can you not imagine the cost of such a facility?" Rudy asked. "Not only to build, but also the cost to run?"

"Astronomical," Earl agreed.

"But, big as it is, this gigantic complex was threatened by the forces of nature!" Dunk found it difficult to put the whole thing into perspective. He looked around at his friends. "Not nuclear attack—not an H-bomb dropping on it—but by natural forces. And guess how much that's going to cost the taxpayer!"

"The thing is," Earl said, *"are* they natural forces? As we've said, we've never known natural forces to pop up on a regular schedule, exactly six weeks apart over the space of nearly a year, and only in the United States."

They all murmured in agreement.

"So what do you think, my man?" Guillemette asked of Duncan. "What's the reason here?"

Looking to Rudolf for confirmation, Dunk tried to summarize the conclusions they had reached.

"These are natural forces, yes. There's no doubt about that—and we felt that, at Cheyenne Mountain. The energy in the air, throughout the whole complex, was almost tangible. But by 'natural forces' I mean it's not artificial lightning, or wind. Water is not being somehow 'manufactured' and released. What is unnatural is that everything's on such a large scale, affecting such an incredibly wide area."

"The whole damn United States," Earl added darkly.

"Right!" Dunk spoke slowly, thinking it through as he talked. "So the question is, rather, who or what's controlling these natural forces? We know—from what research we've done on Witches raising storms and the like—that it's not unknown for someone, or groups of someones, to control the forces of nature." He ran his hand through his hair and looked up at the top of the monument. "We also know that for hundreds—no, thousands—of years, people around the world have been coming together on these special dates, to worship and to give thanks, to *raise power ...*" He emphasized the words, again looking around at his friends. "And from this power-raising over so many millenia, these particular dates have become powerful in themselves."

"And people still do come together on these dates," Guillemette said.

"That's right," Beth added. "Wiccan and neo-pagan groups, Druids, feminists, ecologists, Native Americans, and all sorts of primitive societies."

"If I may interject, *mein jung Freund*," Rudy said. "To continue the analogy of the Wheel of the Year, is it not unlike a flywheel effect, with the festivals? As we know, a flywheel is a wheel with a weight on one side of it. As that wheel starts to turn the weight lends energy, spinning it into turns so that the wheel is then driven by that rotating weight. So, I believe, it is with the energies raised for so long on the wheel of the year. Those energies are intensified to the point where they can be used to drive forces, when directed by those with the knowledge to do so."

"I think Rudy's right," Dunk continued. "Someone is drawing on that energy, knowing it to be there at those times, and is directing it to create havoc with the weather systems. They may not be so tremendously powerful of themselves, but they are working in with the festival power—Rudy's flywheel effect—to blend with it and redirect it to serve their own ends. I believe they've got some definite goal in mind. Exactly what that goal is, I don't know. But I think they have a purpose; I think they're probably working toward some particular goal on one of the upcoming dates."

"Do you think it could be one of these pagan groups Beth mentioned?" Earl asked.

"It's possible. Anything seems to be possible." Duncan stretched out his long legs in front of him and gazed into the reflecting pool. "There have been and still are, I'm sure, any number of Satanic groups and would-be black magicians running around. The question is, who—out there—is powerful enough to do this, and on the scale that we've been seeing? And why are they doing it?"

There was silence for a long time as each of them thought through the catalog of disasters they had been shown by Senator Highland.

"Is there any area of the country that's safe?" Beth suddenly asked. "I mean, anywhere that's not had floods or hurricanes, tornadoes, or earthquakes?"

"Why do you ask?" Earl said.

"I just thought that there would be a good place to start looking for these people. They'd surely see to it that they weren't hurt themselves."

"Good thought, Beth." Dunk smiled at her. "But I think there are actually many places, all over the country, that have come through unscathed so far. Far too many to try checking. The disasters have struck in wide areas, yes, but they've also been directed, it seems, at major concentrations of people. Large cities and towns. Scattered across the country, yes, but still leaving plenty of gaps. Good thought, though."

"I had an idea," Earl said. "You know that grungy little newspaperman we bumped into at Cheyenne Mountain?"

"The one from *American People's News?* Yes?" Dunk nodded his blond head. "What about him?"

"Well, I took the trouble to check up on some of the stuff he's written." Earl hunched forward on the seat—looking something like a conspirator, thought Dunk. "He's been writing junk for that garbage-rag for several years, it seems. But recently—in the last six or seven months—his writing has taken a new twist."

"Twist?" Rudy looked perplexed.

"A new angle; a new emphasis," Earl said. "He's become a Doomsday Prophet. He's picked up on these disasters and he's playing them for all he's worth."

"I'm not sure I follow you, Earl," Guillemette said.

"He's playing up 'the end of the world is coming' almost as though he *wants* people to panic. He's reporting on the hurricanes and floods and things, but leading his readers to believe that this is only the beginning— that there's far worse to come."

"Huh! As if he'd know that!" Guillemette snorted.

"But wait a minute!" Duncan sat forward also. "Perhaps he does know that. Earl, I think you might have something."

"But who reads any of that stuff and believes it?"

"You'd be surprised," Earl said. "Most of the people who buy that rag—and it sells millions of copies— do believe it! They honestly believe that just because something's in print it must be true. And they're the people who could panic."

"Do you think he might be in with the group doing all this stuff?" Beth asked breathlessly.

"Not necessarily that," Earl responded. "Though it's possible. No, rather than being one of them I was thinking that he may just have some connection with them, so that he knows when and where they're going to strike. He was the only reporter out at Cheyenne Mountain, don't forget. And perhaps he knows what their final goal is."

"Perhaps he has just worked out these six week intervals, as we have," Rudy suggested.

"No, I don't think he's that smart." Dunk chuckled. "But you may be right, Earl. He may well have some sort of a connection. How can we follow up on this?"

"Well, I was thinking of going down to their office, and having a talk with the man," Earl said. "They're only out on York Avenue, right here in D.C. According to our theory the next 'attack' should be September 21, the autumnal equinox. Let's see if he's aware of that."

"Yes," Dunk agreed. "And whether he's got any idea as to just what's going to happen and where."

26

Bill Highland sat in his office grimly considering the bulging folder in front of him. It was bursting at the seams. It contained reports, memos, computer print-outs, and newspaper and magazine clippings. Every few weeks, as another natural disaster came, so also came a deluge of reports on wildlife disruptions.

The swallows had not returned to Capistrano, California; the buzzards had not returned to Hinkley, Ohio; the salmon were not spawning; the spotted owl had not been seen anywhere in Washington or Oregon for months; Canada geese were in all the wrong places … it was never-ending.

Now he was starting to get rude letters from hunters. Apparently the deer had all but disappeared from their usual haunts, but were appearing, and causing problems, in areas where they had never been previously. The NRA lobby had been trying to get to him, as had the Wildlife Federation, the Save the American Buffalo people, the Spread the Wolves crusaders and every other special interest group, small and large, that was concerned about the way their pet animals had been disrupted by the changing weather. As if he could do anything about it.

The senator poured an extra package of sugar into his coffee and stirred it abstractedly. He had every confidence in Duncan Webster and his Committee. Somehow they'd figure out what was going on and put a stop to it, of that he was sure. He tasted the coffee and added another packet of sugar. Dunk had intimated that they had some sort of a lead; something to do with that nasty little man they'd bumped into out in Colorado. He hoped it would truly be a lead and take them somewhere positive.

He looked at the other folder on his desk. He dared not even open it. It contained the reports on escalating costs for the recent catastrophes. Aid to the afflicted was in the multi-billions. Millions were needed for the Department of Housing and Urban Development, and for the repair of community health centers. Millions more were needed for the Army Corps of Engineers, the National Guard, the Coast Guard, for highway and bridge repairs, restoration of rail services and federal parks, and for stream monitoring. Multi-millions for disaster-related community development. And this was only related to one of the many such disasters over the previous six months. Total costs so far … in the trillions of dollars. How much more could they take? He shook his head, sipped his coffee, and wondered.

27

"You were one of the people out at that mountain fortress, weren't you?"

Earl nodded. He sat with Arnie Summers, having a coffee and doughnut in a little café around the corner from the offices of *American People's News*. He glanced up at the reporter, taking in his stained fingers with their blackened nails, his rumpled clothing, and seemingly uncombed hair. He wondered why anyone would employ a man who had so little regard for his own self-image.

"It's not actually a fortress," Earl said, sipping his coffee. "It's just a place for gathering information from around the world, stuff coming in on satellites."

Arnie's head bobbed up and down. "Yeh! I know all about that. But if it's so goddamn innocent, why the high security? Why wouldn't they let me in to ask any questions? What are they trying to hide?"

"I don't think they're trying to hide anything. They had some outages, due to that big electrical storm, and were busy repairing their antennas, that's all."

The newspaperman snorted. "Hrmph! I don't believe that one, even if you do. No, I heard that there'd been a big cave-in and dozens of people had been killed."

"Where did you hear that?" Earl asked, innocently.

Arnie airily waved a hand. "Around! It's not important. The thing is, they were being super secretive, so there must be a reason."

"Your sources didn't give you any clue?" Earl bit into a doughnut, trying to appear nonchalant.

"They never do." Arnie also bit into a doughnut, the powdered sugar exploding and liberally sprinkling his shirtfront.

"Oh! So you've received information on this sort of thing before?" Earl pursued.

"Of course! A reporter—a good reporter—has to have eyes and ears everywhere, y'know."

"Then you can hear of what's going to happen before it actually does happen?" Earl tried to make it sound like an innocent question as he picked up his coffee cup and looked at the reporter.

Arnie seemed caught up in his own importance and cleverness.

"You'd be surprised if you knew just half of what I get to know." He gave Earl a broad wink. "The inside scoop! That's what keeps me at the top in my profession."

Earl thought of the *American People's News* and where it rated among top news-reporting journals. He suppressed a smile.

"You certainly seem to have been on top of most of the news stories about this freak weather we've been experiencing," he said.

"Of course!" Arnie preened himself and made a half-hearted attempt at brushing sugar from his shirtfront.

"Another doughnut?" Earl asked. He signalled the waitress. "I've certainly been most impressed with your reporting on all these terrible catastrophes over the last several months, Arnie—may I call you Arnie?"

"You've been following me, then?" The reporter grinned broadly. "Ah, yes! I've been on the ball all right. Had to be."

"What d'you mean?"

"Well, like, it's been worth my while—know what I mean?" He gave Earl a broad wink and rubbed his thumb and first finger together. He gratefully accepted another doughnut from the waitress, sank his teeth into it, and grunted at her to refill his coffee cup.

"Oh!" Earl tried to sound surprised. "You mean, you get paid for putting out these stories?"

"And we're not talking paid by the paper," Arnie said, darkly. "Shit! I'd starve to death if I just had to depend on those bastards."

"I'm sure." Earl chuckled conspiratorially. "They pay well, I imagine; your sources?"

Arnie nodded, his mouth again full of doughnut. "And in American dollars," he finally said. "All I have to do is keep the pressure on."

"Pressure?"

"Shit, man! With all these hurricanes and earthquakes and crap, people are getting the jitters. They're starting to crack. Hey! Did you know that in just the last three months as many people moved out of California as moved in over the past two years?"

"Because of the earthquakes?" Earl asked. "But I always thought they were crazy to live there in the first place. I don't think it's unusual that some of them would now change their minds."

"Huh!" Arnie snorted, blowing crumbs across the table. "This ain't no natural reversal, believe me. And I'm the one who started it."

Earl was silent for a moment. "When's the next one going to happen, Arnie?" he asked.

The reporter opened his mouth to reply then checked himself. He broke into a grin.

"Ah!" He wagged a finger at Earl. "That's where you're going to have to buy my newspaper and read my stories!" He burped loudly then thumped his chest. "And I can tell you—there are some real doosies coming up!"

28

Viale Regina Margherita is a wide, straight avenue running northwest-southeast at right angles across the major Via Nomentana, in the Nomentana quarter of Rome. Two blocks up from Regina Margherita is Via Lazzaro Spallanzani, which borders the garden of the Villa Torlonia. In 1929, the villa became the private residence of Benito Mussolini. Beneath the house and grounds is a vast network of second and third century catacombs, though of the probable five-and-a-half miles of passageways, the vast majority has caved in. In recent years, the property was acquired by the Commune of Rome and opened as a public park, accessible from nine in the morning until dusk.

It was long after dusk, on the night of the new moon, when a number of figures congregated at the south corner of the big house, farthest away from the main roadway. They had all dressed in black, and spoke not a word.

In staggered groups of twos and threes the figures moved quickly and quietly across the manicured lawn to one of the many groupings of trees and rocks scattered about the estate. From there they moved on to a further such rock-strewn copse. Three of the number worked together to move what appeared to be a sizable rock. They swung it on a hidden fulcrum, revealing a dark entranceway into the ground. Within a matter of minutes, the entire group had disappeared underground and the rock had been swung back into position after them.

Incense filled the air and monstrous shadows, cast by the light of flickering candles, danced across the irregular walls of an underground chamber where three passageways came together.

Agara Brachi sat on the ground, facing the wall and wishing she had a rosary with her. But she was naked beneath the flimsy black robe and wore no jewelry of any kind. The admonitions had been strict. She had fasted for three days, taking nothing but black bread and water, and had studied dutifully all that the cardinal had passed on to her.

How they had known her innermost secrets and desires she still did not know, but she had been selected, from the tiny convent in Palestrina on the south slope of Mount Ginestro, to come to Rome and be personally tutored by Patrizio Cardinal Ganganelli, and taken into the Order of the Templars of the Sacred Heart of Belial. For the thirteen male Templars of the order, she knew, there were only three female attendants. It was a great honor to be chosen, though she did wonder what had happened to the previous female whose place she was to take.

This was to be the night of her initiation, and she shivered in delicious anticipation. The chamber they were using was far beyond any open to the public and was, indeed, unknown to the current administrators of the estate. It had been discovered and dedicated in the fifteenth century by followers of the great ceremonial magician Auroelus Philippus Theophrastus Paracelsus Bombast von Hohenheim, better known simply as Paracelsus. At that time, the Templars of the Sacred Heart of Belial (or the "Black Brothers of Belial") had been founded.

Agara had heard rumors of the group for many years—long before her entry into the convent. Mother Superior had insisted that such a group did not exist, and most clergy Agara had questioned agreed. But in her heart of hearts she had always known that they did exist, and that they shared the same exciting feelings and longings that she had. Convent life had always appealed to her; it made her "special," she felt. But to follow the select path of the Templars was even more special—something few could even imagine, let alone experience.

A solid shadow appeared beside her and Agara looked up. She could not make out the face beneath the black cowl, but the head nodded almost imperceptibly. She got to her feet and stood behind the figure, ready to follow it into the central area, which she could now see was bordered by the rest of the cowled figures each facing into the center.

She became aware of a low, mesmerizing chanting that arose from the group. She smelled the sweetness of incense, breathing it in and absorbing it as she would a life-force. A slight sweat broke out under her arms and her throat felt dry. She tried to swallow to relieve the feeling.

"All Hail, Lord!"

A strong, deep voice came from the center of the circle. She recognized it as what she called the "ritual voice" of Cardinal Ganganelli. His normal voice was soft and high, in contrast to the powerful authority of this voice.

"All hail, Lord!" echoed the Templars.

"Ever life unto us all," came from the center.

The circle broke open enough for the figure ahead of her to lead Agara into the ritual area. She followed close behind and felt, rather than saw, the circle close behind her.

Ganganelli stood behind an altar, clothed in a robe of shimmering gold. On his head was a crown of black, red, and gold. In his right hand he held a large, black, Priapic, or phallic-tipped, wand—the head of the wand carved in imitation of a penis. To one side of the altar stood another figure dressed in deep purple and swinging a gold thurible, the smoke of the incense rising from it as it swung. Opposite him she recognized Cardinal della Rovere, in black robes with silver trimmings and wearing a silver and black crown. He held a gold platter of water and an aspergillum: the hyssop branch used for sprinkling holy water. Agara and her guide took their places opposite Ganganelli.

"We stand before the altar of the Lord," sang out Ganganelli.

"The Lord bringing joy to us all!" the others responded.

"Send forth Thy light and Thy truth; they have led me and brought me to Thy temple."

"The Lord giveth joy unto us all!"

"Now may the Lord smile down upon us and be with us, forgiving us our sins and bringing us strength for what is ahead."

"So be it!"

Ganganelli turned to his right and started to walk counterclockwise about the altar. The others, including Agara, also turned and walked about the altar. They circumambulated seven times, returned to their places, and genuflected.

Ganganelli raised both hands and said, "A light shall shine upon us this day, for the Mighty Lord is with us, Ruler in strength and in majesty; His light shining forth."

"So be it!" came the response.

Ganganelli moved forward and kissed the altar three times, then moved around to stand facing Agara. Her leader moved back and was absorbed into the circle of Templars. Ganganelli took Agara's hand and led her slowly around the circle, again counterclockwise, so that she might meet all those assembled. She found herself gazing into many eyes, but the faces were hidden by the depths of the cowls. The eyes that she did meet were uniformly dark and stern, as though judging her.

When they had completed the circle she was led to the center, where della Rovere set down his dish and aspergillum on the altar and then moved toward her. Agara thought she sensed a gleaming in his eyes as he took hold of the top of her robe.

"We bless thee and adore thee, servant of the Lord and of all his followers," he said and he tugged down, ripping the robe from her body and leaving her naked. He again took up the dish and aspergillum and, dipping the latter into the liquid, flicked the saltwater onto her body. She had been prepared for it but still could not suppress a slight shiver as the cold water hit her warm body.

Ganganelli then took her hand and once again led her around the circle for all to see. Back at the altar the tall, black-and-silver clad della Rovere came forward once more. She thought she saw the slightest of smiles touch the corners of his mouth as he moved toward her.

"The Lord grant that our Sacred Grail be ever fruitful," he said, his eyes dropping to her breasts and then lower to her pubic area. "Let her be ever filled with the light of Thy word, a true haven and consecrated receiver ever ready to acknowledge the mystery of Thy Holy Lance."

He asperged her again and then moved closer and bent his head to kiss her breasts. She drew in her breath sharply as he lasciviously ran his tongue over her nipples. Then he took her arm and, on the other side, the figure in purple moved forward to take her other arm. They lifted her effortlessly up onto the altar and she lay back, draping her arms out to the sides and spreading her legs wide.

Agara had been well briefed on what to expect. It was part of her joining with these, her new brothers, and the start of her journey along the Left Hand Path, the path that would bring her all that she desired. She had dreamed of this day; she had yearned for it; she had studied for it. Yet she was trembling as the figure in gold approached and stood between her legs.

"This I do in the name of the Mighty Lord Belial! And of the Unholy Union between the Gods and Man!"

"All glory be to the Lord Belial!" cried the congregation. "So be it!"

"We offer unto Thee, Mighty One, the Chalice of Salvation, the Holy Grail," continued Ganganelli. "In Thy sight may it be opened and filled with the sacred sweetness of the Holy Lance."

Agara could not help flinching at the first touch of the Priapic Wand but consciously relaxed her body to accept all that was demanded of her. Her head was spinning and she seemed to be swept up by a dark cloud from which flashed brilliant splashes of lightning. Thunder seemed to join in the chant that started, and grew, from the people in the subterranean chamber. The wand was withdrawn. Then, one by one, the many figures came to her. Their ritual part enacted, they moved on. It seemed like hours before the last had returned to his place. She could feel the sweat on her body, her genitals felt as though they were on fire, and she ached to be back in her so-familiar cell at the convent.

Yet this was what she had prayed for; this was what she wanted. She had finally found a place in what was almost certainly the most powerful group of people in the world. She had finally been initiated and now was truly "someone special." The ritual continued and she moved on through it as though in a dream.

"*Hosanna in excelsis!*" cried Ganganelli.

"*Deo gratias,*" murmured Agara.

29

Dick Dibell, the president's National Security advisor, hurried into the main presidential Situation Room, located one floor below the Oval Office. It was a small room, spartan by some estimates, and was often decidedly cramped when large attendance was necessary. So much so that, in the late 1980s, a larger facility had been built in the Executive Office Building next door. This—room 208—had been dubbed the Situation Room Support Facility. But today the meeting was small and intimate, and the old Situation Room was adequate. Besides, the president hated the relatively long trip along the subterranean passageways between the basement of the White House and the Executive Office Building.

"Just in time, Dick!"

Dibell spun around to find the president close on his heels, a smile on his face.

They took their seats around the big oak conference table and Dibell looked about him. Chief of Staff Henry "Hank" Tobias was on the president's left and Michael Swaine, Secretary of State, on his right. Senators Highland, O'Cork, and Menendez were there, as was Gerry Fields, Press Secretary. Altogether there were over a dozen people in the small room.

"Senator, let's have it," said the president, turning to Bill Highland.

"Yes, Mr. President."

Bill Highland looked around at all the serious faces.

"As you all know, we've been suffering catastrophe after catastrophe for many months now. We're used to having floods and hurricanes. Earthquakes, of course; tornadoes and the like. But not so many, not so severe, and not hitting on a regular basis, one after another. Pictures, please!"

The lights lowered and a large rear-projection screen came alive. Chair legs scraped as people settled to get a better view. Bill led them through a series of colored still photographs, showing storm damage ranging from earthquakes in the West, through floods and tornadoes in the Midwest, to hurricanes in the South and storms in the East. The reaction was a continuous murmur of surprise and shock.

"We budget for these things, as you all know," Bill continued. "But we only expect to have to stretch that budget so far, for 'normal' catastrophes."

"What kind of demands have we had on the budget in the last six months?" Gerry Fields asked, as the lights came back up.

"In terms of damages covered? You can estimate costs near a billion for every catastrophic occurrence, on average. With some going way above that."

"And what about the number of lives lost, Bill?" the president asked.

"These are well into the hundreds of thousands, sir."

There was silence for a moment.

"But we're here chiefly because of Cheyenne, aren't we?" It was Truman Spears, Secretary of Defense.

There were murmurs of agreement from around the table.

"Can we see pictures on that, Briggs?" the president asked.

The room darkened again and the screen came alive once more with a video of the damage at the Cheyenne Mountain facility. There were shots of the forest of antennas, as they had been before the storm and of the few that were left afterward.

"This is only the outward sign of the problems," said General Briggs Packard, commander-in-chief for NORAD. "We suffered casualties, though thank God the numbers were low. Most alarming is the fact that we were out of contact with all of our satellites, and other facilities transmitting information, for several hours. If this had been under other national emergency circumstances it could have been disastrous for the security of our country. Unhappily, estimates to repair the damage to the facility and the equipment go into the multi-billions."

"Equipment's one thing, General. What about my people?" It was Frank Menendez. "Florida has been very badly hit in the past. This we know. Hurricane Andrew, a few years ago, did incredible damage. But what we've been suffering lately makes Andrew look like a weak windstorm. We've had hurricane after hurricane. Billions of dollars' worth of personal and business property has been destroyed, thousands of people

have been killed, crops—citrus and farm produce—
have been literally wiped out ... that's something that's
going to affect the food supply for the whole country.
Here's a long-term result—the crops will never recover
this year, or for I don't know how long!"

"Meaning what, exactly?" Dibell asked.

"Meaning that there goes the economy of the state.
Meaning that there goes the livelihood of the people
and, in case you haven't realized it, there go the food
prices for the rest of the nation!" His voice rose.

"Easy, Frank, easy!" said the president. "Yes, we
know. We know only too well. What happens in one
part of the country can have repercussions throughout
the nation. It's a snowball."

"Mr. President?"

"Yes, Pat?" He acknowledged the only woman in
the room, Budget Director Patricia Jackson.

"The bottom line seems to be that we are facing
bills, or a total bill that has got to be paid. But that bill
is already into the trillions of dollars and is still climbing! If this continues, then there go all our other bud-
gets—including defense. This country could very
quickly find itself bankrupt!"

"It could very easily destabilize the nation," said
the Secretary of State. "This is a serious problem. As
serious a one as we've ever had to face, and that
includes past decisions of going to war."

"I thought my colleague, here, had someone working on all of this?" Senator O'Cork looked questioningly
at Bill Highland. "Won't you share with the president
what you have discovered so far, Mr. Highland?"

Bill squirmed in his chair.

"Of course," he said. "Of course. Actually there's not a great deal I can tell you … yet. Nothing that answers any real questions. But … " he raised his voice as he heard a few murmurings from the others.

"Give him a chance, now," the president said. "Let's take this one step at a time. What have your boys found out, Bill?"

The senator tried to get comfortable in his chair, though he knew any comfort wouldn't last long, not once he tried to explain what he had to explain.

"My Committee has found out one or two things, some of which you may have difficulty accepting, but I ask you to bear with me." He swallowed, then continued. "First of all, we believe that all of these disasters have been caused — brought about — initiated — by human means."

"What?"

"What do you mean?"

He held up his hand for silence.

"I asked you to bear with me for a moment. Yes, all these storms of various types have been brought about by human means. They are natural phenomena, of course, but it's just a question of how they were sparked. And we believe they were sparked by a person or persons, as yet unknown, who are deliberately trying to bring the United States to its knees."

"Well they've damn near done that all right," muttered Dibell.

"Further," Bill Highland continued, "we believe that these people are operating from a foreign country, though as yet we're not sure which one."

"I guess we can't automatically blame the Russians this time," the president remarked. "Assuming for the moment—and I'm not saying I accept it, yet—that someone *is* causing these catastrophes, Bill. Why do you think it's a foreign power?"

"We've made contact with someone in their pay, Mr. President. He let slip that he was being paid and said he was pleased that it was in American dollars, implying that he'd half expected to be paid in some other form of currency."

"Can't we bring him in and make him talk?" Spears demanded.

"On what charge?" Hank Tobias asked. "Presumably he hasn't done anything illegal, yet? Has he, Senator?"

Bill shook his head. "No, he's clean. But we—the people on my Committee—do believe that he may be the key. They do think that they may be able to zero in on the real culprits through this man."

"Well, let's hope they can do so before we go for broke," the president said.

There were murmurs of agreement.

30

"It's just a question of listing everyone we can think of who's working the Left Hand Path," Duncan said. "Then, from there, we can narrow down to the people we think might have the power to do this sort of stuff."

"What do you mean by 'working the Left Hand Path', Dunk?" Beth asked. "I've heard the term before, but I'm not sure what it is."

"They're the bad guys," Earl said, looking up from where he sat at a small table, scribbling on a sheet of yellow paper.

"Earl's right," Dunk said, "putting it into the vernacular. They're the ones who work negative, or 'black', magic, as opposed to positive, or 'white', magic. Nothing to do with race, of course. They're magicians who are only interested in their own enrichment, even if it's at the expense of everyone else. And, especially, they're the Satanists; the worshippers of the powers of evil."

"We, on the other hand, *meine Leibling*, follow the Right Hand Path," Rudolf said, smiling at the redhead. He sat beside Earl and was also writing on a yellow

145

pad. "We are the Champions of the Light, and they are of the Darkness."

"The forces of Good and Evil," Beth murmured. "That's what I thought. So how do we make a list? I certainly don't know anyone who falls into that category."

"I can think of one or two," Guillemette said. "Down in the islands there are a lot of *Bokos*, though why any of them might try to bankrupt the U.S. I don't know."

"Don't worry about motive right now," Duncan said. "Let's just get the list together of everyone we can think of who works magic negatively. Then we can narrow it down to those with the power and those with a motive."

"But it may be someone we've never even heard of," Earl protested. "Between us I'm sure we can come up with a lot of names—we've all kept up with occult matters around the world for a few years now—but we obviously don't know everyone who's into the Black, let alone who's got a grudge against Uncle Sam. Let's face it, they're the types who really try to keep out of the limelight."

"It's a start," Duncan said, lamely. "We have to start somewhere. At least we know that it *is* a 'someone', and can try to pinpoint them. We'll just have to hope we can get lucky. If we draw up a list, then narrow it down, we can start checking on these people astrally, and who knows … if it's not them, perhaps they'll lead us to the culprits."

"As you say, it's all we can do," murmured Guillemette.

"Dunk, what was the name of that Canadian we heard about back in the early '80s?" Earl asked, pushing his spectacles up on his nose. "You remember, we came across an ad he was running in the occult press, offering to initiate young women and girls for a large fee? Claimed he was part of the *Illuminata*, but was really into sex magic."

"Oh, yes. Wasn't it Milburn or something?"

"Melbourne! That's it. Rex Melbourne. He's on my list!"

"But I thought he got killed in an auto accident the year after we exposed him?"

Earl scratched out the name he'd written, muttering darkly.

"Do any of you know who was the source of the psychic attacks on Prime Minister Thatcher, at the time of the Falklands fiasco?" Rudolf asked.

"Good point!" Dunk said. "I don't know if they ever did find who was responsible, but I know the poor woman suffered tremendous headaches and lack of sleep because of it. They say she lost thirty pounds."

"I never heard anything about that." Beth looked surprised.

"No. They kept it out of the newspapers," Earl said.

Beth shook her head. "I don't know! You guys seem to really be in the know about these things."

"Which is why I think we may be able to come up with some interesting names, if we put our minds to it," Dunk said. "Rudy, now that I think about it, didn't the French psychics finally suspect that group in Sweden and work against them?"

The old German thought long and hard, slowly beginning to nod his head. *"Ja!* You are right, *mein Freund.* They did not really prove that the Swedish group was responsible but, as soon as they focused their energies on them, the attacks came to an end."

"Might be worth checking them out," Earl said, his brow wrinkled. "Think we could track them down?"

"Possibly. Going astrally by way of the French," Dunk said thoughtfully. "I've been thinking of Etienne Macé recently anyway. Perhaps I'll give him an astral call. And I have to make contact with my old Gypsy friend, Reg Lee, in England, and find out what he knows."

They worked steadily for most of the afternoon.

Duncan's suite made an excellent headquarters, with plenty of room for them all to spread out and be comfortable. In mid-afternoon, Earl called room service and had coffee sent up. By early evening they all felt drained, but had compiled a long list and whittled it down to no more than a dozen names.

"All right," Duncan said. "I suggest we take a break and get some dinner. We can get back together here at, say, eight or eight-thirty to start checking. Beth, I'd like you to get your E.S.P. pot boiling and see if you can hone in on them. Guillemette, you do the same with skrying. You do have your crystal ball with you, I take it?"

"Wouldn't go anywhere without it, my man!"

"Good. Rudy—you, me, and Earl will go out on the astral. We'll break the list down into three, and that way we can get to them all tonight. We'll consolidate our notes when we get back."

31

Beth settled herself comfortably in the big armchair, her feet flat on the floor, her hands loose in her lap, and closed her eyes. She breathed in and out deeply and slowly, by stages relaxing her whole body. Then, as she continued the deep breathing, she imagined energy flowing up from the ground deep down beneath the hotel. She felt the energies of the earth, far below, as they surged upward through the structure of the building, into the floor where she sat. She felt them entering her body through her feet, moving up to fill her body with every breath she drew in. As she exhaled, she sensed the negativity leaving her body, the tiredness easing out and dissipating. She breathed in the positive energies of the earth and breathed out the negativity.

She saw the energy flowing in as a bright, blue-white light. Soon she could "see" her whole body filled with the light. Then she concentrated on expanding that image, until the light encased her in a brilliant globe: a ball of positive protection. This, she had been taught by Duncan, was the way to start all metaphysical exercises. This would ensure that no negative forces of any sort would be able to invade her or even be attracted to her.

When Beth was finally satisfied that her preliminary work was done, she tentatively sent out her mind to make contact with the first name on her list. She knew that the person lived in Vermont, and so focused for a moment on that part of the country. Then she gradually brought her focus down to the actual name, finally excluding all else from her thoughts.

"Otto Downsfend," she thought. "Otto Downsfend … Otto Downsfend … " She repeated the name over and over in her mind.

Otto Downsfend lived alone in a log cabin in the middle of Vermont. Beth could sense both the man and his surroundings. She somehow knew that there was no living being within five miles of his home. She could also sense that he was not a happy man. Far from it; he was in a rage. She picked up that he had been in a long and drawn-out argument with the local sheriff over fishing rights. Otto had been fishing illegally and threatened with arrest.

With a little gasp, Beth realised that Otto was working magic against the lawman. He was making a poppet—a cloth doll representing the sheriff—and was about to stick it with long, sharp spikes cut from a wild blackthorn. She could feel the anger and the palpable evil that pervaded the whole cabin where Otto worked his spell. For not only did Otto cast his spell, but he called upon the darkest forces of evil to join with him in punishing the man he wished to harm. With a shudder, Beth broke contact.

Guillemette sat cross-legged on the floor and followed much the same preliminary relaxation and protection discipline that Beth had gone through. She
cradled a large, black, obsidian crystal in her lap as she
closed her eyes and erected her psychic defenses.
When she was ready, she came to focus on her purpose. She concentrated on the name she was to check
and slowly opened her eyes, bringing them to bear on
the obsidian orb.

Her back was to the low light in the room, and
there was nothing around to distract her eyes; the orb
itself sat on a circle of black velvet held in her hands.

The globe seemed to be a living thing, its shape
and depth lost in a gentle pulsation of energy that
throbbed in her hands. It was impossible to see into the
solid blackness of the orb, and yet she gazed at its very
center. It was as though she were being drawn down
into the globe, as a movie camera slowly and inex-
orably zooms forward, bringing its subject into sharp
detail from a start far distances away.

There was the man, Carlton Marshall, a real estate
broker who specialized in old buildings. He stood in
the center of a huge, bare room that must have been
sixty feet long. Down the center was a colonnade of
three wooden pillars rising to the high, vaulted ceiling.
The walls were wainscoted. A scattering of mounted
animal heads decorated the otherwise bare walls above
the high paneling. They were mostly deer, elk, moose,
and caribou. The room was dark, its only light coming

from behind the heavy drapery hung on mullioned, leaded windows on the far end wall.

Guillemette watched as Marshall started to walk around the edge of the room. He paused at a large alcove and ran his hand over the intricate fretwork of the surround. Then he continued on to the French windows at the far end of the room, the source of the light which filtered in. He turned to look back at the room, as though appraising it. Then, as though making up his mind, he marched down the full length of the room and out the Norman door at the far end.

Guillemette followed him down a long, dark hallway and finally out to the circular driveway that prefaced the big, Gothic-revival house. She watched him take a real-estate FOR SALE sign from the trunk of a car parked there and hammer it into the ground near the high wrought-iron fence that encircled the property.

When Marshall drove back to his office and started going through listings, Guillemette gave up on him and pulled back from the crystal. She would return to him later, after checking the others on her list. Closing her eyes again, she broke the contact, allowed her mind to settle back, and centered herself on visions of her original home in Haiti. Smiling at remembrances of Voudoun rites and hounfors—the Voudoun churches—she then brought her focus back to the next name on her list, and once again opened her eyes.

Across the room from Beth and Guillemette, Duncan lay on the bed; Rudolf stretched out on a rose-and-gold, silk-covered Chippendale sofa; and Earl rested on the floor on a thick, pliant Persian rug. The room was quiet and dimly lit. All three were entering states of self-hypnosis preparatory to astral projection.

Duncan had done his introductory psychic-defense-building and now felt himself slipping down into unconsciousness. Almost immediately he experienced the slight shuddering he had come to associate with astrally extricating himself from his physical body. With a sudden release, and the sensation of a remote "wooshing," he slipped up out of the position of his third eye and found himself—his invisible, astral double—floating up near the ceiling. He looked down on his friends below, seeing them as though there were full light in the room. He saw his own physical shell lying on the bed—always a strange sensation. Then he saw Earl's astral shape suddenly separate and, with a casual wave, disappear up through the ceiling. He guessed that Rudolf had long since departed, being the experienced practitioner that he was.

With a last glance at Beth, and blowing her an astral kiss, Dunk soared up effortlessly through the levels of the hotel and emerged in the night sky above.

He hovered for a moment, as always completely fascinated by the view of the myriad stars (which seemed unnaturally bright in his altered state), and thought to clothe himself in an astral jogging outfit, rather than float around in the nude. Not that it mattered one iota, he knew, but somehow it made him more comfortable.

The first name on Duncan's list was a woman who lived in Ireland. No sooner had he thought of her name than he was there beside her.

Late evening in Washington D.C. was the very early morning hours in western Europe. Dunk was surprised to find that Clodagh Byrne was far from sound asleep. She stood in the center of an ancient, ruined building. He guessed it had once been a small church, many centuries before. He squatted down on a pile of tumbled granite blocks and watched her. There was no need to sit; in his present state he could as well have hung suspended in space, as it were, yet he found old habits died hard. It just seemed natural to sit, so he did.

Clodagh Byrne seemed to be in the middle of a ritual. Dunk could see fine blue lines of light marking three concentric circles around where she stood. The consecration she had obviously done was responsible for the twinkling blue light he was able to see in his astral state. Seven black candles burned at intervals about the circles. The woman was alone, which surprised him. He had understood that she usually worked with a group—what she termed her "Scarlet Sisters," better known to others as the "Sisters of Satan." She was dressed in a flowing crimson robe and carried a silver drinking horn, which she held high before her as she circumambulated in a widdershins, or counterclockwise, pattern.

Going to the center of the circle, Clodagh spilled some of the contents of the horn onto the ground. It was a dark red liquid. She then brought it to her lips and drained the horn. Suddenly she spun around and flung the silver cup as far as she could from her. As it passed through the glittering light of the consecrated circles, Dunk saw a crackling flash, like static electricity. He had no idea what the Irish woman was doing; it was a rite with which he was totally unfamiliar, and he watched in fascination.

She raised her hands high and started a soft wailing keen in the ancient Irish tongue. Then, as she sang, she started to move once again widdershins about the circle, lowering her arms and moving faster and faster. As her speed increased, so did the volume of her lament, until she seemed to be screaming at the top of her lungs as she raced about the sacred space.

Suddenly she stopped dead and dropped to the ground. An eerie silence filled the area. Duncan felt chilled; he was glad he had envisioned the jogging suit.

He shook himself. What was he thinking of? He should not be feeling cold on the astral plane! Whether or not he wore clothing would not affect his astral body temperature! With a gasp he realized that the only way he would feel such a drop in temperature would be in the presence of evil.

No sooner had he realized it than Duncan became aware of a shape materializing in the center of the circle, where Clodagh had spilled the blood—and he was now certain it was blood that had been contained in the drinking horn. Dunk quickly dropped down behind the pile of rocks so that whoever, or whatever, was appearing could not see him.

In a matter of moments, a frightening, squat, bestial figure had materialized and stood, arms crossed on its thick chest, glaring down at the crouching woman.

Small goat-like horns sprang from the forehead of the creature and a grey-black, spiked beard stuck out from its chin. Its eyes gleamed bright red and its flesh was dark brown in color. It was naked, and from its matted hair-covered torso an erect phallus thrust out and up. Duncan almost expected to see a tail and cloven hooves, but neither were in evidence. The feet were human in shape, though covered with coarse, dark hair. A fearsome roar came from the figure, and Dunk wondered that it seemed not to affect the crouching woman.

"For what reason dare you disturb my rest?"

The words seemed to ring about the dark ruins, without actually being said by the creature. Certainly its lips had not moved, thought Duncan.

Clodagh Byrne seemed to take a deep breath, then come slowly to her feet. She, too, folded her arms across her breast and stood with feet planted firmly apart.

"I ordered you here!" she suddenly snarled, glaring directly at the figure.

Immediately there was a change in the creature. It seemed to lose its assertiveness and, dropping its arms, almost cringed.

"I await your orders," came the unuttered response.

"That's better!" said the robed woman. "Listen carefully, and follow my orders. You are to appear in the dreams of Molan Walsh. You are to be a nightmare to him. He has dared to reject me as a lover! I told him he would pay for that. You will be my tool to wreak vegeance on him! No man spurns Clodagh Byrne! No man!"

Duncan gave a sigh of relief and slid further down out of sight. A woman with the power to conjure up demons, albeit minor ones — but who was engrossed in tormenting lovers who had spurned her — was unlikely to be bent on breaking the United States of America. It was possible, certainly, but unlikely. He would keep her on his list for further scrutiny, but for now would pass on to others.

Leaving Clodagh Byrne and her demon to their plans, Duncan concentrated his thoughts on the next name on the list and immediately found himself in Switzerland.

32

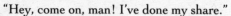

"Hey, come on, man! I've done my share."

Arnie's voice took on a pleading tone and he clenched the telephone tightly. He glanced about him, as much out of habit as any real fear that he was being overheard. He stood at a pay phone outside a convenience store and dragged hard on a Camel cigarette.

"No I'm not squeamish!" he snorted. "I can stomach anything you care to throw my way. Ask anyone. No, it's ... well, for one thing that fuckin' MacKay is getting on my case. Says enough already on the doomsday stuff."

The voice on the other end spoke slowly and forcefully. Arnie listened.

"Yeh, sure! Yes, I know I'm one cog in your whole damn machinery, but ..."

He listened again.

"Look, I've done a damn fine job! You should come over here and see for yourself ... What? You're going to do just that? Fuck! When?"

He nodded as he listened. He flicked away the cigarette stub and dug into his pocket for another. Slowly a smile spread across his face.

"Well, yes. I mean, if you're willing to up the ante of course you can depend on me … Yeh, sure! … Oh, don't worry about MacKay; I can handle that bastard. Listen, I mean I used to be Catholic, when I was a kid that is. I know all about the power of the Catholic Church. Shit! Yes, I used to be an altar boy. Can you believe that? Me? Arnie Summers, a fuckin' altar boy! So you see, I can relate to you, Your Eminence."

He listened for another few minutes and then hung up the phone. He lit his cigarette and leaned back against the side of the building, drawing deeply.

So the old man was coming to the States, was he? Wanted to get a good look at the writhing body before putting the death shot into it. Wouldn't be long now. As for Arnie, when it was all over he'd be off up to Canada. To hell with the United States! He'd had it with the country ever since they'd shipped him off to 'Nam. Stole the prime of his life from him, they did. He bit down on the cigarette. He'd teach them, boy! He'd show them who'd have the last laugh.

He pushed himself off from the wall and stalked over to his car. He should have gone to Canada all those years ago, like the other guys, running out instead of going to Viet Nam. They'd shown some sense; why hadn't he gone with them? Well, it was never too late to learn.

He punched his foot down and the Cougar spun its wheels, leaving tiremarks across the parking lot as it roared onto the street in a cloud of blue-black smoke. He headed back to the newspaper office. He'd work his way around MacKay all right; he'd done it before. It seemed there wouldn't be a lot more to do. Before the end of the year, the cardinal had said. He could hold on until then and, hell, the money was damn good!

At the back of his mind was the thought of how powerful his employer was. Arnie Summers was one for self-preservation, whatever the cost.

33

Duncan settled back in the seat and tried to sleep. He was seldom successful sleeping on airplanes, but perhaps the Concorde would be different, he thought. He closed his eyes and relaxed his body. Beside him Beth was already sound asleep. Across the aisle, Rudy was very softly snoring.

Bill had not batted an eyelash when Dunk had said that three of them needed to make a trip to Europe. It was vital, Dunk thought, that he meet with Reg Lee, the old Gypsy. And Rudy had suggested they look in on Etienne Macé in Paris, and perhaps even stop by Rudy's own place in Hamburg, to pick up what he referred to as "one or two bits and pieces that might come in useful."

Earl and Guillemette, meanwhile, were going to visit her aunt in New York, to consult on Voudoun matters, and then make a quick trip down to the Caribbean. All five of them were feeling frustrated, and found the very act of running around gathering necessary information comforting.

At London's Heathrow airport, the three parted company, Rudolf going into the city and making for the Reading Room of the British Museum, while Duncan and Beth rented a car and headed for Hampshire, southwest of London.

"I love the English countryside," Beth said as they drove along the hedgerowed lanes. "Parts of it look a lot like north-central Ohio. Gently rolling farmland with lots of green and plenty of trees. Beautiful!"

They drove down through Woking and Guildford, and then onto the A31 highway out to Alton. There Dunk turned off again onto local roads and made for the little village of Selborne.

Reg Lee was a full-blood Romany who had spent the first half of his life traveling the roads and lanes of England in a Gypsy *vardo*—the colorful, horse-drawn, house-on-wheels now fast disappearing from English life—and the last half of his life settled in an old showman's waggon, in a yard at Selborne restoring vardos. His work was known the length and breadth of the British Isles. He had been responsible for repairing and restoring numerous bowtops, square bows, Readings, Ledges, Burtons, Lambert drays, and Bradford flatcarts for museums, private collectors, and the few travelers who still roamed the land.

Reg was in his eighties, though no one would ever have known it. Streaked with just a bit of silver, his hair was still mostly black. His dark brown eyes flashed from beneath black eyebrows, and his skin was a deep mahogany brown. There was a perpetual pipe in his mouth, old and curved, hand-carved in the shape of a horse's head.

When Dunk and Beth came into the yard they found Reg flat on his back working on the front axle of a splendid green and yellow bowtop and blowing clouds of smoke from the pipe clenched between his teeth.

"Ah! Be handing me that spanner, *pral,*" he said to Duncan, as though the two had been together all morning. He removed the pipe from his mouth long enough to point its stem toward a large, old-fashioned wrench lying by his toolbox. Dunk bent down and gave it to him.

"Got to get this out today," said the old man, tightening the wrench on a massive axle bolt and puffing more smoke.

"Reg, this is Beth," Dunk said.

"Aye! The *odjus chai;* the lovely girl," he grunted, his attention on what he was doing. "A pleasure to meet you, *mi pen.*"

"He likes you," Duncan murmured to Beth. "He just called you 'sister'."

The redhead stood with her mouth open in amazement. "But isn't he surprised to see you?" she gasped. "I mean, you were in America the last he knew and now, suddenly, here you are in his workyard in England and he doesn't even blink an eye!"

A low chuckle came from under the vardo.

Dunk moved forward to help Reg up as he rolled out from under the waggon.

Once he was on his feet, the Gypsy beamed at Beth and took her hand in his. She was surprised to find he was tall—close to six feet, she guessed. Slim and muscular, she would have been hard put to believe him more than sixty years old. His hands, despite their hard surfaces, held hers gently. He had the high cheek-bones typical of his race and wore an elegant mous-tache turned up at the ends and, she believed, waxed.

"Any friend of my brother Duncan is doubly wel-come beside my fire," he said, speaking carefully in full English. Then he grinned. "Y'see? *Mandi* can *rokker Angitrakeri!* I can speak English instead of Romanes if I have to."

Beth couldn't help smiling at him.

"So, what brings my brother all the way here?" he continued, turning to Duncan. "Come! Let's sit around the fire and have some *pimeskri*—you can't beat a nice cup o' tea, y'know."

He led the way across the yard to where a small fire was burning in a circle of stones on the ground before a large, solid-wheeled waggon. Over the fire was a tripod with an iron hook, from which hung an old iron kettle, steam issuing from its spout.

The three sat down on large wood logs laid around the fire as seats. Reg busied himself making the tea. He poured it into three mugs he pulled from a bucket full of crockery, standing to one side of the fire.

"So y'got my message." It was a statement rather than a question. He finally laid down his pipe and picked up one of the mugs.

"Yes." Dunk nodded. "A bit surprised, I don't mind telling you. But, yes, I got it. Now I'm here to get the rest of the story."

Duncan told the Gypsy all about the Committee, what they had accomplished in the past and what they were now up against. The old man nodded under-standingly, not in the least surprised by the metaphys-ical happenings Dunk described.

Beth studied the two men as they talked. They were totally different in their physical appearances, yet she could see that they were brothers beneath the skin—or father-and-son might have been more appropriate, she thought. Obviously Duncan adored the old man and Reg, in his turn, greatly respected the younger man.

"Just about a week ago I was *dukkerin'*," Reg said, then glanced up at Beth. "That's 'fortunetelling' m'dear. I was *dukkerin'* a *rawnie*—a lady; an American tourist, as a matter of fact—when all of a sudden I got this terrible sense of ... of ... *waffedopen.*" He looked at Dunk.

"Evil," the young man said. "Or evil actions of some sort."

Reg nodded. "Aye! That's it exactly. It came out o' nowhere. It'd nothing to do with the *rawnie* I was reading. Somehow I knew it was you, *mi pral.* I had to let y'know, but how?" He took a long drink of tea. "I was worrying the rest of that day and when I went to m'bed. I suppose it was while I was asleep I made it through to you, by way of our *pen* here." He smiled again at Beth, who returned the smile.

"You said you felt I was in danger," Duncan said.

"Aye! That I did. And you still are. Oh, I've no doubt you can handle y'self, but you did need to be warned, so's you'll be on y'guard."

"Can you float the needles and spin the *chiv*, to find out more?" Duncan asked.

The old Gypsy gave it some thought.

"Aye! Aye, we'll do that. I'll get *m'putsi.*" He got up from beside the fire, taking his beloved pipe with him, and ambled off to the big *vardo*, disappearing inside it.

"What's he getting?" Beth asked.

"His *putsi*. It's a bag in which he keeps all his for-tunetelling 'goodies'," Dunk replied. "I've asked him to use a couple of old Romany tricks to try to see who's threatening us. Needles and a knife. You'll see."

Reg returned carrying a beautifully decorated, and obviously very old, pouch made of worn green and purple velvet. It was decorated with miniature white beads, strung together in bunches so that it looked like wildflowers hanging from the bag. He reached inside and extracted a piece of folded maroon silk, which he unrolled to reveal a number of silver needles.

Reg placed the needles side by side in the bottom of a flat plate. Then, from a metal jug standing on the ground near the fire, he gently poured some water into the plate. To Beth's surprise some of the needles floated momentarily, while others moved and rear-ranged themselves.

The old Gypsy studied them carefully, puffing on his pipe, with Duncan leaning over his shoulder.

"You've got several crossing," Dunk said. "And those two have quite separated from the others and are truly crossed, over on the left side there."

"Aye! That's your ringleader," Reg muttered. "There must be a whole tribe—a gang—working against you, *Lavengro*. See? He's on the left ... a fol-lower of the Left Hand Path."

Beth had heard that before. A follower of evil, she knew.

"What else can you see?" Dunk asked.

The old Gypsy stared at the needles for the longest time until Beth realized that he had gone into some sort of trance. Finally he shook himself and looked up, his eyes slightly teared.

"It's *waffedi, mi pral.* Bad! Really bad. A whole group that's in league wi'the beng; the old mullo-mush!"

"Well, it so happens I don't believe in the devil—your *beng,*" Duncan said, his face serious. "But I do believe in evil, and I do believe that others might believe in the devil and act accordingly."

"They're powerful, Dunk. Really powerful." Reg's eyes searched the younger man's face. "And whether it's really the *beng* or no, it's something fearsome!"

"That I believe! Let's see what the *chiv* says."

Along with the pouch, Reg had brought out from the vardo what looked to Beth to be a circular wooden breadboard. This he now lay on the ground in front of them. She saw that in fact it had been carved and wood-burned with a variety of words around its rim. Reg took a slim, hiltless dagger from a sheath at his waist and laid it on the board. With his head bowed, he seemed to meditate for a moment and then spun the knife.

It spun around and around, their eager eyes following it, till it slowed and finally stopped, its blade pointing at one of the words.

"*Mokkadi!*" Reg spat out the word. "'Unclean'! Aye, that we know."

He spun the knife again. This time it stopped at a different place, its tip between two words.

"*Chiriklo* is to the left of the blade. How strange," Dunk said. To Beth he said, "That means 'a bird'."

"Aye! And *Wavvertem* is on t'other side. That means a foreign land."

"Then that must be the one it means," Dunk said. "We'd found out that they're probably outside the

U.S.A. This confirms it. The question is, which foreign country? Any ideas, Reg?"

The old man again laid down his pipe and sat quietly for a long time, his hands in his lap and his eyes closed. Finally he opened his eyes, shaking his head.

"All I seem to be able to get is the *prals:* the Rom," he said. "And we know it's not Romanies that's agin you, *Lavengro.* It would never be Rom."

"Rom," Beth said. "For a moment I thought you said 'Rome'." She laughed, then stopped as she saw their faces.

"Rome!" Dunk cried. "Do you think it could be?"

The old Gypsy beamed at the redhead. "I knew you were a *pen;* a sister," he said. "You fine-tuned what I was picking up. Aye! Rome it is."

34

They kept the rental car and took the "Chunnel"—the newly opened Channel Tunnel—across to France. On the way, Dunk and Beth brought Rudy up to date on what had transpired with Reg Lee.

"Rome, you say?" said Rudy, his eyebrows rising. "Hmm! That is extremely interesting, and makes a certain amount of sense."

"It does?" Beth asked.

"Insofar as the group—and I think we can now assume it to be a group rather than an individual—is working on hallowed ground: ground that has for centuries been associated with power and also with sadistic pleasures. If such a group could find the right site from which to operate, they might draw tremendous additional power to supplement their own basic energies. And, I might add, I did mention the Vatican Library as a source for incredible reference material of this kind. Very handy to have that at their fingertips, if they can get access to it."

"You did indeed mention it, Rudy," Dunk said. "So what do you mean by 'the right site'?"

The old German shrugged. "Perhaps one of the ancient Roman temples—one dedicated to Zeus or Ares, perhaps. Cronus, Hephaestus or Hades are other possibilities. Perhaps even Eris, the goddess of strife and discord."

"Nemesis, the goddess of vengeance, if they've got a particular axe to grind," Dunk added.

"*Ja*, that too. *Mein Gott!* That is a wonderful place to work, if you are going to attempt something so awe-inspiring."

They traveled through Amiens and south toward Paris, enjoying the small lakes and woodlands, the rich farmlands and many orchards they passed. Anemones and camellias were everywhere.

"What did you do at the British Museum, Rudy?" Beth asked.

"Ah!" he said, his hands out, fingers spread wide in ecstacy. "The Reading Room of the British Museum is the equivalent of your Library of Congress, *nein?* It has books and manuscripts going back to the beginning of printing and beyond. What an incredible source for material—magical material especially!"

"You got some good stuff then, eh?" Dunk chuckled.

"*Ja!* 'Good stuff' indeed," said Rudy with a smile. "Almost as good as some of the 'stuff' our friends have been studying in the Vatican Library, I do not doubt. There are so many variations on ancient magical rituals it is not always easy to determine the most practical yet the most effective. The books I was able to consult helped me to determine what was most suitable for our purposes."

They entered Paris on the Avenue de la Porte de Clignancourt, turning right onto Bessières Boulevard.

"I think it's the First Arrondisement that Etienne lives in," Dunk said. "I know it's not far from the Arc de Triomphe; just south of it."

They merged into the mass of traffic circulating Place Charles de Gaulle, and got out again to drive down Avenue d'Iéna.

"Rue Boissière," Beth said, reading the address from her notebook.

Dunk found the elegant house on the corner of Boissière and Avenue Kléber. Etienne rented the top floor studio of what was once a private residence and was now apartments.

"Dunk! And Beth and Rudy! *Magnifique! Quel plaisir!* It has been a long time. Come into my humble abode." Etienne Macé looked like a caricature of a Frenchman, with his beret—which he wore every-where—and his pencil-thin moustache. He was short—five feet tall at most—with a round face and dark hair. He hugged them each in turn. His ruddy face beamed as he ushered them inside.

They were soon settled, each with a cold drink, and catching up on old times. Duncan had phoned from Washington before they left, so they had been expected. Quickly Dunk and Rudy updated the Frenchman on their present problem.

As they talked, Beth looked around the studio. The entire top floor of the building was one big room, with three skylights set into the ceiling. There was a bed in one corner of the room and a kitchen area in another. There was a plain wooden table, about which they all now sat, but little else in the way of furniture. Paintings were stacked along most of the wall space. One large, blank canvas sat on an easel facing a small dais on which rested an elegant chair.

The paintings were mostly metaphysical. Etienne painted a lot of scenes for book covers, but his major income came from paintings he did for private collectors. He was earning a name for his esoteric work. Beth recognized a representation of Dr. John Dee and his assistant Edward Kelly, standing in a necromantic circle and working magic—a scene she had noticed in many occult encyclopedias. Another canvas showed what seemed to be a companion piece, of Kelly gazing into a crystal ball while Dee wrote on a scroll. There were pictures of Arthur and the Grail Knights, of Merlin, of Stonehenge, and of the Witches on the Brocken. She saw portraits of people she recognized—such as Aleister Crowley, Nostrodamus, and Madame Blavatsky—and others she could only guess at. There was a realism to the paintings that made her gasp. The faces were so expressive, and the backgrounds held such tremendous detail.

"Like what you see, Beth?"

She turned at the sound of Etienne's voice.

"I love them! You're really talented, Etienne."

He gave an expressive shrug.

"It is not me," he said. "I go into a light trance when I paint. I am taken over by Mauricio Chavez, a nineteenth-century Spanish painter."

Her mouth dropped open. "You're kidding!"

Etienne laughed. "Non. I assure you I do not kid."

"He's right, Beth," Dunk said from where he sat at the table. "Take a close look at the signatures on the paintings."

She did, studying the scrawl on the bottom of the canvas closest to her. It read "Chavez-Macé."

"Credit where credit is due, *n'est ce pas?*"

They spent a couple of hours with their friend and then left to check into a small hotel a block or two away, on Place des Etats-Unis.

"You'll like the old Majestic Hôtel," Etienne said. "It used to be Gestapo Headquarters during the war!"

That evening they got back together again at the studio and took seats around the kitchen table. It had been decided to hold a séance.

"I still don't understand how communicating with the dead is going to help pinpoint the people we want to locate," Beth said as she settled herself.

"This is one of Etienne's specialties," Dunk said. "He is an excellent medium."

"Oui. I have some small success at it," the Frenchman said modestly. "And you will see, *chère* Beth, that it can be useful even in such circumstances as we now find ourselves."

His dark eyes gleamed in the light of the candle he had placed on the table, and she couldn't help smiling back at him.

All other lights were extinguished, and the four sat quietly and held hands around the table as they completed their psychic protection and erected their barriers. They then sat patiently and waited, but not for long.

"Good evening, my friends."

"Good evening," they all murmured.

"My name is Barrister. I am Etienne's Doorkeeper."

The precise, clipped, British accent seemed strange coming from the little Frenchman, Beth thought, but they had been told what to expect. She saw that Etienne had his eyes closed tightly. In fact they looked as though they were screwed up. He leaned slightly forward, one hand held by Rudolf, on his right, and the other by Dunk. Beth sat opposite him. Rudolf had elected to act as spokesman for the group.

"Welcome, Barrister," he said now.

"And how may I help you?" asked the voice.

"We would like to make contact with a person familiar with the city of Rome," Rudolf stated. "Someone who may be able to determine what a particular group of magicians is doing there at the moment."

"I see. Hmm. Yes, I think I may be able to help you. One moment."

There was silence for awhile. Beth caught Dunk's eye. He winked at her. She quashed an urge to giggle.

Barrister was there again. "I have here an elderly gentleman who claims he can help. His name is Professor Chiaramonte."

"Thank you for coming, Professor," Rudy said.

"It is my pleasure."

Beth was startled at the change. The new voice was entirely different from the English of the Doorkeeper. This had a heavy Italian accent to it and sounded as though it was an old man speaking.

"I am familiar with *Roma* and I think I can answer whatever you may ask," said the old man.

"Our questions concern a group of men—or men and women—who are working high magic of the Left Hand Path," Rudy said. "We would like to pinpoint who and where they are, if possible."

"There are many such groups, it pains me to say," came the reply. "My beloved city has for generations— for centuries—been a hotbed for those who would distort the indicated scheme of things. From the time of the ancient Romans this area has gathered to it special energies that, over the years, have grown and accumulated exponentially. Like moths to a flame the power-seekers have flocked to *Roma* to tap into this power—to distort and refocus it. Many of the dignitaries of the Christian Church were seduced by these forces. Bishops, archbishops, even popes. It is sad but true that…"

"Professor!" Rudy interrupted the old man's lecture. "We do have to get on with it. Would you mind…?"

"Oh! Oh, yes, but of course. Let me see … Hmm! There are, as I have said, many groups scattered about the city who work on the negative side. But I think I can see the ones you mean … Yes! Yes, I can. They gather in one or two different places. Most recently they have been working in the tunnels beneath Villa Torlonia but they have also done much work in the catacombes along the Via Appia."

"Catacombs! *Jawohl!* Of course," Rudy cried. "I should have thought of that myself."

"They are led by a man of the cloth; a cardinal," the professor continued. "A short, fat man who is a lot more agile than his figure would suggest. He is a shrewd character. Very dangerous. I see very strong contacts with the Powers of Negativity. Very strong. Be very careful, all of you … Wait a minute, I … "

"Do you have his name?" Rudy asked.

There was silence.

"Professor?"

After a long silence the British accent of Barrister returned.

"I'm dreadfully sorry, but something seems to have happened to Professor Chiaramonte. I - I have never experienced this before. It's as though he were suddenly whisked away … "

"Barrister?"

Beth couldn't mistake the apprehension in Rudy's voice as he called for the Doorkeeper.

"Barrister … ?"

"Ah! Yes. My apologies. I have never … " The Englishman was back but sounding disturbed. "The stench here, if you'll pardon me for mentioning it … No, I've never experienced this … Forgive me. I must go!"

There was a long silence.

"What's going on, Rudy?" Dunk asked.

"I do not know." The old German shook his head. "But I think we had best awaken our friend Etienne."

The little Frenchman took a long time to regain consciousness. He asked for water, which they quickly gave him. For a long time he sat hunched forward over the table, his head in his hands. Finally he seemed to shake himself and looked up and around at all their faces.

"What happened?"

Rudy told him all that had transpired.

Etienne shook his head. "That is strange. Very strange. *Mon Dieu!* In all the years I have been working as a medium I have never known Barrister to run off. And certainly never heard of a spirit suddenly disappearing like that. You say he was talking about the Satanic group?"

"Yes. He was about to start naming names," Dunk said. "I kind of got the feeling that they tuned into him and didn't want their names given. What do you think, Rudy?"

The tall, thin man nodded his head. *"Ja.* You are right, I am sure. I think our friends in Rome picked up on the connection and, shall we say, severed it!"

"Then, do you think they now know we're onto them?" Beth asked.

Rudy and Dunk nodded in unison.

"Yes, I think they do."

35

Earl and Guillemette flew from New York to Santo Domingo. They traveled west, by taxi, along the coast to the little town of Barahona. There they rented a big, twenty-foot Seacraft, the only ocean-going boat of any size to be found in the area, it seemed.

"I thought you were never going to go to sea with me again, Earl Stratford?" Guillemette looked up at him from under long black lashes as she dropped the line and pushed off from the rough wooden dock.

Earl grinned as he thought of their last trip together, almost drowning when their twenty-six-foot Chris-Craft had sunk in the middle of nowhere.

"Well, it's true you're a jinx," he said. "But you're such a beautiful jinx I thought I'd give it another try!"

He ducked as she threw a lifevest at him.

"Just keep the coast in sight this time," she said. "If we do that, my man, we should be all right."

They cruised through the smooth waters, away from the land, out until the shoreline was still in view but distant and generally appearing featureless. Earl couldn't help thinking that the loud engines disturbed what could otherwise be a beatific setting. He turned southwestward, moving down and eventually around the little island of Isla Beata, the southernmost tip of the Dominican Republic. There they turned and headed northwest up the coastline toward Haiti.

"How far across into Haiti are we going?" Earl asked.

"There's a little village between Marigot and Belle Anse, about forty-five miles along the coast," Guillemette said, joining him on the bridge. "If we pull in there, my people will meet us."

"You called them, then?"

She smiled her mystifying smile. "They don't have telephones there."

"But - but you say they'll be expecting us?"

"Oh, yes!"

And so they were. Some two hours later the engines of the big seacraft dropped in volume as Earl eased back the throttle and guided the boat in toward the shore. He saw a half-dozen people on the rocky bank, one of them signalling for him to steer into a cleft in the shoreline. He found it opened up into a small natural harbor just large enough for the boat.

Once they had safely tied up their boat, the two friends came ashore and were immediately surrounded by the Haitians. Guillemette seemed to know them all, and chattered away in the French *patois* of the Republic.

"Last time we landed on Haiti it seemed that everyone was a relative of yours," Earl said.

The black woman smiled broadly. "We are all brothers and sisters here, Earl. You should know that by now."

They set off inland through the pine forest. Two tall black men lead the way, Guillemette and Earl followed, and four or five men and women brought up the rear. There was no path that Earl could see, but the men led the way unhesitantly through the trees and undergrowth, seeming to know exactly where they were going. In a very short time, the ground rose and they started climbing.

After almost an hour they stopped for a brief rest. Some of the women produced gourd containers of a pinkish liquid, which Earl sipped hesitantly, and then gulped delightedly. He didn't know what it was, but he knew he liked it. Guillemette finally put a hand on his arm.

"Easy, my man. Too much of that on a hot day and you'll get a very upset stomach."

They moved on again and soon the ground began to slope down. Suddenly they broke out of the trees and Earl found they were on a well-worn trail along the treeline, approaching a small village.

"Is this where we're headed?" he asked.

"This is it," Guillemette said.

Earl sat on a rough wooden bench in the shade of a big satinwood tree. He polished his glasses on his shirt-tail as he watched Guillemette and another woman directing a group of people dressed all in red. He knew that they were *hunzi-kanzo* — in training to be initiated into the Voudoun religion. He guessed that the woman with Guillemette — a small, emaciated creature dressed all in white—was the *mambo*, or priestess of the local *hounfor*.

They were heaping wood to form a huge bonfire in the center of the village, and bringing benches and chairs from neighboring huts to form a circle about the fire. They left plenty of room inside the circle of seats for the religious ceremony to come.

Earl knew that normally all religious rites took place in the peristyle of the *hounfor*, or church, itself, which was usually a short distance away from the village. But Gulliemette had told him what was planned.

"The local *mambo* has agreed to come down into the village and work here for us. I think it's important for what I'm trying to achieve. We need to be in the midst of the everyday surroundings, the homes of the people, to pick up their daily energies."

"And just what are you trying to achieve?"

"I'm planning a massive onslaught by one of the *loa*," she said.

"Which god would that be?"

"Ogoun."

"Isn't he a warrior god?"

She smiled. "You're doing all right, my man. Yes! Ogoun is a warrior *loa*, much like your Saint George. I figure with all the stuff these Satanists are sending out, we need someone with a bit of punch to fight back."

Earl nodded his head. "I think you're right, Guillemette. But will this be enough, do you think?" He scratched his beard.

The black woman shook her head.

"No way. Not by itself. But this is just going to be the start, Earl. From here, other *hounfors*, other *mambos* and villages, will pick it up. They'll repeat the ritual and keep repeating it, sending a massive wave of energy rolling across the ocean!"

"To where?"

"Ah!" She held a finger up along the side of her nose. "That's where we have to hope our friends and fellow Committee members come up with something. I've got a feeling, my man, that they are on the verge of discovering just where our enemies are holed up!"

36

"All right, Summers, ye've made your point." MacKay glared at Arnie over the top of his half-glasses. "Yes, these terrible disasters are continuing, so your stories have to continue too. But can't ye see, man, that you're fanning the flames wi' your rhetoric? The newspaper had three sacks of mail this week after your 'Run for the Hills!' outburst! These people are scared to death, and you're scaring them more."

"Three sacks of mail?" Arnie grinned broadly. "Say, that's not bad."

"I understand that a very large number of people have purchased one-way tickets to Australia," MacKay continued. "You know the last time that happened?"

Arnie shook his head.

"Nineteen and sixty-two! When we almost went to war with Cuba."

"Is that a fact, boss?"

"Aye! It is. Now get out! ... Wait! What are ye putting your doubtful talents to now, if I might ask?"

"I'm off up to New York. I'm meeting with that Italian cardinal who arrived at JFK this morning."

"The one the pope sent to tour our disaster areas?"

"That's right, boss. That's the one."

MacKay rubbed his chin thoughtfully.

"Well, I guess ye canna get into too much trouble wi' that. Off ye go then. And don't forget to put in your expense chits as soon as ye get back!"

Patrizio Cardinal Ganganelli was not impressed with New York. To him the massive skyscrapers were just another sign of American ostentation. With their expensive suits and their big, fancy cars, they were a decadent people. After his meeting with Cardinal Josephs of New York—an ugly, scheming, obviously power-hungry man—he directed his limousine to drive south on Fifth Avenue and then make a right on Forty-Second Street.

He stared out the window at the dozens of porno movie houses and live sex shows. He nodded to himself at the sight of the many beggars and homeless people. He even witnessed a purse-snatching, watching as people stepped back rather than interfere and allowed the thief to run down the street and disappear safely down a subway entrance.

The limo made a wide circle around the theater district and then moved uptown toward Central Park. The cardinal had half an hour to spend before he was to meet with the newspaper reporter who worked for him. Tomorrow he would fly down to Florida to look at hurricane damage, and then on to New Orleans, Dallas, St. Louis, and the West Coast. A tiring trip, but one which would give him a great deal of pleasure. He understood that the damage and devastation was so widespread it was unprecedented. Billions upon billions of dollars' worth of damage and the loss of an unbelievable number of lives ... very satisfying! He smiled, then chuckled quietly to himself. Things were working out better than he had ever dared hope. The Americans were suffering, in torment, beginning to panic—and they had no idea why these terrible things were happening to them or who was behind it. He almost laughed out loud. An eye for an eye and a tooth for a tooth. If only his long-deceased mother could be here now, he thought.

37

It was dark when Earl heard the drums start. He left the hut and made his way, with the rest of the villagers, to the circles of seats around the bonfire. The fire had already been lit and there was enough wood to one side to keep it going for hours.

The five drummers were set up at one side of the fire, on a small improvised platform. There was one very large drum, the *maman*, lying on its side. The drummer sat astride it and beat its goatskin head with his hands. Next to him was a slightly smaller upright drum, the *seconde* or *papa*, which another drummer beat with a stick. Then came the small *boula* drum, beaten by its drummer's hands, and beside it another *seconde*, this one beaten with the drummer's hands rather than with a stick. On the end was the *ogantier*, who sat and struck a chunk of metal with an iron spike, producing a rhythmic "chinking" sound.

The assembled people hadn't been seated long before a procession came into sight. It was led by standard bearers: two women carrying the colorful silken flags of the local *hounfor*. Behind them came *La Place*, the master of ceremonies, who proudly bore an old military sabre. He was followed by the priest and priestess — *houngan* and *mambo* — the *mambo* being the small, thin woman Earl had met earlier. Both were dressed in white, with long strings of colored beads looped across their bodies, from shoulders to hips, in the form of a cross known as a *sautoire*. The *houngan* carried a ritual gourd rattle, or *asson*, decorated with colored beads and snake vertebrae, a small silver bell hanging from its handle. The *mambo* carried two bottles of rum. Behind the leaders came the white-attired initiates and the red-dressed neophytes.

The *houngan* began the ritual by shaking the *asson* to the four quarters. He was followed by the *mambo*, who took a mouthful of rum and then spit it out at the four corners, to consecrate the area. The drums and drummers were then saluted and libations poured.

Earl noticed small differences from the Voudoun ritual he had witnessed the previous year. Guillemette had told him that, since there was no set standard — Voudoun being an oral tradition — there would be differences from one *hounfor* to another. He wondered where Guillemette was and then spotted her, dressed in white, with the group of initiates. He tried to catch her eye, but she was intently watching the mambo.

The ceremony started with the litany. The *mambo* cried out and everyone else responded:

> *Papa Legba, Papa Legba, open wide the gate!*
> *Papa Legba, Papa Legba, open wide the gate!*
> *Papa Legba we are here;*
> *Open up the gate to let us pass.*

Open up the gate for we are here.
Papa Legba, open wide the gate so that we can pass!

The priest and priestess were on their knees, facing one another. The others started to dance around them, clockwise, to the rhythm of the drums. The chant was repeated, over and over, as they danced.

Then everyone stopped moving and the drums fell silent. Earl leaned forward to watch as the *mambo* got to her feet and started to draw the *vévé*. She dipped her hand into a jar of cornmeal and allowed the meal to trickle through her fingers onto the ground as she moved around, "drawing" with the white flour. She moved very quickly, and it did not take long for a large, intricate design to appear on the ground before the blazing bonfire. It was the *vévé* for Ogoun, the warrior god.

When the *mambo* finished, Earl thought he heard a collective sigh of relief from the watchers. Everyone knew how the design should look, and it was considered a very bad sign if the *mambo* made a mistake in drawing it. He caught a smile from Guillemette and smiled back, nodding his head in appreciation.

The *houngan* walked around the design, pouring a little rum onto the ground about it. Suddenly the drummers started up again. Everyone remained still except for the frail-looking *mambo*. With eyes closed she started to move, swaying first to the left and then to the right. Slowly she danced around and around the *vévé*. When she next came to the end of the line of white-dressed *hounsi*, she started to dance along the line. Since her eyes were closed all the time, Earl couldn't understand how she knew where she was. He was even more surprised when she stopped immediately in front of Guillemette. The two black women bobbed to one another and Guillemette, eyes also closed, took up the beat and the dance. They circled one another, exchanging places, and then Guillemette danced back to the *vévé*.

When she reached the place in front of the *vévé*, Guillemette opened her eyes and held her arms high as she danced. The others immediately started dancing too. The beat of the drums increased, and everyone milled around. Some feet started to encroach on the design on the ground. Then, rapidly, the whole *vévé* disappeared under the dancing feet. It was trodden into the ground as the pitch rose and the dancing became more abandoned. One woman—a *hounzi-kanzo* dressed in red—started spinning like a top and a wild scream came from her lips. She clawed at her clothing and soon the frail dress hung in tatters from her waist. Her bare breasts gleamed in the firelight as she twisted and turned. The other dancers seemed not to notice her as they continued dancing, though one or two of them became more frenzied and some tore at their clothing as though to be free of any restraints.

The audience leaned forward, Earl with them, as though expecting something. Then he saw Guillemette, completely naked, in the melee of dancers. Suddenly she let out a piercing scream and dropped to the ground. If Earl hadn't been prepared for it, he would have panicked. She rolled from side to side of the area where the *vévé* had been drawn, beating the ground with her arms and fists and kicking with her legs. The others stopped dancing and the drums went silent. Slowly the black woman's gyrations subsided and she lay still. The *houngan* approached and stood over her.

He shook the *asson* rattle and spoke to Guillemette in a language that Earl did not recognize. There was no response. He spoke again, louder, and shook the *asson* up and down the length of Guillemette's body. Suddenly she spoke, but it was a strange, deep, male voice that responded. She spoke in the same curious language that the *houngan* had used.

They conversed back and forth for a few moments and Guillemette came slowly to her feet. Her eyes, which had been tightly closed, suddenly opened wide and her face lit up with a huge smile. She spread her arms wide and ran in a circle around the fire, looking out at the people on the benches.

"Ogoun!" they all roared, recognizing the male deity who now inhabited her body.

"Mais oui!" responded the beautiful Haitian, in her man's voice. *"Alors—venez!"*

Everyone leapt up and clambered over the seats to get to the center area, where they all began to dance as the drums once again began to sound in a wild, frenetic beat. Earl found himself being swept along with them. At first he found it strange the way the beating drums and vibrant *ogan* worked on him. He was suddenly aware that he was dancing, and wasn't too upset to find himself coming into contact with naked female bodies. But he had no time to dwell on it. His body, rather than his feet, seemed to respond to the heavy drum beats and he twitched and turned, spun and bobbed, his arms swinging out and up, his feet stomping the ground. For a moment he caught sight of Guillemette's beautiful face in front of him and felt a tremendous urge to tell her he loved her, but then she was gone and he was caught up again in the rhythms and counter-rhythms of the dance.

Above the beat and the cries of the dancers, Earl occasionally heard the shouting of Guillemette as she was "ridden" by Ogoun. Her strong, male voice was bellowing out encouragement for the dancers to let themselves go. And this they did. He remembered taking off his glasses and sticking them in his pocket, as he was swept along with the tide of black bodies. And that was the last thing he remembered.

■

38

They had reached Rudolf Küstermeyer's house on Grabenstrasse, in the northwest corner of Hamburg, not far from the Platen un Blomen Park, and it was all that Duncan had expected. It was a large, older house, with a great many rooms spread through three floors and an attic. Built in the early 1800s, it was one of a small neighborhood of such buildings that had survived the Allied bombs of World War II and now stood, grand and dignified, in contrast to the ugly, modernistic, glass-and-steel boxes that had become the major part of post-war reconstruction in Hamburg.

Rudolf, Beth, and Dunk sat in Rudy's library, on the ground floor, admiring his more than five thousand volumes dealing with every imaginable aspect of the occult.

"I wouldn't think even the Vatican Library has much that you don't have, Rudy," Dunk said, perched precariously on the library ladder that rolled around all four walls of the room, giving access to the upper shelves.

"Oh, do not you believe it, *mein Freund,*" Rudy replied. "My poor collection is as nothing compared to what they have amassed over the centuries."

"But you've certainly got a lot of rare volumes," Beth said. She sat studying a small, thin, leather-bound volume of magic entitled *Le Véritable Dragon Rouge plus la Poule Noire,* dated 1521. Its illustrations were printed in black and red.

The tall German shrugged. "I have a few small gems, I do accept," he said. "But, books ... it is like an addiction—one can never have enough!"

"Amen to that," Dunk said, climbing down to the oak parquet floor. "Okay, Rudy, when do we eat?"

Rudy smiled a tight smile. "When does Elizabeth eat, you might ask, Duncan. For you and I are on a short fast."

"What? What d'you mean?"

The German closed a large, hand-illuminated volume of mediaeval magic he had been looking at and glanced at the blond young man.

"Tomorrow night you and I shall enter the hallowed circle, and I will initiate you into the mysteries of ceremonial magic, *Brüder Duncan.* If we are to battle the forces of evil, it will be well for you to be consecrated for the work. In preparation for that event it is wise that we cleanse our bodies with a minor fast. Nothing but whole-wheat bread and water until tomorrow night, I regret."

"What?!"

"Until that time we shall study together the ritual we will perform, and I will instruct you in the preparation of certain requirements," Rudy continued.

"Hey, wait a minute," Beth said, her cheeks glowing. "What about me?"

Both men looked at her with eyebrows raised.

"Well," she said, "I don't see why I should be left out."

"But this could well be dangerous," Duncan said.

"So could crossing a road in this day and age," Beth retorted. "Now, if you're taking Dunk through this because of what we're up against with these Satanists, Rudy, then it would certainly be best to take me, too, because the more of us who're properly prepared, the better!"

The two men looked at one another.

"She's got a point," Dunk said.

"I suggest we all go and find some bread and water," Rudy said, smiling.

It was the sort of thing Duncan had seen and enjoyed in movies: a whole section of bookshelves in Rudy's library swung silently back on well-oiled castors, allowing them to slip through into a hidden room.

He found himself in a windowless area with concealed and subdued lighting. There were cupboards along one wall and a huge black mirror, covered with a hanging tapestry, in the center of another wall. Various ritual tools—swords, wands, masks, sceptres, etc.— hung on another wall, and a gigantic map of the world covered the fourth. In one corner, on a small, raised dais, sat an ornate, gilded, throne-like chair. In the opposite corner was another small dais painted black, though this one had nothing on it.

In the center of the room stood two pillars, one black and the other silver, with an altar between them. The altar was covered with a gold cloth on which sat a number of magical implements. On the floor, glowing as though they had been marked with luminescent paint, were three concentric circles with an inset pentagram. Various words, which Dunk recognized as timeless words of power, were inscribed between the circles and along the lines of the pentagram. Tall white candles stood at the four cardinal points of the outer circle, each in its own little pentagram.

"Wow!" was Duncan's comment.

"Double wow!" Beth said, her voice hushed.

"Welcome to my inner sanctum." Rudy moved around to the cupboards. "You are the first people who have ever entered here, other than myself."

"We're honored, Rudy."

"Really. How long have you had this?" Dunk asked.

"Oh, some twenty years or more. This area was originally part of the library, but then I had a wall constructed to section this off and make it completely separate. It may seem a trifle melodramatic, perhaps, but believe me, it saves lengthy explanations to my cleaning lady. Come! We have much to do. I came here ahead of time while you were both taking your ritual baths, and I set up the altar, so we are almost ready."

He busied himself taking incense and charcoal from one of the cupboards. The charcoal block he placed in a large, elaborate thurible, decorated with wild boars and surmounted by a centaur. He lit the charcoal and scattered incense on it, swinging the censer to get it started.

Dunk and Beth were both dressed in simple white robes, edged with silver. The robes opened down the front and were encircled with silver girdles from which hung parchment talismans that they had made earlier in the day. They were naked beneath their robes. Rudy wore a magnificent robe of deepest purple trimmed with green and gold and bound around the waist with a solid chain that Dunk guessed was pure gold. They all wore parchment crowns on which they had carefully written certain names of power and drawn sacred symbols.

"We will assemble in the circle," Rudy instructed. "Dunk, you will stand beside the black pillar and Beth beside the silver."

They did as he said. Dunk watched carefully, mentally noting everything his German friend did.

Rudolf set down the thurible in the center of the altar and then, from the various working tools assembled, took up a gleaming sword and walked to the eastern point of the circle. There he held it, point up, in front of himself and spent some moments in meditation. He then called out some words in what Dunk thought was Latin and, turning the point of the sword down to almost touch the outer circle, began a slow perambulation. Arriving back at the easternmost point, Rudy again raised the sword and said:

"Ab ovo usque ad mala, ad majorem Dei gloriam."

He returned to the altar and laid down the sword. In front of the thurible sat a crystal dish of water and a matching one of salt. Rudy dropped three pinches of salt into the water and stirred it with his right forefinger, saying *"Anston, Cerreton, Simulator, Adonay."* Taking up the salted water and a horn-handled aspergillum, he again went around the circle, this time sprinkling it with the sacred water. Returning to the altar, he picked up the thurible and went a third time around the circle, this time calling out:

"Damahil, Lumech, Gadal, Pancia, Veloas, Meorod, Lamidoch, Baldach, Anarethon, Mitatron, Most Holy angels, be ye wardens of this circle."

Rudolf took up a silver bell, rang it three times at each corner, and returned it to the altar. It was close to where Dunk stood, and he was able to make out the letters *A.V.O.B.Y.* and certain mystical characters engraved around the bell.

Alongside the sword was a hazelwood wand, about thirty inches in length and with a forked end. There was a silver band around the end of one fork and a gold band around the other. The handle end of the wand was bound in what looked like copper wire, extending about seven inches up the length. Along the length Dunk could make out strange runic characters carved into the wood. Rudy now took this wand and stood before the altar, facing outward, with it raised above his head.

"In the names of the Most Holy proceed we in these mysteries to accomplish that which we desire. We therefore consecrate this piece of ground for our defense so that no spirit whatsoever shall be able to break these boundaries, neither be able to cause injury nor detriment to any of us here assembled; but that they be compelled to stand before this Circle and answer truly our demands. Bless, O Mighty Ones, this creature of earth on which we stand. Confirm, O God, Thy strength in us so that neither the adversary nor any evil thing may cause us to fail. So Mote It Be!"

"So Mote It Be!" Dunk and Beth joined in.

Rudy turned and laid down the wand. He then signaled Dunk and Beth to come and stand before him.

"We will now bring you into the Brotherhood and Sisterhood of Ceremonial Magic," he said. "By my knowledge of you both, and what you are capable of, I take it upon myself to initiate you and raise you both to the level of Fifth Degree, Panch Grade, in the Most Sacred Order of the Shining Light."

"How many degrees are there?" Beth whispered.

He smiled. "Twenty-one, in this Order. Then you may go on to the three highest degrees of Master of the Right Hand Path."

"Wow! A long way to go."

"I am just placing you here to start," the magician said. "I believe you will both advance very rapidly, as I teach you. Now, to work!"

From the altar he took up a small gold dish containing sacred oil. The two removed their girdles and opened their robes. The German magician anointed their breasts and genitals then drew the sign of the pentagram over the heart, with the words *"In hoc signo vinces."*

Dunk felt a surge of energy much like he experienced whenever he filled himself with the light of protection before any psychic exercise. He was surprised to see the oil absorbed into his skin almost immediately. Yet there remained a tingling and a glow which was to stay with him for several hours.

They refastened their belts, and then all joined hands and knelt. Rudolf spoke the words of the sacred oath and they repeated them after him. Then they spent a moment in silent prayer.

The magician went on to present to them certain magical tools and instruct them in their uses. They each, in turn, took the sword, the sacred salt, and the thurible, and went through the steps of erecting the temple.

The ceremony seemed to pass quickly to Dunk and he was surprised later when he found that they had been in the circle for over two hours. Much of it seemed like a dream to him, yet it would never leave him.

After all the instruction had been given, Rudy again took up the forked wand and held it above his head.

"Domine dirige nos!" he said, in a loud, clear voice. *"Amor vincit omnia!"*

He turned and hugged each of them, kissing Beth on the forehead.

"Blessed be both of you. May you always tread the way of the light; may you ever be on the Right Hand Path. So be it!"

"So be it!" they responded.

39

"How is this George going to help with our investigations, Rudy?" Earl asked, vigorously polishing his glasses and peering near-sightedly at the tall German.

They had all returned from their overseas journeys and were now traveling to the north of New York state. A limousine had met them at the Albany airport and was taking them westward toward the Finger Lakes region.

"He may not," Rudolf replied. "But, as you know, George Ravenfeather expressed concern to Duncan about the changing animal behavior patterns. He has been keeping records of what he has observed. We must talk with him about it. We cannot chance missing anything that might be of help."

"George is an old acquaintance," Dunk said. "He's a Shawnee. I met him in L.A. when he was there doing something for some movie. George left a message at the hotel yesterday—don't ask me how he tracked me down—and asked me to get in touch with him."

"George says that the Native American people are becoming greatly concerned about the disturbance in the weather patterns and what that is doing to the animals and birds," Rudy added.

"But what's this ceremony we're going to see?" Earl held up his glasses to the light and inspected them closely. Satisfied, he put them back on.

"It's a very rare one," Duncan said. "And we should feel honored that George received permission for us to attend."

"It is the initiation ceremony of a shaman into a cross-tribal medicine society," Rudy said. "This is the Midéwiwin, or Grand Medicine Society, of the Ojibwas, Potawatomis, Menominis, Sauks, Foxes, and other Woodland and Prairie tribes."

"I didn't know they had any shamans," Earl said.

"Not many people do," Dunk replied. "The shamans were virtually extinct for the last hundred years, so far as most anthropologists knew."

"I know that few Woodlands tribes had priests at all," Earl said, thoughtfully, "but I didn't think there were any shamans in the Algonquin/Iroquois."

"Didn't the Iroquois have the False Face Society?" Beth asked. "I read that somewhere."

"That's right." Dunk nodded. "But these shamans—this 'Grand Medicine Society' as Rudy puts it—seem to be something else."

"They are something like the kachina societies of the Southwest," Rudy said. "They have a system of degrees of advancement ... "

"Like in Wicca?" Guillemette asked.

"Like in some traditions of Wicca," Dunk agreed.

"The Ojibwas have four degrees or steps," Rudy continued, "and they are open to both men and women.

But each degree involves a large payment of money to the healer who heads the medicine society. And, as with the ancient Keltic Druids, there is a tremendous amount of knowledge that has to be learned by heart, for it is an oral tradition."

"In fact, the payments are so high and there's so much to learn that it seems very few make it through to the fourth degree," Dunk finished.

The limousine turned off the main highway onto a minor road, and from that onto a dirt road. It slowed and finally came to a stop at a barrier across the road. Beside the barrier was a hand-painted sign which said: "WINABOZO RESERVATION—NO ADMITTANCE WITHOUT AUTHORIZATION."

The limo driver looked back at the group, his eyebrows raised questioningly.

"Just hold on," Dunk said. "Someone should be out in a minute." To the others he said, "George said he'd meet us at the gate."

They sat there for five minutes before anyone showed up. Then a tall man in well-worn jeans, a red flannel shirt, and white Reeboks sauntered out of the woods and lifted the barrier, waving the limo through. When it was inside, he dropped the barrier again and came to the door that Rudy had opened. His jet-black hair hung loose and fell below his shoulders. On his hands he wore wide silver rings, one with a red coral stone set into it. A single, thin strap of leather with a cowrie shell hung around his neck.

"Hey, Dunk!" he said. "How's it going, man? You made it okay, I see." He grinned around at the others.

"Good to see you again, George." Dunk made the introductions. The Shawnee's eyes settled on Guillemette.

"You're a fine looking lady," he said.

"Why, thank you, kind sir," she replied, with a wink at Earl.

"Get in, George," Dunk said.

They drove into the reservation. Dunk noticed an assortment of small, poorly-kept houses tucked in amongst the trees along the winding road. The universal means of transportation seemed to be the pick-up truck; mostly old, though he did see one new one as they drove by.

"As you can see, we're not a wealthy tribe. Problem is we don't do bingo games. P'raps we should." George chuckled. "Some of the younger guys have been trying to talk the elders into bring in slot machines. 'We'll all be rich', they cry! Huh! I don't want that sort of money, and I don't think most of us do."

They finally pulled in beside a shack with a sign saying "General Store" and parked. As they got out Dunk told the driver what time to come back for them, while George made for a Coke machine beside the store entrance.

"Anyone for a Coke?" he asked.

They all shook their heads.

"Well then, anyone happen to have an extra quarter?"

Dunk gave him one. He got his drink, popped the top, and took a long draw on it. Wiping his mouth on the back of his hand, he beamed around at the group and motioned for them to follow him. He sauntered across the road towards an old Jetstream mobile home sitting on concrete blocks.

"Come and meet the chief," George said.

"Many villages of the Ojibwas belong to the Midéwiwin," said Chief Owlcries. He pronounced it "mee-DAY-wee-win," Dunk noticed. They sat with the chief on a bench to one side of a clearing in the woods, not far from the back of the general store. He was an old man—in his eighties, Dunk guessed—and was dressed in his ritual regalia, complete with feathered headdress.

"What's the Midéwiwin?" Guillemette asked.

"It's a medicine society, mainly. All important for curing the sick. The members are experts at healing disease."

The daylight was fading, and a group of half a dozen men sat in a circle about a large drum, each with a drumstick, beating it rhythmically and singing in loud voices. At the back of the clearing stood a wigwam made mostly of birch bark. People were scattered all around the clearing, and a large table, heaped with food, stood off to one side.

"That is the wigwam of the chief Midé," Owlcries continued, nodding toward the wigwam. "The chief Midé is the head of the Midéwiwin."

"What are the men singing?" Beth asked.

"All the songs, chants, and prayers of the medicine society come from the spirit *Winabozo*," the Shawnee chief said. "*Winabozo* is the Great Rabbit who directed the Otter to teach our people how to make drums and rattles."

"*'Winabozo'* is also the name of this reservation, isn't it?" Earl asked.

He nodded. "The Great Rabbit is also known as *Mana Boshu*, or *Nana Boshu*. It was he who became the Brer Rabbit of your folklore."

"You said earlier that the Midéwiwin is mainly a medicine group," Rudy said. "What else are they involved in?"

Owlcries smiled knowingly. "It is said they are sorcerers," he said softly. "Able to change their shapes and work much magic."

"Is that true?" Earl asked.

Owlcries again smiled but said nothing.

"Who is being initiated tonight, Chief, besides George?" Duncan asked.

"Only George Ravenfeather. A young man with much potential, the chief Midé believes. I remember the days, many, many moons ago, when there were initiations such as this on a regular basis, when many young men received the vision and were led to join. In the old days a messenger would take the news to all the Ojibwa villages, so that all might attend. It was an exciting time. They would come and set up their wigwams about the Medicine Lodge."

"How long has Ravenfeather been training?" Rudy asked.

"For seven years now he has been working with his teacher," replied the old chief. "He has been through all of these woods, learning each and every plant and its properties, and how to gather it."

Rudy nodded toward the wigwam across the clearing and they all turned to look. A small group of people were hanging things on the half-dozen poles stuck into the ground outside the wigwam.

"That is George's family," Owlcries said. "They are hanging gifts for the members of the Midé council."

"And where's George all this time?" Beth asked.

"He has been taking a ceremonial sweatbath to cleanse his body and clear his mind. He should be here any moment now. Ah! Here come the Midé."

Indeed, at that moment a group of five men, wearing brightly colored paint on their faces and carrying medicine bags, entered the clearing and sat down on the ground in a large circle. George himself appeared next, though the Committee didn't immediately recognize him. He was dressed in suede leather shirt and pants, with a headband pulling his hair back. A large feather hung from the headband. On his feet were moccasins. His face was unpainted. He moved to stand in the center of the circle of Midé.

The drummers changed the beat and paused in their singing. Beth leaned close to Dunk, and he took her hand in his.

The five Midé came to their feet and began to shuffle around in a circle, chanting as they went. Dunk counted as they walked around four times. Then they stopped and George took his turn, walking around and chanting.

When he had returned to the center the Midé pointed their medicine bags at him.

"The bags are made of otter skin," explained Chief Owlcries. "They contain many sacred objects."

The encircling Midé then each put a hand into his bag and pulled out a cowrie shell, which he threw at the initiate.

"They are symbolically showing their willingness to transfer some of their power to the new Midé," said the chief.

As the shells hit George he reeled and staggered, as though mortally wounded, finally falling to the ground. Then the chief Midé got up and went to him. He spoke sternly to the figure on the ground, in words which the group did not understand. Slowly, George seemed to recover and stood up. The chief Midé then handed him a medicine bag of his own.

George waited until the chief Midé had returned to his place and sat down again. Then he, in turn, reached into the bag and pulled out cowrie shells.

"The cowrie shell is the most sacred item," explained Owlcries. "It is the main emblem of the Midéwiwin Society."

George threw the shells at the men around him. They then prostrated themselves on the ground. Slowly the initiate advanced on them, touching each with his new medicine bag, and they gradually revived.

Having thus proven his medicine power, the initiate then had his face painted, to show his level in the Great Medicine Society of the Midéwiwin.

"Now for the feast," Owlcries said, his face breaking into a grin. "I always did like this part best."

They laughed and joined him as he got up and headed for the table of food.

"Hey, man! Pretty moving, eh?" George came over and joined Dunk and Beth as they piled their paper plates with food.

Dunk smiled into the newly-painted face. "Very impressive, George. So now it's all over?"

"Uh-uh," George responded. "After we've eaten, the main Midé has to go into the wigwam. Secret stuff! You'll see. And from now on, for many moons, I'll be further instructed in some of the, shall I say, more esoteric practices. Sorry I can't talk much about them."

His broad face was serious, but Dunk could see the happiness there. He nodded understandingly.

After everyone had eaten their fill, there were a number of speeches by Chief Owlcries, the chief Midé, George's teacher, and his father. Then the chief Midé excused himself, walked over to the wigwam, and entered. Soon the sound of a drum came from inside.

The drum beat faster and faster. The walls of the wigwam started to sway. As Dunk looked at it, the top of the structure seemed to bend, backward and forward, swaying to the beat of the drum. Strange howls came from inside, and the mumble of many voices followed—even though the chief Midé was alone inside. Throughout the clearing everyone stood transfixed. The sounds, together with the beating drum, continued for a long time.

"This is like a Voudoun ceremony called *'retrait de l'esprit de l'eau'*," whispered Guillemette. "I can't believe how similar it is! The voudoun mambo goes alone into a tent then many different sounds and voices are heard coming from inside. Just like this."

The wigwam continued to sway backward and forward. Slowly the energy seemed to dissipate and the wigwam became still. The voices faded away and eventually the drumming stopped. People started moving about again, and going back to the food table.

"Now it's all over," said George. "Pretty impressive, huh?"

His face glowed with pleasure and excitement, Beth noticed. She felt he was a strong yet gentle man. She could understand his concern about the animals.

"When this is all over we must sit down and talk," Dunk said. "We need to study your records of animal movements and how they tie in with certain dates."

"Something big brewing?" George asked, a look of concern on his face.

Dunk nodded. "Very big," he said.

40

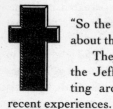 "So the Shawnee celebrate the seasons at about the same time," Guillemette said.

They were back in Duncan's suite at the Jefferson Hotel in Washington, sitting around and discussing their most recent experiences.

"That is correct," Rudy said. "Our friend Chief Owlcries said that they still do the traditional dances around the Wheel of the Year."

"He was really concerned about the disturbance of the wildlife population," Beth said. "The Shawnee still rely a lot on hunting for food, quite apart from the tradition attached to it."

"Yes," Dunk agreed. "He said that the deer have simply disappeared from that region. And, as you say, the tribe depends a lot on venison, for getting through the winter."

"George said he hasn't seen a deer in almost a year," Guillemette said. "Where have they all gone?"

"There are reports they've moved down into northern Pennsylvania and even across into Ohio," Dunk replied. "And a number of them apparently have gone north into Canada. Bill Highland says they've been getting many reports about wandering herds all across the U.S. Deer and moose and caribou. They all seem to be completely confused."

"Well, we have, all of us, gathered together much important information over the past several weeks," Rudy said, filling his old, curved, briar pipe as he spoke. "We have determined that the catastrophic weather, hitting at regular intervals, is human-controlled and that those humans are situated in Rome. They appear to have some sort of a vendetta against the United States as a whole and are learned in the ways of the Left Hand Path. If we are to face them, to fight them, and to defeat them, we must be exceptionally cautious. Now we need to pinpoint just who this enemy is—names and faces, *nein?*"

"Right!" Earl agreed. "And let's not forget that the autumnal equinox is fast approaching. That means another onslaught by this enemy, unless we can get to him first."

"You know," Dunk said, "I've been thinking. We've made a lot of contacts recently. A large number of groups know what we're trying to do. Why don't we draw on some of them to help us pinpoint these guys?"

"What do you mean, exactly, Dunk?" Beth asked.

"Well, let's say we haven't stopped them by the autumnal equinox. Okay, so we can be pretty certain they'll be continuing their onslaught—perverting the forces of nature to devastate and destroy, maim and kill. They'll continue to draw on the seasonal powers built up over the centuries and direct them to bring about even more cataclysmic occurrences. But while they're working, we—and dozens of others like us—can be honing in on where they are: the exact location! Instead of sitting and waiting for them to finish their dirty work and *then* going after them, let's go while they're working."

"*Gut!* Excellent, *mein Freund,*" Rudy said, drawing on his pipe. "We will contact many of the groups we know and ask that they try to 'ride back the beams', as it were, back to the source."

"There certainly has to be a hell of a lot of psychic energy buzzing our way at that time," Earl agreed. "Now that we know the direction it's coming from, yes, we should be able to ride it back, as you say, Rudy."

"Meanwhile," Dunk said, "I read that some Italian cardinal, who's been touring the disaster areas, is returning to Rome this afternoon. Why don't we go out to the airport and see if there's any chance of getting a word with him? I mean, he might know of some negative group there; he just might be able to give us some clue. It's a slim possibility, I know, but I think it's worth a shot."

"Good. Yes!"

"Great idea, Dunk."

41

 "They'll be boarding in twenty minutes," Dunk said. "Which means that he should be arriving in the building any time now. It's probably timed so that he doesn't have to sit around waiting; he'll get here and more or less go straight onto the airplane."

"So do you think we'll be able to get any time with him?" Beth asked.

"Oh, sure," Earl said. "It's not like we want a long interview. We just want to ask him a couple of questions. You'll see."

"This is the right gate?" Guillemette asked.

"Sure!" Earl nodded.

"Here he comes!" Dunk cried. "Rudy, stand by. I'll approach him and you be right behind me. I'll introduce us and then you can ask him the questions."

"Sehr gut!"

They caught glimpses of a short figure, in the black and crimson robes of a Roman Catholic cardinal, being escorted through the airport toward the gate where they all stood. They moved forward. There were a number of people apparently also waiting to see him off.

"Your Eminence!" Dunk called out as the entourage drew near and pushed forward. The round face with the gold-rimmed spectacles turned in his direction.

"Your Eminence, if I may just ... "

Behind him Dunk heard Rudolf exclaim. The cardinal looked past Duncan to the German. His eyes grew wide, and he made a quick movement of his hands. Later, Beth said she thought he'd been making the sign of the cross.

"Mein Gott! Vade retro me, Sat ... !"

There was a crash, and someone bumped hard against Dunk. He half-turned as Beth and Guillemette both cried out. He saw Earl lunge forward to try to catch the tall German as he fell, clutching his heart, bumping against Duncan and then sliding to the ground. In the commotion that followed, the cardinal disappeared down the boarding ramp to the airplane.

The ambulance raced through the streets, its siren screaming. Dunk and Beth were squeezed in the back, watching the paramedics work on Rudolf. An oxygen mask covered his face, and one of the men was thumping his chest.

"Is he going to make it?" asked Beth, tears rolling down her cheeks.

The men didn't answer; they were too busy.

42

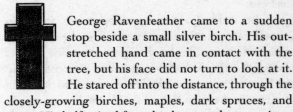 George Ravenfeather came to a sudden stop beside a small silver birch. His outstretched hand came in contact with the tree, but his face did not turn to look at it. He stared off into the distance, through the closely-growing birches, maples, dark spruces, and pines. His half-raised foot slowly came down again to settle on the ground. To an observer it might have looked as though he had gone into a sudden trance.

Two mourning doves flew close to him through the trees. There was a scramble to his right and a wild turkey made off at a half run. A gray squirrel sat on a branch and studied him for a while, then turned and scampered away.

The trees were tall, towering over several layers of shrubs, both evergreen and deciduous. The sun's rays broke through the tops of the trees and fought gallantly to get down to the floor of the woods. The Shawnee's face was in shadow.

His eyes closed, George found himself seemingly melting, descending into the earth. It was as though he had become a red fox, and he sniffed the air as he dove into his den at the base of an old tree. But he did not stop in the den beneath the roots. He found a tunnel and continued on down—deep, deep down into the ground. The passageway twisted and turned, and sometimes he found himself wondering if he should turn back. But he kept on.

The damp earth tickled his nose and he sneezed. The low roof caused him to crouch and squeeze himself forward, closing his eyes as the dirt tumbled about his head.

Then, suddenly, he was in an open area, an underground cave. A slight light came from he knew not where. He turned his head to peer, from side to side, though the gloom. Fallen rocks were scattered about the floor of the cave and he heard the thin trickle of an underground stream to his left. The roof seemed high, but he couldn't see it in the dim light.

Softly he padded forward, then stopped again and sniffed the air. There was a stillness, as of anticipation.

With hardly a sound a dark shadow broke from behind a rock to his right and dashed across the open space, passing right in front of his forepaws. He was taken aback but quickly recovered and gave chase. What it was he couldn't make out. It could have been a large rabbit, or a hare. But somehow he knew it wasn't that. It was something else: something that he needed to catch. He bounded from rock to rock, bruising himself as he tried to turn sharply and hit a sharp stone edge. The object he was chasing seemed able to stay ahead, just out of range.

They left the cave and climbed rapidly up a steep, winding tunnel. The thing he had to catch remained one turn ahead of him, though he managed once or twice to get a glimpse of jet black fur. Abruptly, he found himself out on the forest floor again, darting through the underbrush and scraping past trees and thorny bushes.

Ahead of him, breaking out from the roof of the woods, was a black grackle, and the fox suddenly became a red-tailed hawk. They climbed high into the sky and then swept down, over the trees and toward the rising mountains. At over a hundred miles an hour he swooped down on the grackle, gaining rapidly, but the small black bird reached the safety of the trees.

Suddenly, George was sitting on a branch, in the form of a raven, looking down to see a smooth, black, rat snake slithering into a hole. And then he was himself again, standing beside the birch tree.

George had no idea how long he had been standing there. He blinked his eyes and moved on.

43

They sat around the hospital bed, eyes fixed on the face of their friend. His usually pale face was chalk white, his eyes sunk into deep, dark hollows. His normally prominent cheekbones seemed to stretch the thin skin, and his thick eyebrows met over the beak of his nose. His breathing was short and raspy. Beth said they would only stay a short while, to let him get some rest.

"I feel fine," Rudy protested. He pushed the oxygen mask he'd been using to one side. "All I have done is lay resting since I got here. I need to talk to you all."

"Can you tell us what happened, Rudy?" Dunk asked.

The gaunt head nodded. "I remember it distinctly and I blame myself entirely. I should have been prepared."

"Prepared for what?" Earl asked. "How do you prepare for an unexpected heart attack?"

"Is that what the doctors said I had?"

They all nodded. Rudolf chuckled, a cracked, dry sound without mirth. He reached for the mask and took another long breath of oxygen.

"Are you saying it wasn't a heart attack?" Dunk asked, leaning forward.

"Oh, it was a heart attack, in the strict sense of the words," Rudy said. "But it was induced; it was forced upon me."

"Did the cardinal have something to do with it?" Guillemette's face was grave.

"*Ja!* That is it *genau.* Exactly!"

"But ... but the cardinal?... " Dunk found it hard to comprehend.

Rudolf's eyes found his own and managed a smile.

"Do not be deceived by the appearances, *mein Freund.* As soon as my eyes met his I recognized him—and he me. He may wear the cloth of the Roman Church now, but I recognized him for who he is."

"You know him?"

"*Ja!* He is my old nemesis. Patrizio Ganganelli is his name, though he is sometimes known as Patrick Ganelly, Paolo Gallo, or whatever. He and I have been at war for many years. And he recognized me as surely as I did him, only he was quicker to react than I was. I must truly be getting old!"

"How did he do this to you?" Earl asked.

The old German gave a slight shrug. "It is not difficult to throw a shock wave at someone. It can hit the heart like a bolt of lightning. I should have been prepared! But at least we now know who our adversary is."

"You think he's behind the weather attacks?" Dunk asked.

"Not he alone, *nein.* It is too much for one man, even one of his caliber. But, *ja,* I believe he is the leader of the group that works against the United States."

"What can you tell us about him, Rudy?" Guillemette asked.

"Without tiring yourself," Beth added, smiling.

He reached out and squeezed her hand.

"I am fine. Thank you, *Liebling.*" His eyes moved around them, from one anxious face to the next. "Patrizio Ganganelli was born in Sicily in near poverty, but quickly developed a taste for power and riches. He was taken to Rome by his mother when his father deserted them. There, as a child, he watched his mother being viciously raped by a group of drunken American soldiers. That was when he swore to take revenge. He has worked all his life to rise to a position where he can manipulate and destroy as he, and he alone, sees fit. He came to see the Church as a tool toward that end."

"The Church?" Beth sounded amazed.

"Oh, the Church has long been a powerful, manipulating force," Earl said.

"Just look back over history," Guillemette agreed. "Especially the Middle Ages. Take the Spanish Inquisition, for example: sadistically torturing and destroying people, in ways worse than Hitler's Gestapo, to impose the Church's views on everyone."

"I suppose you're right." Beth slowly nodded her head. "They certainly have tried to cram their views down everyone's throats with no regard for others' beliefs and feelings."

"But where did magic come into it?" Duncan asked.

"Ah! There you have it." Rudy sighed. "As our beautiful Haitian lady has said, look back at history. The Church has always been into the occult."

"Yes, I know you're right there," Dunk agreed. "We certainly know that throughout the Middle Ages it was the high dignitaries of the Christian Church who were the major practitioners of Ceremonial Magic. They had the time to study and practice, they had the knowledge necessary for the study, and they had the funds to pay for the expensive equipment. But what I meant was, where does our 'friend' the cardinal fit in, so far as magic is concerned?"

"I have spoken many times of the magical tomes available in the Vatican Library," Rudy said. "What better place to study the Arcane Laws? But our 'friend', as you put it, Dunk, was drawn strongly to the Left Hand Path. He did not want to practice positive magic in any way. He desired power, wealth! He wanted to rule! He was naturally attracted to the Powers of Darkness."

"He's a Satanist?" Earl asked.

"Most certainly. And a Satanist of the highest order. I have crossed swords with him in the past. Even in his younger days—for I have not encountered him in recent years—he was formidable. Some people have a 'natural bent', I think you say, for certain things. Some are ideally fitted to become actors or musicians, others to be politicians or diplomats. He, *meine Freunde*, is the perfect Satanist."

"But I thought most so-called Satanists didn't really worship the Devil in true sincerity," Beth said. "I thought most were in it for the thrill of it, if you like—for the excitement, without really believing in and worshipping Satan?"

"That is true of most, I have to say," Dunk said. "But there've been certain ones, over the ages—Francis Dashwood, the Abbé Boullan, perhaps Aleister Crowley—who've signed a pact, and who do worship, in all sincerity, the Powers of Darkness."

"It really doesn't matter whether or not we believe in Satan as an all-evil entity, in the Christian sense," Guillemette said. "The thing is, there *is* evil, per se, in the world, and we have to battle it. It's the ages-old war of Good against Evil."

"Yes, that I know." Beth nodded.

"Do not underestimate our Ganganelli," Rudy said. "He is a magician of the first order. As a young man he was initiated into the Order of the Stella Matutina, an offshoot of the old Order of the Golden Dawn. He quickly rose through the ranks of that and found it too tame. I first encountered him when I was a young man in the Collegium Pansophicum, a newer magical order, in Berlin. I was impressed with his knowledge at that time and felt he would go far. I did not realize on which Path he would travel, however."

"Wasn't the Collegium Pansophicum connected, in some way, to the O.T.O., the *Ordo Templis Orientalis?*" Dunk asked.

The German nodded. "It was founded by a friend of my father's, Heinrich Tränker, who was supposed to have obtained much of the ancient Rosicrucian knowledge, and certainly it showed in the rituals. Tränker was acquainted with Theodor Reuss, who appointed him head of the O.T.O. for Germany shortly after the first World War. As you know, the infamous Aleister Crowley was leader of the British branch of that Order. But meanwhile, our friend Ganganelli moved on to a Special Lodge of the Fraternitas Saturni."

"That specialized in sex magic, didn't it?" Earl interjected.

"*Ja!* And, in the case of Ganganelli's Lodge, of the worst kind—using young children! From there he returned to Italy and founded his own group, the O.H., or Order Honorius. This was his training ground for Satanism and his recruitment center for many who were to later stay with him. For all I know, they may still be there, a part of this present insidious group."

"All these Latin names and initials," Guillemette sighed. "They're not easy to keep up with."

"Do you know the name of this current group?" Dunk asked.

The old German frowned. "Let me see ... it was generally known as the Black Brothers of Belial—or the B3—but I think its 'official' name was the Templars of the Sacred Heart of Belial."

"Belial, of course, being the Demon of Lies," Earl said. "Along with Beelzebub, he was once a major evil figure in Jewish belief. What an unholy entity to choose to worship!"

44

"It's so good to have you home again, Rudy."

Beth busied herself arranging pillows behind the old German, who sat propped up in his bed at the Hotel Jefferson. It was one of the hotel's typical antique four-poster beds, and somehow Rudy looked right at home in it, thought Duncan, who stood at the foot of the bed and smiled.

"Don't go fussing over this old man too much, Beth," he said. "We don't want him getting into the habit of being waited on hand and foot."

"Now Dunk! I'm more than happy to do this," Beth said.

Duncan saw the gentle look in Rudolf's eyes as he allowed her to plump up his pillows.

"You are just jealous, *mein Freund*. You wish you were here in my place, I can see." He gave Dunk a warm smile and a broad wink.

"Well I know I'd like to have someone fussing over *me* like that." Earl sat on a chair by the window, polishing his glasses. "Sometimes I feel badly neglected."

Guillemette threw a cushion at him.

"We're all really glad you're back, Rudy," Dunk said. "The doctors said that you should take it easy for a few days, so *we'll* all put up with this nonsense if you will. Now … " He sat on a Georgian loveseat and Beth moved across to join him. "What's next on the agenda?"

"I want to know a little bit more about this Ganganelli," Earl said. "What sort of stuff has he done, that we might know about? You know, to give us an idea of his power."

"Let me tell you a story," said Rudy from the bed. "It is a true story, and you may well be acquainted with it. On August 26, 1978, Albino Luciani was made Pope John Paul I. On September 28, less than four weeks after his inauguration, he was dead. Rome—and Vatican City especially—was rife with rumors of foul play."

"What was given as the cause of death?" Earl asked.

"He was found dead in his bedroom, apparently of a heart attack. There was much talk around Rome of *jettatori*—the evil eye. Though there was also talk of the then-common Mafia-type assassinations, and even of a Vatican cabal."

"Are you saying Ganganelli had a hand in this?" Dunk asked, intrigued.

"I am not saying anything as yet," Rudolf replied. "But let us go back a little further. The death of Pope Pius XII, in 1958, was one of questionable circumstances, and a poison plot was very strongly suspected when Pius XI died in 1939, just before he was due to deliver a speech critical to the fascist regime. There was also talk of poison connected with the deaths of Pius X, Leo XIII, and Pius VIII, but they were all before the period in which we are interested."

"So was Ganganelli involved in the Pius deaths and the John Paul one, or not?" Earl asked.

"I am certain he had a hand in all three," Rudy replied. "The John Paul heart attack … well, you have all witnessed what has happened to me."

Earl whistled softly.

"He would certainly have been in a position to get to those popes," Dunk said. "Though I guess with his means of working, direct accessibility isn't a real factor."

"*Nein!* As you know, when working by occult means, geographic location has no bearing. He could as easily attack someone halfway around the world as he could someone next door."

"And now he knows of you, Rudy." Dunk felt worried. "What can we do to protect you?"

"Not just myself, Dunk. He will by now know of every one of us. But to start with, you have all been erecting your psychic barriers, *nein?*"

They all nodded. They had all long since got into the habit of visualizing the protective globe of light about themselves every night before going to bed and every morning on rising. They knew it was one of the very foundation stones of psychic defense.

"But from what you say, we need a heck of a lot more than that," Dunk said.

"You are right, of course. That is why I asked you to obtain that parchment." The German nodded toward the material Dunk had earlier set down on a lacquered coffeetable. "We will construct talismans of protection."

"You taught us about those when we were in Germany," Beth said excitedly. "I know I'll feel a whole lot happier with one. When do we make them?"

"There is no time like the present," Rudy said. "Duncan, you will lead the others in constructing a magical circle and preparing the necessary tools." He pointed toward the wardrobe. "You will need my bag—the large black one I brought back from Hamburg with us."

"Right, Rudy!"

The furniture was all pushed back against the walls and Duncan carefully laid down a length of white clothesline, in a circle on the Persian carpet, nine feet in diameter. At each of the four quarters—north, east, south, and west—stood a tall white candle alight. In the center of the circle was the coffeetable, acting as an altar. On it rested another white candle, with two red ones at either side. A small brass incense burner gave off a pleasant smell, a stream of blue-gray smoke rising from it to the ceiling. Earl had had the foresight to disconnect the room's smoke alarm—"It'd never do to have the sprinklers come on in the middle of the ritual," he said.

They helped Rudolf out of bed and into the circle. Not having the appropriate robes, all were naked, having first taken ritual baths—of clear water with a handful of salt—in Rudy's bathroom ahead of time.

"You don't have to be too obvious about admiring Guillemette's body!" Beth hissed at Dunk, her eyes daggers.

"Don't be silly," he replied, and busied himself adding more incense to the thurible.

"The tools on the altar have all been consecrated," Rudolf said when they were all ready. "I brought them, and a few other items, back from my house in Hamburg. But I did not think we would be using them so soon."

He took up the sword and handed it to Duncan. *"Bruder* Duncan, will you please consecrate this circle?"

The blond Californian was taken by surprise, but took the sword and advanced to the east. As he stood with the sword raised, he quickly went over in his mind the instructions he and Beth had been given in Rudolf's inner sanctum. Then, swinging the sword down to point at the clothesline circle, he started the ritual.

When the circle and everyone in it had been appropriately cleansed with salt, water, and incense, they all settled down to sit on the floor and discuss what was to be done.

"As you can see, the parchment has been cut into small squares," Rudolf said. "On the altar, along with it, there is the Pen and Ink of the Art. These we will use to draw sigils, protective symbols, on the parchment squares. We will then consecrate the squares, and from now on you will each wear one, as a protection, on your person at all times. Is that clear?"

They murmured assent.

"What's the ink?" Earl asked. "Just any old stuff?"

"Nothing, in ceremonial magic, is 'any old stuff'!" The German's eyes flashed and Dunk couldn't help noticing that his voice had gained back much of its old power. "Like everything else here, it has been made from the specific ingredients of a time-honored recipe. This is why it's referred to as the 'Ink of the Art' … the

Art of High Magic, of course. The ink is, in fact, made from peach kernels that are put into a fire and reduced to carbon. That carbon is then mixed with soot from the fire's chimney, in equal parts. That, in turn, is mixed with two parts of crushed gall-nut and two parts gum Arabic. All are mixed, sieved, and then stirred into pure, clean, river water. The ink is then exorcised."

"Jeez! I'm sorry I asked!"

They all laughed.

"And dare I ask about the pen?" Guillemette looked anxious.

"Of course, *meine Liebling*." Rudy's voice softened. "That is a feather taken from the right wing of a gander. Before plucking the feather one must say, *'Arboy, Narboy, Naray, Tamarav, Eyonar, Atamar, Elyo, Daamaar, Expollatis, ab hac poine omnum fallacia et in retinae veritatum'.*"

There was silence for a moment.

"What does that mean—and how on earth do you remember all this?" Guillemette asked, breaking the silence.

Rudy chuckled. "It is a traditional, time-tested blessing utilizing various magical names of power. When you have been doing these rituals as long as I have, it is no problem to remember these things."

The German had brought into the circle with him an example of the symbols that were to be written on the talismans. They all examined it carefully.

"These are called 'sigils'." Dunk said.

"Correct. They have special occult significance, in this case for protection. You will each copy these onto your own parchment talisman. Then, on the reverse, you will write your own name in the Theban script."

"Theban?" Two voices spoke together.

"*Ja!* Again, a time-honored form of magical writing. Here is the alphabet I have written out for you."

"Would it matter whether you used Theban, Malachim, Angelic, Passing-the-River, or any of the others?" Dunk asked.

"*Nein.* They are all good. I just prefer the Theban."

"You know about all these?" Guillemette seemed impressed.

"Both Dunk and I have come across a lot of this stuff in our research," Earl put in. "There are a lot of these so-called 'magical alphabets' shown in many of the old books on magic. They have many applications."

"Why can't we just use everyday English?" wondered Beth.

"I can tell you that," Dunk said, glancing at Rudolf. The old man gave a slight nod of the head. "If you used an alphabet with which you were really familiar, you wouldn't really put much thought into it as you wrote it. Using an unusual form of writing, you have to concentrate and really think about what you are doing."

"So you're putting 'power' into it," Earl added.

"Right!" Dunk agreed. "You are putting in your *mana*, or *prana*, or whatever you want to call it. So when you write the word PROTECTION, it really becomes a magical word of power."

"And then the consecration seals it?" asked Guillemette.

"Right," said Dunk and Earl together.

They made their talismans and Rudolf examined each one carefully. At last he seemed satisfied.

"*Gut!* Now, in turn—why don't you start, Beth, then Duncan, Guillemette, and lastly Earl—take your talisman and sprinkle it lightly on both sides with the sacred salted water. Then turn it over and over in the smoke of the incense. So! You will have then 'sprinkled and censed' it."

"And it's ready to wear?" Beth asked.

"Almost," Dunk said.

"*Ja.* We will say a few words over them, and then they are done."

They followed his directions and laid the finished talismans in a line on the altar. Rudy took up the sword and laid it down again so that its blade lay across all the pieces of parchment. Keeping his hand on the handle of the sword, he said:

"*Yod, He, Vau, He, El, Elohim!* By the great and mighty Adonay, by the virtue of the Heaven and the stars therein, by the gracious goodness of Our Lady and Her Lord, by the trees, flowers, and herbs, by the winds and waters of the Earth, by the power of the Great Ones and of all past and to come, O Great One, deign to bless and to consecrate these instruments in perfection, in purity, and in all that is true, to their purpose in the Art and their power through the Word, I entreat Thee. So Mote It Be."

"So Mote It Be!"

45

Beth and Rudolf sat at the side of the Reflecting Pool in West Potomac Park. They sat in silence for awhile, enjoying the sunshine and watching the many tourists. They turned and looked out at the wonderful view of the Potomac River and the mass of cherry trees around the tidal basin.

"It is very pleasant here," Rudy said finally. "I am feeling much better now."

"I'm so glad, Rudy. We were all so worried. We all love you, you know."

"*Ja.* I know. And I thank you for it. You are all my family."

Beth dabbed at her eyes. "Now stop that, Rudy, or you'll make me cry."

Rudy cleared his throat. "Tomorrow is the autumnal equinox," he said, to change the subject.

She shivered and wrapped her arms around herself.

"I wonder how many more people will die this time," she said. "It's all wrong that anyone can have such power, to manipulate the forces of nature so evilly like this."

"From the beginning of time humankind has been trying to alter nature," Rudy said. Beth noticed the German pull out his pipe and start to fill it. She smiled to herself, thinking he must be feeling better. The doctors had told him not to smoke for awhile, but Rudy had totally ignored that advice. Beth knew there was no arguing with him on that score.

"From the beginning of time?" she asked.

"*Ja.* In those earliest of days, when we lived in caves, we were trying to manipulate nature so that we could survive and so that we could go out and hunt when we needed to. We prayed for good weather and did magic to try to ensure it. Later, when we learned to grow our food, we wanted to control the weather so that we could regulate our crops. We have always been trying."

"Yes, but how successful were we, in the past?"

"We had our moments," he said, flicking his big, bulky lighter and drawing on the pipe. He puffed clouds of smoke into the air. "And ever since those very early times we have kept dabbling in magic, later—into the Middle Ages—getting into the ceremonial variety."

"Yes. You said something about popes and bishops and all sorts doing that."

"That is true. And, as I think I mentioned, some of the popes were even into Satanism."

"Satanism! Popes?" She was incredulous.

"*Gewiss!* Certainly. It may seem incredible to you, but it is, nonetheless, true. I have told you of those who were very much into ritual magic—Leo, Sylvester, Honorius and Urban. But there were also two who were out and out Satanists: Pope Gelasius II and Pope Honorius V."

"When did they live, Rudy?"

"Gelasius II was pope from June 1292 until May 1294, and Honorius V from January to March of 1670."

"He wasn't around for long, then."

"*Nein*. He hanged himself."

"Oh!"

They sat quietly and Rudy puffed on his pipe.

"What else can you tell me about those popes?" Beth asked.

He examined the burning tobacco and tamped it down with his thumb.

"They were both members of the same magical order, the Bogomils—spiritually descended from the Manichees. They were both condemned by the Church as Satanists and struck from the records."

"Struck from the records?"

"*Ja.* If you look at any list of Roman Catholic popes you will find no mention of them. Yet you will see that there is no pope listed from June 1292 until May 1294 or from January 1670 until March 1670. Just two gaps in the papal list."

"Well, now we have a Satanic cardinal," she said. "I wish we could strike him from the record!"

46

The road led out of Charlottesville, Virginia, winding up into the hills, past Monticello, the home of Thomas Jefferson, and on toward the little riverside town of Scottsville. Somewhere along the way a trail led off to the right, passing a farm raising "beefalo"—a cross between beef-cattle and buffalo—and a couple of pig farmers. The dirt road dipped down through a shallow ford and up the other side, where it divided. The left-hand fork wound on to come into Scottsville by the back way. The right-hand fork ended in the yard of a small orchard farm. At the back of the time-worn old farmhouse, in the middle of the orchard, was a small clearing. In the center stood a group of men and women. They were Witches.

Tanya Demidas wore a thin white robe with a green belt. Her feet were bare. Around her head she wore a narrow band of silver with a silver crescent moon at the front. A wide silver bracelet was about her right wrist, and a silver ring on the middle finger of each hand. Around her throat was a necklace of amber and jet. Her thick black hair hung down almost to her waist. She tossed it back as she turned to speak to the others.

"Okay, let's get started. Promos, get the incense going, would you? Justine, make sure there's wine in the goblet. Thanks."

The others moved about. They were dressed in similar long robes of different pastel colors. The one Tanya had called "Promos" was the only other person wearing a white robe. He was the priest to Tanya's priestess.

"My lady," he called to her. "The incense is burning and we're all ready."

The sun was setting in a magnificent blaze of red which extended across the sky in all directions. The breeze, which had blown gently all day, dropped off and the air became still. Somewhere an early owl called across the area.

All the Witches stood to one side against the trees while Tanya moved in and approached the single old oak tree stump in the very center of the clearing. This was their altar, and on it lay their working tools. It was decorated with autumn flowers, acorns, pine cones, and gourds. A bowl of fruit from the orchard lay on it. From beside the stump Tanya took up a sturdy staff and walked slowly out to the east. About six feet from the altar she pointed the end of the staff at the ground and stood still.

The others watched intently as their priestess started the consecration of the area. She pressed the end of the staff into the ground and walked slowly around, marking a discernible circle and finishing where she had begun. As she walked she focused her energies to flow down the staff and into the ground.

She walked around twice more: once sprinkling salted water and once swinging the thurible. Then she moved to stand in the east of the circle she had cast. There the others had assembled.

From her belt Tanya drew a straight-bladed, double-edged knife, or athame. She used it to ceremonially cut through and make a temporary opening in the sanctified circle she had just constructed. Through this opening came the coven members, one at a time, led by the priest. As they entered they were kissed by their leaders and consecrated with oil.

When the last had entered the hallowed space Tanya drew the lines of the circle together again with her athame and sealed the join with a pentagram.

The God and Goddess of Wicca were hailed and invited to attend the rites. The priest, priestess, and all coven members drew their athames and held them high.

"All hail the four Quarters and all hail the gods!" cried Promos.

"We bid the Lord and the Lady welcome," said Tanya, "and invite that they join with us in these sacred rites of autumn, witnessing that which we do in their honor. All hail!"

"All hail!" responded the coven.

"Now do we enjoy the fruits of our labors," the priest said.

"Now do we celebrate the harvest," responded a covener.

"As we sowed in the spring, now do we reap," the priestess said.

"Now let us pay our dues and enjoy our just rewards," responded another covener.

A bell was rung three times and the whole group took hands and started a slow dance, clockwise, about the altar. To an ancient tune they began to sing:

> *Here is the balance of day and night.*
> *At narry a point doth time take flight.*
> *Ever turns the wheel anon,*
> *Children are born, and years pass on.*
> *Death will come as doth the sun*
> *Each morning when the night is done.*
> *Yet Death is here as only a friend,*
> *And greets you when your life doth end.*
> *Remember 'tis he who opens the door,*
> *That we may advance forevermore.*
> *Balance and harmony, ease and strife,*
> *Life to death and death to life.*

They danced about the circle, slowly increasing their speed until they let go their hands and spun around and around. Some took hands again with a partner and some spun individually. Then, gradually, the pace slowed and they stopped.

Three of the number moved forward and the others sat around the edge of the circle. The three proceeded to act out a centuries-old play symbolizing the planting of the seeds, the turning of the Wheel of the Year, and the gathering of the harvest.

Then Tanya moved up to the altar and took up a silver goblet filled with wine. She turned to face the others and, as she did, Promos came and knelt before her. He took out his athame and held it, with both hands, its blade pointing down into the wine-filled cup.

"Now is the time to give thanks to the gods for that which sustains us." Tanya's voice rang loud and clear about the circle.

"So be it," Promos replied. "May we ever be aware of all that we owe the gods." He slowly lowered the blade of the athame into the wine. "In like fashion may male join with female, for the happiness of both."

"Let the fruits of union promote life," responded Tanya. "Let all be fruitful and let wealth be spread throughout all lands."

The priest raised the athame. With a muttered "To the Gods!" the priestess spilled a little of the wine on the ground as a libation, then offered the goblet to the priest. He drank and then she did the same. The goblet was then passed from hand to hand, until all of the coven had drunk from it. What wine remained was spilled out upon the ground.

Tanya replaced the goblet on the altar and took up a home-baked loaf of bread. This she offered to Promos. He stuck the wine-wet athame blade into the loaf and said: "This food is the blessing of the gods to our bodies. Let us partake of it freely."

Tanya continued: "And, as we share, let us remember always to see to it that aught that we have we share with those who have nothing."

They each tore a piece of bread from the loaf and ate it, passing on the loaf to the coveners who did the same.

"As we enjoy these gifts of the gods let us remember that without the gods we would have nothing," Tanya said.

"Eat. Drink. Be happy," Promos added. "Share and give thanks. So Mote It Be."

"So Mote It Be!" cried the coveners.

Later the coveners all sat about the altar, each with a goblet of wine and bread, fruit and nuts, enjoying the feast of the autumnal equinox. Tanya spoke to them.

"You all know what problems we have been having across the country these past several months," she said. They nodded and murmured. "We have all been wondering, 'when will it end?' Well, it seems there is far more to this than you or I imagined. There is evil at work here."

"What do you mean, my lady?" asked a young blonde girl in a soft, green robe.

"I have a friend—some of you may know him by his books—Duncan Webster ... "

Again there were murmurs of assent.

"Well, Duncan has asked our help on something to do with this crazy weather. He's been in touch with a lot of groups such as ours."

"Just Wiccan, my lady?" Promos asked.

"No. All types of pagans and neo-pagans; Native American groups, Voudouns, and earth-conscious groups. Even Freemasons, Rosicrucians, and the like. Apparently tonight, in addition to being one of our Sabbat dates, is the night when these Enemies of the Light are working against us. Duncan says they have been drawing on our energies, on the energies that have been built up, through these rites, over thousands of years. And they're turning these positive energies into negatives. They're diverting them to harm that which we love—nature and all parts of our Mother."

There were cries of protest from the coveners.

"What can we do?" someone asked.

"The Sabbats are for celebration, not for magical work," Promos said dubiously.

"I know." Tanya nodded. "But this is important enough that we need to act. Even as we sit here, these Satanists are sending out their energies to meet with and distort ours. We have to try to sabotage them. We have to build up one of our great Cones of Power, and direct it as pure white light, such that will sear anything negative that it touches."

"And that will stop them?"

"I doubt it'll stop them," she said. "But it *will* dilute what they can do. If Duncan can get enough groups to work at this tonight, in unison, it will severely dampen what they've been able to do before."

"Then let's get to it!"

They planned their strategy: how they would raise the power and how and where they would focus it. They discussed what precautions they needed to take to protect themselves, and put those into action.

Across the country similar groups were working with the same focus. Some raised their power by dancing, some by chanting, some with ritual tools and instruments, and some with nothing but their naked bodies. Traditions and practices varied, but all had previously been proven effective. Groups and solitary practitioners who had received the word all worked together with one aim in mind: to stop the Satanists in their perversion of the seasonal power.

47

The walls of the underground chamber echoed with the beating of sandaled feet upon the hard ground. Black-robed figures moved backwards and forwards to a strange, syncopated beat, advancing and retreating around a fiery circle of light glowing in the floor of the catacomb. The sonorous chanting reverberated around the irregular walls and echoed back in counter-rhythm to the cadence of the ancient *collects*, short prayers for specific purposes. Latin liturgies gave way to Enochian calls and the sounds of gong and bell intermingled with the rising, resonant voices. Incense lay thick and heavy across the upper reaches of the chamber and beneath their robes sweat ran down the bodies of the celebrants.

Agara Brachi lay naked on the altar once again. Indeed, she *was* the altar for these sacred Rites of Belial. At her side stood the imposing figure of Patrizio Cardinal Ganganelli. Gualtiero Cardinal della Rovere stood at her head. Her arms and legs were spread wide so that her body formed a five-pointed star. A thick black candle burned at her head and at each of her feet;

in her hands she held two burning red candles. A gold plate, on which sat a gold-handled knife and a gold chalice, rested on her stomach. She could feel its weight and found herself consciously controlling her breathing so as not to disturb it.

Two figures in grey robes stood at Agara's feet, a covered basket on the ground between them. These were the other female members of the Order. Both stood with their robes open, exposing their bodies in the shimmering candlelight. Their voices blended and harmonized with those of the black-clad men encircling the central tableau.

Agara closed her eyes and let her thoughts wander back over the weeks that had passed since her initiation into the Templars of the Sacred Heart of Belial. She had felt buoyed-up for many days after that ritual. She could hardly believe that she was now a member of the most powerful secret society in the world. She had settled comfortably into the position of paramour to the cardinal, and to whomever of his associates he indicated she should give her attention. After the ascetics of the convent it was a welcome duty. In fact, far more pleasure than duty, she had no trouble admitting.

But this was her first major role in ritual. She had asked Patrizio for the honor and he had given it. She was the altar; she was the platform through which the celebrants would connect with their deleterious deity. Over her naked body a connection would be made to discharge the energy raised and blast it across thousands of miles to do its work. Over her naked body would the Satanic Grand Master make the sacrifice that would culminate the power-raising ritual. Over her naked body would the spectre of the Lord Himself materialize and receive obeisance from His followers.

The figures around the circle raised their hands high above their heads and then swung them down, bowing low. They raised them up again and repeated the movement. Time and again the wall of limbs rose and fell. Then they were still. All was silent, a silence intense in its contrast to the foregoing buildup of sound and movement. The figure on the altar was aware of the splutter of the candle at her head, as a draft blew unexpectedly into the circle.

Ganganelli turned to the two women at the foot of the altar. One of them bent to the basket at their feet and uncovered it. She straightened up, a small, naked baby in her hands. She walked around, handed the child to the cardinal, and returned to her place.

"Ad extremum; ad majorem Satanus gloriam!"

Ganganelli held the baby high above his head. Its eyes were open but it lay quiet and still, as though drugged.

"Ad majorem Satanus gloriam!"

The response came in a roll of sound that echoed and re-echoed around the underground cavern.

Rovere moved around to stand opposite Ganganelli. He reached out his hands and took the baby from the Grand Master, holding it suspended over the golden ritual objects on the body of the altar. Ganganelli picked up the gold-handled knife. Its razor-sharp blade glinted in the candlelight.

"Lord Belial!" cried Ganganelli. "Once more we meet to honor Thee. Once more we bring Thee that which You desire. Once more we raise the powers with which Thou hast imbued us, to turn the tide of Positive

Light and throw it back upon its perpetrators. Raise up the storms! Throw down the lightning! Stir up the winds and seas that none shall be immune! Here, Mighty Lord, is our offering!"

The Satanist reached out and drew the blade of the knife across the throat of the child. Blood gushed from the wound, flooding down into the chalice and overflowing onto the plate.

Blood spattered over Agara's breasts, and she smiled at its warmth. "The Eucharist of Belial," she murmured.

As the blood ceased its flow, della Rovere passed the lifeless body to the nearest woman, who callously dropped it back into the basket on the ground. The Grand Master took up the cup of blood and held it high.

"Lord Belial!" he cried.

"Lord Belial!" came in a roar from those about him.

He sipped from the cup and passed it across to his partner. As the golden goblet was passed around the circle, the two women moved forward on either side of Agara. She watched them take the plate and pour the overspilled blood onto her body. There they rubbed it over her stomach and breasts and then their own naked bodies. Agara gloried in this and closed her eyes, praising the Dark Lord for His blessings.

She opened her eyes again as she heard a murmur from the assembled Satanists. There, above her body, the smoke of the incense had drawn together and was swirling around like a miniature tornado. As she watched, it seemed to thicken and take shape. Slowly it took on the form of a man, though only from the waist up and almost twice normal lifesize. The red-brown face was twisted in fiendish glee, the fire-red eyes wide and blazing. Black hair hung to the shoulders and matching black eyebrows met over the beak of a nose. Saliva drooled from one corner of the creature's mouth, a drop falling on Agara's body. She stifled a cry as it burned like acid.

The creature was naked, with coarse black hair sprouting in tufts across its body. Its arms were disproportionately short but incredibly muscular. Its fingers were long, hairy, and gnarled, with large joints and long, sharp, black fingernails. Agara couldn't help being repulsed at the sight, yet she knew He was the giver of power; He was the one who could make all things possible for her ... and because of it she worshipped Him.

"Master!" murmured Ganganelli, lowering his head.

The creature turned its eyes on the cardinal.

"The sacrifice is acceptable."

The voice was low-registered and sepulchral, echoing around the cavern. The pointed teeth flashed, but the lips seemed somehow out of synch with the words that sounded. Agara couldn't help thinking of a Japanese film she had once seen where the dubbed-in voices did not quite match the movement of the actors' mouths.

"But you have a problem, it would seem."

Ganganelli's head snapped upward and he looked at the figure over the altar.

"Problem? What do you mean, my Lord?"

Hollow laughter rumbled around the cave.

"A challenge, it seems! The forces you draw upon are not content to sit quietly and be abused."

"My Lord?" Ganganelli still seemed unsure of what was meant.

"Oh, I have directed the forces you have raised, fear not! But they have met opposition. They have been diluted. Now, if you were to give me that which I demanded … "

Ganganelli seemed to suddenly comprehend.

"Rudolf Küstermeyer!" he snarled. "So! The old fool survived, did he?" He turned his full attention back to the figure before him. "My Lord, it will be as I have said. We will continue to follow the timetable I set. Yes, you will receive that which you desire … at the time I originally stated."

There was a long, drawn-out hiss from Belial.

"So be it, then! You have made the pact. I will stick by it. We shall meet again, my friend!"

Even as he spoke, the figure began to dissipate. It faded away until the column of smoke broke up and wafted once again about the cavern. There remained a cold dampness in the air, together with a mildly sulphurous smell. Agara could see the goosebumps on her body and shivered slightly. She noticed the other two women pull their robes tighter about themselves.

Ganganelli seemed lost in thought and stood silently for a long moment. Finally della Rovere coughed and mumbled something. Ganganelli looked up.

"What? Oh, yes!" He raised his arms in the air and spread them out to the encircling Satanists.

"Ave atque vale," he said.

"Ave atque vale!" came the response.

"Domine dirige nos," della Rovere sang.

Agara sighed and congratulated herself on how well her first major rite had gone.

48

It was the end of a two-year voyage. The Beyerly family was elated. They had sailed their schooner, the *Global Kestrel,* around the world. The end was in sight. Morgan Beyerly stood at the wheel, his wife Deidre by his side. The twin girls, Dawn and Jody—only twelve years old when the voyage started—were up for'ard with their older brother, Pete. Long Island was in sight, and before the end of the day they would be entering New York Harbor. It had been a wonderful, incredible experience, but it felt good to be returning home.

The *Global Kestrel* was a Beelsden-designed schooner built by W. J. Woodard at Northwich, Cheshire, England. The gaff foresail and the Bermudian mainsail, with the sleek hull lines, lent a hint of old-time glory to the 1976 gaff rig. Forty feet six inches at the waterline, twelve feet eight inches beam—with a seven-foot-four-inch draught, she set 1,820 square feet of canvas.

As they swept along, Fire Island off to the starboard, for the twentieth time Morgan went over in his mind what he would say at the dinner the New York Yacht Club was certain to give him. He'd tell them of their being becalmed for eleven days in the Indian Ocean; of losing the working and storm jibs in a murderous storm in Le Maire Strait, while rounding Cape Horn; of spending nine successive days at an angle of heel of 35° to starboard; of crashing through the South-East Trades, closehauled for ten consecutive days.

"What glorious weather to end the trip with." Deidre snuggled in tight against him.

Morgan slipped one arm around her shoulders and smiled down at her. They'd had their trials in the last two years. There'd been times when each had longed for access to a lawyer and a divorce court, but they'd come through it all right; if anything, closer than they had ever been before. And the kids had been great. They had really matured. Pete was now sixteen, but had the bearing of a young man in his early twenties. He'd do all right for himself, Morgan thought with a smile.

He glanced up at the sun. It had been out all morning but had just now gone behind a cloud. There had been no clouds the last time he'd looked up. Deidre caught his glance and looked up also.

"That's funny," she said.

"What's that?"

"Those clouds—where did they come from so suddenly?"

Morgan chuckled. "I guess we've been too wrapped in our thoughts to have noticed them building. They're nothing, though. Radio says all's fair for the rest of the way in. Then it can do what it likes."

She joined him in laughter.

An hour later there were no smiles on their faces. All five of them wore their heavy-weather gear. The rain had swept in unexpectedly and the wind had risen rapidly to a force of 80 knots. The ship's barometer had plunged to 28.31 inches. Waves towered above the sailboat and it labored through the high seas. Land was no longer visible through the curtain of rain. Lightning flashed directly overhead and the thunder sounded as though it was all around them.

Morgan had the auxiliary engine going and had lashed the wheel, to keep the boat heading into the wind, as he and the rest of the family fought their way across the decks and frantically tried to stow the sails.

Before they could bring down the foresail, a sheet parted and the canvas was grabbed by the wind and ripped away, snapping off the top twenty feet of the foremast. Deidre screamed as she saw a whipping sheet from the masthead snap around Dawn's ankle. She lunged toward her daughter but the girl was snatched, screaming, off the deck and disappeared into the foaming water. Pete managed to grab his mother and hang on, or she would have gone over the side as well.

Morgan's deeply-tanned face turned to chalk white as he helped tie his remaining daughter and son to the main mast and struggled with his wife toward the stern.

The wind howled and snapped the rope; the wheel broke free and spun like a roulette wheel. With a tremendous crack, the rudder gave way and Morgan felt the ship heel to starboard as it turned side on to the sea.

A tremendous wave picked up the stricken ship and hurled it shorewards, tipping it and snapping off both masts and the lower third of the keel. Rolling over and over, sideways, the sailboat rode with the waves to the shoreline, where it smashed into a beachhouse tottering on stilts, striving to maintain its balance against the fury of the storm. House and boat, in a tangled mass, crashed to the ground and were swirled across the narrow stretch of Fire Island Beach, coming to rest temporarily against similarly broken homes. The storm howled and shrieked. Pieces of wood, metal, and unrecognizable parts of houses and boats tangled and untangled along the ravaged stretch of sand.

49

 At 11:53 a.m. Pacific Standard Time, on the morning of September 21, the top blew off Mount Thielsen, Oregon's 2,796-foot high mountain in the Cascade range. It was an eruption the equivalent of four hundred megatons of nuclear explosions—or thirty-two thousand Hiroshima-size atomic bombs. The top 850 feet of the mountain were blown off, sending a cubic mile of debris into the atmosphere.

In the immediate area, visibility was reduced to less than twenty feet. In the city of Eugene, eighty miles to the northwest, fifteen inches of ash were later measured on the ground. The ash cloud attained an altitude of fifteen miles. Two hundred and five people were killed, and seventy-five thousand left homeless. It was the worst disaster in the area since Mount St. Helens had erupted on May 18, 1980.

An hour before the Oregon volcano erupted, an unexpected tornado touched down in Nebraska, just south of the town of Taylor. Traveling over the ground at over sixty miles per hour, with a wind speed of more than 300 mph, the tornado moved northwest into the neighboring town of Brewster. Both towns were razed to the ground. The move to Brewster was unexpected, since tornadoes are generally steered by the jet stream and move in a northeasterly direction. The result was 242 lives lost in Taylor and 313 in Brewster. Total property damage was placed at more than $150 million.

At ten minutes after noon on September 23, three coal-slag dams in southern West Virginia, saturated from the unusually severe rains of the previous two days, burst and sent two-and-a-half miles of back-up water surging down onto a lower dam. The lower dam exploded, and fifty billion gallons of water spewed out onto the low-lying land beneath. Hundreds of homes were swept away, with a loss of 729 lives. Over 4,000 people were left homeless.

50

"It's some small consolation that there don't seem to have been nearly as many disasters this time as at the previous Sabbat dates." Dunk sat with a worried look on his face and a stack of computer printouts in front of him. "Bill sent over everything he has from the last few days. All seems to be quiet again."

"Till next time," Earl said morosely.

"I know, my man," Guillemette said, squeezing Earl's arm. "It's all very well to have cut down on things, but we haven't stopped them yet. There have still been a tremendous number of lives lost and properties destroyed. Volcanoes, hurricanes, tornadoes again." She shook her head sadly.

"Nevertheless," Rudy said, glancing at one of the newspaper headlines on the coffeetable beside him, "we have made a difference, and for that we should feel gratified. In fact, if you compare figures, we have actually made a substantial difference. Much fewer casualties this time compared to last. We still have a way to go, *ja*, but at least we are, how you say, 'off and running'."

They were all once again in their usual seats in Duncan's suite, reviewing the events of the autumnal equinox attack.

"Rudy's right," Beth said, looking around at her friends. "With something of this magnitude we couldn't expect to stop it abruptly. It'll probably be a very long battle."

"I don't know," Dunk said. "I think you'll agree with me, Rudy, that when it comes down to the wire we're going to have a hell of a skirmish with these Satanists, and it'll probably all be over in one big fight—albeit in favor of either the Forces of Good or the Forces of Evil."

"You are right, *mein Freund,* of course. It will be one big battle: the biggest any of us has ever had to face, including myself. These Satanists—and this Patrizio Ganganelli especially—are not novices. They are seasoned followers of the Left Hand Path. They have no qualms, as we have seen from the thousands upon thousands of deaths they have already caused. Their aim is no less than to destroy the United States of America! I will be frank, *meine Lieblinge,* I do not think well of our chances."

There was a long silence eventually broken by a knock at the door. Dunk crossed the room and opened it.

"Tanya! You got here faster than I expected. I didn't think you'd be here for another couple of hours at least."

The dark-haired Wiccan high priestess gave him a hug and a kiss and came into the room.

"Blessed be!" she said. "Your senator Highland had everything arranged. He flew me on a special charter plane from the airfield at Earlysville into Washington's National Airport. There I was met by a limo and brought straight here. I tell you, I feel like a princess!"

Duncan introduced her to the Committee and she took a seat beside Beth.

"To get straight to business, Tanya," Dunk said, "why don't you fill the others in on what you told me over the phone?"

"Of course." She smiled around at them. "I tell you, this is not what I'm used to. I'm a Witch because I believe in the Old Gods: the Goddess of Life and Love and the God of the Afterlife. It's my religion and I just want to be left alone to worship with my friends, as we always have." She shrugged her shoulders. "All of this is a bit beyond me."

"We know exactly how you feel, girl," Guillemette said. "We've all been dragged into this one against our wills."

"Well," Tanya continued. "Duncan asked us to work on building a cone of power and sending it out, even though we don't usually do work at Sabbats. Esbats are for that sort of thing, as I'm sure you all know." Several heads nodded. "Anyway, we're a coven in the Robatian tradition and the way we work is something similar to Gardnerian. We build up the energy through chanting and dancing and then, when we feel we've got as much power as we can generate, the coven directs it into me—the High Priestess—and I, in turn, direct it to the target."

"And you've all agreed on the target ahead of time," Earl said.

The Wiccan nodded. "And exactly how we're going to raise the cone. It's just that I'm the one who pulls the trigger, as it were, rather than having everyone firing off individually. We think it makes for a more powerful projection."

"What happened when you did this at the autumn equinox?" Beth asked.

"Ah! This is what I was telling Duncan on the phone. Normally the power is projected and then some sort of an image appears in my mind's eye—feedback, if you like—which seems to give me a symbolical indication of how successful it's been. But this time it was as though I was pulled along with the power. It's very strange; never had anything like it happen before." She smiled around at them. "D'you remember that wonderful scene at the end of the movie *Dr. Strangelove*, where Slim Pickens is riding down sitting astride the bomb they've dropped? Well, it reminded me of that! I felt I was flying through space alongside this projectile, though I couldn't really see any projectile. And the next thing I knew I was pitching forward and catapulting out of the sky toward the target—just like the man on the bomb."

"You could see where it was aiming for?" Dunk asked. All eyes were on the black-haired woman.

She nodded. "I could see the whole city of Rome laid out before me. I glimpsed the Vatican and St. Peter's over on the left bank of the river, and the Colloseum—I'd recognize that anywhere—way over on the other side of the river and south, I guess, of me. But we went in further north. I'd know that place anywhere. I could see this building; a big house. I thought we were going to hit it, and then we veered off and missed. We landed on the grounds—like in a big park. But we plunged on through the earth and into an underground cave, like a big room. I had a fleeting glimpse of people in black robes. I'd swear they were around an altar with something white on it, but it all happened so fast. Just as I burst in everything spun around and every imaginable color flashed in my eyes. The next thing I knew I was lying in the circle back in Virginia, in front of our altar, and my coven was bathing my face with water and trying to ground me."

"Wow!" Earl said.

"But you don't know where the building or the cave were?" Dunk was anxiously trying to pinpoint it.

"Yes," Tanya said. "Yes, I do. It made such an impression on me that I went to the library and got out a guidebook to Rome, with a full city map. Duncan, I landed in—under—the old villa where Mussolini used to live during the Second World War! The Villa Tor-lonia, it's called. It seems there are catacombs under-neath it."

Earl whistled.

"I … I don't understand exactly what you were trying to achieve," Beth said. "I know about raising energy to work magic—to make things happen that wouldn't normally happen—but just why, and where, were you directing this energy?"

"We're part of the network that Dunk and the rest of you got in touch with," Tanya explained. "We were asked to raise lots of positive energy and direct it out-ward, to counteract any negative energies being directed our way. To reflect back what was coming at us. Isn't that what you said, Dunk?"

The blond Californian nodded. "That's it exactly, Tanya. That was all we could ask. We didn't know exactly where they were located—though you seem to have found them—so we couldn't be more specific."

"But now we know they're in Rome," Guillemette said.

"Right! But we didn't even know *that* for certain when we first alerted all the groups around the country. Though Beth had suggested it, when we were with Reg Lee in England," Duncan said.

There was another knock at the door. Dunk glanced at his watch.

"I don't believe it! That must be Etienne."

51

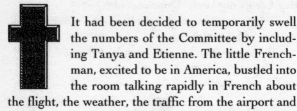It had been decided to temporarily swell the numbers of the Committee by including Tanya and Etienne. The little Frenchman, excited to be in America, bustled into the room talking rapidly in French about the flight, the weather, the traffic from the airport and the pleasure of seeing them all again. Dunk finally got him to sit down and be quiet.

"It's getting on for lunchtime," Dunk said. "I suggest we let Etienne bring us up-to-date on what he's just come up with, and then we'll all go out to eat … on Bill Highland, of course!"

Everyone laughed and agreed.

"Okay, Etienne. What is it you've discovered?"

The suntanned face beneath the ever-present beret beamed at each of them briefly and then became serious.

"When you were over in Paris, recently, Rudolf mentioned that you thought there was some special date; some *occurrence* that was to be the goal at which these Satanists aimed, *n'est ce pas?*"

"Right," Earl said. "We think they must be working up to some special date when they're going to really 'let slip the gods of war'."

"*Bon!* As I thought. Then, *mes amis,* I think I have found that date!"

There was a murmur of excitement.

"Well done, Etienne," Dunk said. "Tell us all about it."

The Frenchman's eyes gleamed as he looked around at them, stroking his moustache.

"As you know, Dunk and Rudy, I am an astrologer but of a—what you say?—*particularité.*"

"A specialist," Rudy said. "You specialize, do you not, Etienne, in the stars rather than the planets?"

"*Oui.* That is it *exactement.* Most astrologers work with simply the relative positions of the planets, but not I. I look at the greater picture."

"Is this accurate?" Earl sounded doubtful. "Not to be skeptical, Etienne, but I really don't hold much brief for those newspaper horoscopes."

"I'd hope not!" Guillemette said. "For goodness sake, Earl! Nobody in their right mind believes in those things. They're far too generalized to be of any use to anyone!"

"Don't you need to know a person's date and time of birth, to cast an accurate chart?" Beth asked.

"And place of birth," Dunk added. "All three. As Guillemette says, a newspaper or magazine's little paragraph can't possibly fit everyone everywhere who was born anytime throughout the entire month!"

"But let us get back to Etienne, here," Rudy said anxiously. "We can discuss horoscopes over lunch. What news does our friend bring?"

"*Bon! Merci, mon ami.*" Etienne's eyes were bright as he looked around the circle of friends. "I will first tell you what I have found, and then I will try to explain it."

They all strained forward. He cleared his throat.

"On the date I have found, coming up soon, Saturn is conjunct Pluto in Scorpio, opposing the Pleiades in Taurus and squaring Regulus in Leo. Also squaring Uranus and Mars in Aquarius, creating a critical twenty-nine degree Grand Square. Not only that, but we will also have the Moon conjunct Neptune at twenty-one degrees Virgo conjunct Denebola. Denebola, as you know, is the fixed star of natural disasters and catastrophes."

He sat back. All faces remained blank and fixed on him. Etienne gave a typically Gaulish shrug.

"On November Eve," he said, "the sun will oppose the United States's natal sun, creating the trigger point."

Dunk cleared his throat.

"I don't know much about astrology," he said. "Although I certainly recognize Pluto and Scorpio and Taurus and Aquarius. But I'm damned if I've ever heard of this Regulus or, what was it, Denebola? Can you explain a bit, Etienne?"

"*Certainement!* There are certain fixed stars that have been recognized as significant over the centuries. Lilly used about fifty of them in his horary delineations. They are significant in that they have what we call 'malefic' degrees. For example, the star Hamal, at seven degrees thirty-one minutes Taurus, is an indication of violence and cruelty. Hyades at five degrees forty-one minutes Gemini is tied in to scandal, violence, evil and even imprisonment. Caopus, at fourteen degrees fifty-one minutes Cancer, is associated with quick tempers and specifically trouble with one's father. There are many such stars."

"Ach! I begin to see," Rudy said.

"Good for you!" Earl muttered.

"So, you're saying that on November Eve—that's the Samhain Sabbat coming up—there's going to be an especially bad arrangement of planets and stars?" Dunk asked.

"Not just 'especially bad'," Etienne replied. "It is directly connected to the natal sun—the birth configuration—of the United States. If I were wanting to harm this whole country, that is exactly the sort of configuration I would look for to time my attack!"

"So it's to be at Samhain?" Guillemette said. "We might have guessed it, I suppose."

"Ja! It is the most important, and therefore the most powerful of the Sabbats of the year," Rudy agreed. "And for it to coincide with these things Etienne has been detailing—*mein Gott,* but that is frightening!"

"Well, at least we do have the date now, and the place … assuming they always operate from the same temple." Dunk got up and paced the floor, running his fingers through his hair. "We'll have to get word out to all the groups again. We'll give them the whole story so they can direct power as they see fit. And I think we'll have them all work at exactly the same time, so that it'll be a huge surge of energy that's directed at the Satanists."

"And what do we do?" Beth asked.

"We?"

"The Committee. The seven of us sitting here?"

Dunk thought for a moment.

"I think we should go to Rome," he said.

52

The raven kept the crow in sight as they winged their way across the treetops. They had been flying for several hours with only occasional rests on upper tree limbs and fenceposts. The raven had flown an erratic course so that the crow would not know it had an escort. They had left Cooperstown, in upper state New York, and were now on the outskirts of the city of Albany.

Suddenly the crow made a diving turn to the left, which became a full circle. It swung around over the top of a group of old stone buildings which were encircled by a tall stone wall. The raven climbed high into the sky and looked down.

Seeming assured that it was alone, the crow settled down on the top of the wall and then dropped to the ground inside. The raven flew lower.

Where the crow had stood was now a nun in a black habit. She looked about her and headed for the heavy oak door to the rear of the nearest building. She opened the door and disappeared inside. The raven swept down and alighted on the gutter of the same building.

Sister Joseph addressed the small group of nuns gathered in the chapel.

"We must keep this meeting short, sisters," she said. "We don't have a lot of time that we can count on being alone here, and I have many more of you to talk to before I'm through."

Her gaze traveled around the room. They were only half a dozen there; a mixture of young nuns and old, she noticed. Typical. The young ones were frustrated at being kept in the convent when they wanted to be out among the people, doing things. She found that there were invariably a few new nuns in every convent who became increasingly frustrated and disillusioned with their calling. Whereas the older ones had seen it all and were tired of having achieved nothing. They felt their lives had been wasted and wanted, somehow, to strike back, though they didn't really know at what. They just wanted to see some return for their energies before life ended.

"I'm here to report that all across the country there are groups such as yours—all frustrated with the slow-moving, tradition-steeped lack of action of Mother Church—who have taken it upon themselves to join the greater band of Our Lord Belial. He it is Who will answer our prayers; He it is Who will guarantee that which we desire most in this life! It's all very well to profess dedication to the so-called Savior, to claim to be 'the brides of Christ', but what does that bring you? Sleepless nights, hard work that's never appreciated, bad food and abominable living conditions! Well, I'm here to tell you that there is a better way. You've all responded to my initial contacts and have shown your-selves as willing to try 'the other side', as it were. Good! You've shown courage and it will be rewarded."

An elderly nun at the back tentatively raised a hand.

"You say there are others who have turned to Satan?" she asked.

"The Lord Belial!" snapped Sister Joseph. "Satan is an old, over-worked name that we don't use. Yes, there are many more of you."

"Throughout the country, you said?"

"That's right. I've personally been in contact with those in New York state. I can vouch for there being other followers in every other state."

"Does the Reverend Mother know about this, Sis-ter?" asked a young nun in the second row.

The nun at the front sniffed in contempt. "Do you see her sitting here?" she asked. "Do you see any of her cronies sitting here? Of course she doesn't know!" She looked hard at each of them in turn. "You are special! You have been invited to join us because of what you truly desire, and because of what I've learned about you. Because of how you feel about what you want to accomplish. You don't want to be slaves to Mother Superior, do you?"

There were murmurs from the small group.

"You don't want to waste your entire lives singing psalms and muttering prayers; scraping the barren ground outside to grow vegetables to eke out a dry existence here. Do you?"

"No!" They all responded.

Outside the raven sat on the gutter and listened to the voices filtering through the half-open window. He sat there for a long time before finally spreading his wings and soaring up into the sky. He headed west, back toward the Finger Lakes region.

"Your friend George Ravenfeather has been filling me in on some sort of plot within the Church," Bill Highland said. "God knows how he found out the details." He switched the telephone to his other ear and reached forward to the dish of M&M candies on his desk. "It's right up your alley, Dunk. Satanists, if you can believe it. Satanists right inside the Church! How about that?"

"That fits, Bill," Dunk's voice came over the phone. "I've been telling you about it." His voice sounded tired.

"Yes, but you said a group of 'em in Rome, didn't you?" The senator filled his mouth with the candies and chewed contentedly.

"That's where the main bunch is, yes. But we figured there had to be satellite groups all across this country. Has George found them, then?"

"Several of them, apparently. Though he's only been covering New York state. But he's given me the details of the ringleader. A nun, for god's sake! We're picking her up, and she should be able to lead us to others. Probably make contacts for other states."

"I doubt you'll do more than scratch the surface, Bill, but every little bit helps."

"So when are you off to Rome?"

"In a couple of weeks. We've got lots to do before then, though. Contacting groups around the country and apprising them of the situation. Tying in everyone as to what we want them to do and exactly when. We're all working hard at it and burning the midnight oil, believe me. I'll keep in touch, Bill."

"You do that. And Dunk … ?"

"Yes?"

"Good luck."

"Thanks, Bill."

The senator put down the phone and picked up more M&Ms. His brow was furrowed. He was worried.

"Our friend is off somewhere, fast," Earl said.

Dunk raised his eyebrows in question.

"The reporter. Arnie Summers."

"Where's he going, Earl?"

Earl was on his way to the door. "I don't know. I just got word from the newspaper. I got friendly with a copyboy there and paid him a couple of bucks to keep an eye on Arnie; to tell me when he left town. Apparently he's about to leave now. The copyboy says there don't seem to be any assignments that should send him off in any sort of a hurry. Want to come with me?"

Dunk made up his mind quickly.

"Sure! We can call Rudy from somewhere along the way. We probably won't be gone long, anyway."

They spotted Arnie's beat-up old green Cougar, with its one brown door, just a block from the newspaper office. It was heading north out of town.

"You got enough gas?" Dunk asked.

"Oh, yes. I always keep it full. It's a habit I've had for years. You just never know when you may need to go somewhere."

The smoke-blowing Cougar wound its way through the busy city and got onto the Beltway going around to connect to I-95 North.

"We know he's in cahoots with the Satanists," Earl said, keeping a discreet distance behind the newspaperman. "It's my bet he's going to rendezvous with them."

"The principals are in Rome, don't forget," Dunk said.

"Right. But there must be some heavyweight here. I'll bet you a subscription to FATE magazine that he's going to some important meeting to do with this Samhain planetary alignment, or whatever it is."

"You're on," said Dunk, grinning. "But if we don't hit paydirt within a few days, we're going back. We've got to get ready to go to Rome for the showdown, don't forget."

The trail led them up through Baltimore, Md., Harrisburg, Penn., and Binghamton, N.Y. In Harrisburg Arnie stopped to eat. Dunk seized the opportunity to call Rudy and tell him where they were and what they were doing.

"You think it is worth following him?" the German asked.

"Well, we've got a little time before we leave for Rome," Dunk said. "At least this way I feel I'm doing something constructive. And besides, I do think Earl might be right. There might be some important meeting this guy is going to."

"Mmm. *Gut!* All right, Duncan. The ladies and I have enough to keep us busy. Good luck, *mein Freund.*"

After his meal Arnie got back on the main road and continued on, still heading north. They went through Binghamton, and some time later the Cougar finally pulled into a motel on the outskirts of Syracuse.

"Over there, Earl." Dunk indicated a second motel, almost opposite the one Arnie had checked into. "This is going to be a short night."

"What d'you mean?"

"Well," Dunk said, "we'll have to be awake by six at least, so we can keep an eye on the Cougar and be ready to leave when he does."

As it happened Arnie slept late. He didn't leave the motel until nearly ten in the morning, and then drove less than a block to a McDonald's, where he had breakfast. Finally he emerged and got onto I-90 westbound.

"Canada!" Dunk said.

"What?"

"Canada. I bet he's going to Canada. I-90 leads into Buffalo and Niagara Falls. He's running away, Earl!"

"Son-of-a-gun, I think you're right. Now why would he do that, d'you think?"

Dunk sighed. "I think he knows only too well what's in store for America in the next couple of weeks. He's getting out while he can. Oh, by the way … you owe me a subscription to FATE magazine!"

53

On a suggestion from Guillemette, the Committee decided to split forces, with half of them going to Rome and the others proceeding to Haiti, to work on coordinating and building Forces of Light there. So, a few days before Dunk, Beth, Rudy, and Tanya were to fly to Rome, Earl, Guillemette, and Etienne took a flight to New York.

"I have a love-hate relationship with this city," Earl said.

"I know what you mean Earl, my man," Guillemette said. "I love the botanicas, the little stores that deal in herbs and powders, candles, and incense. They're all over the city. And if you know what you want, so that you can ask for it by name, you can get anything. But I hate the bums, the traffic, and the crime."

They had taken a checkered cab downtown to see Mirari Jauregi, Guillemette's aunt. Earl paid the driver and followed the Haitian and the Frenchman up the stairs to the apartment.

After they'd been introduced, the old black woman looked Earl up and down. "So this be he?"

He turned red under her scrutiny. "What have you been saying about me?" he demanded of Guillemette.

"Now, now! Hush, my man!" said Mirari. She turned to the younger woman. "He don't seem too bad, child."

Guillemette exploded in laughter. *"Mamaloi,* I swear you'll be the death of me!"

Earl huffed and found himself a seat. Etienne watched the exchange with an amused smile on his lips.

"We're on our way down to Haiti," Guillemette said. "But I wanted to stop off here first, on our way, to let you know the exact date for everything."

"Oh, don't you worry 'bout me, girl. I knows all 'bout it. I'll fit in all right."

"I know you will." Guillemette smiled at her aunt. "And I had guessed you were onto the date—even before we got it, I bet. Have you talked to the other mambos?"

"Uhuh! You know we can get the word out if'n we has to. We's all set, girl, don't you worry none."

"May I ask what you have planned?" Earl asked.

The deep-set black eyes turned to him. "We's got a nice surprise planned for these Satanist people, Earl, my man. We going to invite the 'Big Three' to visit wi' them."

"The 'Big Three'?" Etienne asked.

Guillemette grinned. "That's pretty heavy medicine, believe me. There's Ogoun, who's a warrior loa. Then there's Gédé."

"Ah, yes!" Earl nodded his head. "I remember him. God of the dead, isn't he?"

"And who is the third?" Etiene asked.

"The third is the main man," Mirari cried. "The ancient and venerable father hisself. It's Damballah."

"Pardon. I am not too clear on all this," Etienne said.

Guillemette smiled at the Frenchman. "Damballah-Wédo is the father figure of the Voudoun pantheon. He is looked upon as the source of all wisdom, the origin and essence of life. To his followers he is represented as a serpent. Gédé—also known as Baron LaCroix, Baron Cimitère and Baron Samedi—is a chthonic god: very powerful, though he can get pretty crude in his language and gestures in his earthly appearances! Ogoun, or Ogu-Balindjo, is a storm god also known as the blacksmith of the loa. All three are very powerful deities."

The four of them discussed the plans of the Committee: the idea of the many various groups across America working to send their energies hurtling back at the Satanists, all at exactly the same time. Guillemette told her aunt that the others of their group would shortly be going to Rome, hoping to actually locate the evil cardinal and somehow defuse the situation on the spot. But, if all else failed, they would have a battle to end all battles on their hands by November's Eve, the end of the month.

"Don't you worry, child," Mirari said, her face serious. "You won't be alone in that battle. By then I'll have everyone ready! New York, New Orleans, Chicago, Miami, Los Angeles, San Francisco—we'll all be working with you. We ain't goin' down without a fight! The loa'll see to that."

⚡

They flew on to Santo Domingo and then followed the same route that Guillemette and Earl had previously taken. They rented the same 20-foot Seacraft at Barahona and sailed south and then northwest into Haitian waters. Past Anse-à-Pitre, Saltrou, Belle Anse—near where they had landed last time—on past Marigot and Timo village until they came to Jacmel.

Jacmel had been cut off from the Haitian capital of Port-au-Prince for the longest time by the fact that the only "highway" between the two was a riverbed filled with boulders and prone to flash floods. But in 1978 the French government presented Haiti with the gift of a magnificent mountain road, turning travel between the two towns into a pleasurable one-and-a-half hour drive.

The little town of Jacmel then sprouted a hotel and a number of *pensions,* some of which became well-known for their cuisine. Restaurants, art galleries, and nightclubs quickly brought prosperity to the previously impoverished community.

Earl brought the Seacraft into the hill-town's harbor and they disembarked. Guillemette led the way through the bustling streets of balconied townhouses, many with wrought-iron balconies and gardens across the roofs. Between the cathedral and the wharf, some of the streets were so narrow and steep that they became long stretches of steps, climbing higher and higher and totally precluding motor traffic.

Guillemette led her companions to one of the town's "coffee palaces," set high up behind the cathedral and overlooking the waterfront below. It had been built in the 1880s out of cast-iron columns, balconies, and doors shipped from France and Germany as ballast for the freighters. There were Corinthian-style columns with fluted bases, ornamental brackets forming shallow arches, iron railings of interlocking squares, circles, crosses, and arabesques. The doors were massive things set into Romanesque and Gothic portals. Colorful tiles covered the floors of the courtyards and piazzas.

As the trio approached the building, a distinguished-looking Haitian gentleman with silver hair and wearing a fine linen suit got up from the table in the courtyard, where he had been drinking iced tea, and waved to them.

"Guillemette? Is that you, my dear?"

"Robert!" she cried and broke into a run. "Robert Vital! I didn't know if you'd still be here or not."

They embraced and then he stepped back and took her hand, kissing it. Earl felt slightly annoyed, though he wasn't sure why. Guillemette turned to indicate her companions.

"These are my very good friends," she said. "Professor Earl Stratford, of New York, and Etienne Macé, from Paris, France."

"Enchanté!" Robert Vital inclined his head to them and spread his arms to indicate the other chairs at the table. "Won't you sit down? Tea?"

"Please!" Earl was sweating and only too ready for something cold.

"Merci," said Etienne.

The older man clapped his hands and a tall, thin, black manservant appeared in the doorway.

"Now, tell me all about it," Vital said, when they were all settled with their drinks. "What brings you home, Guillemette? It's been too long, you know."

Robert Vital was the wealthy owner of a rum factory in Haiti. The house in Jacmel was only one of three he owned. Although outwardly a refined, upright, Christian businessman, Robert Vital was houngan at the hounfor in the hills above Jacmel and a Voudoun drummer of some repute. Stories of his pounding a favorite *seconde* drum for four or five hours at a time, without a break, in past Voudoun rituals were whispered from one end of the Republic to the other. At one time Guillemette's mother had been mambo to Vital's houngan.

Soon the four of them were laughing and joking, and even Earl was coming to like the suave businessman in the impeccable suit. Gold flashed from the several large rings on his fingers as Vital poured them more iced tea.

"So, while the rest of your friends are off to beard the lion in his den, you are here to organize the loas' presence against these Satanists?" he said.

"It's a very important part of our offensive," Earl agreed. "I've seen, myself, what the loa can do."

"This is not Earl's first time in Haiti with me," Guillemette murmured. "We have had to draw upon the power of the loa before."

"Then you will be here for some time?"

They nodded.

"Exactly how long we don't know," Guillemette said. "Much depends on our friends in Rome, and how they make out."

"And you will be staying where?" Vital asked.

They hesitated. Earl and Etienne looked to Guillemette.

"I was thinking of one of the pensions here," she said, "or we might even go into Port-au-Prince. We have to make contact with a number of hounfors while we're here."

"Then you shall stay here," said Vital, matter-of-factly. "I shall arrange it. No more to be said!"

54

 "I *am* being reasonable," Earl said petulantly. "There's just something about the man I don't like."

"What?"

"I don't know, Guillemette! I can't put my finger on it. Just ... something!"

Guillemette turned back the covers and sat on the edge of the bed. They were in the room she had been given in Robert Vital's house. Earl had a room next to her's but had slipped in to talk. Although it was still early evening, both were preparing for bed. Guillemette was wearing a delicate, lacy, red silk nightdress cut very low. Earl was in neatly pressed blue and red striped pajamas.

"I've known him for years," Guillemette said. "He was my mother's houngan for the longest time. He's known throughout the Republic."

"I dare say he is,"

"So what do you want me to do, Earl?"

He was pacing the room, tugging on his beard. He stopped at the foot of the bed and looked hard at her.

"I guess nothing. Just ... just be careful, all right?"

She smiled up at him through long eyelashes.

"Why I do believe you care about me, my man."

"Well of course I do."

He moved around and sat down on the bed close beside her. She took his hand.

"Guillemette … "

There was a soft tap on the door. Earl sprang up and away from Guillemette as if he'd received an electric shock. She laughed.

"Come in," she called.

The door opened part-way and Etienne peered around it.

"All right if I come in?" he asked.

"Of course it is, my man. Come and join the party."

"Oh! Hope I am not interrupting anything?"

"Not anymore," muttered Earl.

All three sat on the bed and talked in hushed voices.

"I have to let you both know that I am getting very negative vibrations from our host," Etienne said. "I was doing my meditation before going to bed and I slipped into an out-of-body condition."

"You astrally projected?" Earl said.

"*Oui.* I found myself floating above my physical body, so I decided—out of curiosity you understand?—to quickly run around the house and see what the rest of it was like."

"And what did you find?" Guillemette asked.

The Frenchman shrugged. "It was pretty much as one would expect: large living room, dining room, kitchen, servants' quarters. But when I went into Monsieur Vital's study I received a shock."

The other two leaned forward expectantly.

"His study is part library and has bookcases around three walls."

"That's it?" Earl snorted.

"Un moment, mon ami. It was the books that were in these bookcases that attracted me."

"What were they, Etienne?" Guillemette hesitantly asked.

"Black magic. Many, many books on black magic and Satanism. Others on ceremonial magic, *oui,* and on Voudoun of course. Witchcraft, divination, herbology—the rest were as you would expect from anyone interested in this field at all. But, as I say, the majority were on the Left Hand Path, and they looked as though they had been well handled."

"You're saying you think Robert's a Satanist?" Guillemette sounded incredulous.

"I do not know." Again a shrug. "However, my curiosity was piqued. I continued my inspection and went down into the basement of the house."

"And … ?" Earl sounded impatient. Guillemette put a hand on his arm.

"This is why I have come to you," the Frenchman said. "I found a temple, a ritual set-up, down in the cellars and I must call upon your expertise to tell me whether or not it is one for Voudoun. I am not too familiar with that practice."

"But how did it look to you?" Earl asked. "From your knowledge of other forms of magical practice?"

"I would think almost certainly that it is Satanic. But, as I say, I know nothing of the Haitian religion."

"What shall we do?" Earl asked, looking at Guillemette. "All astrally project down there?"

"I don't know," she said thoughtfully. "The only problem with projecting is that you can't easily open things, like cupboards and boxes and, especially, books. I'd love to go down there in the physical and have a thorough look around. Any idea where our host is, Etienne?"

"Mais oui. He is in the study I spoke of. That was the other thing ... he was very busy studying an ancient tome on Satanic conjuration. Reading and taking notes."

"Mmm. Could be tricky," Guillemette said. "If he should catch us ... "

"I'm game if you are," Earl said.

"I myself also, of course," Etiene added.

The black woman made up her mind. "All right. Give me five minutes to get dressed—you too Earl—and we'll meet at the top of the stairs."

They easily found the door to the basement. It was beneath the staircase and was unlocked.

"He wasn't expecting guests and probably didn't think to lock it after we arrived," Earl whispered. He glanced back down the hallway to where a crack of light appeared from under the door to Vital's study. Cautiously Earl opened the cellar door and led the way down.

It was pitch dark, and Earl ran his hand down the rough wall alongside the staircase. There didn't seem to be a handrailing on the other side, so they moved slowly and cautiously. Eventually they reached the bottom.

"Which way, Etienne?"

"Let me see. The staircase above is in this direction, *bon!* So we must go toward the back of the house. Try to move to the left, Earl, if you can."

"Ouch! Damn!"

There was a dull thump as Earl walked into something.

"Are you all right, Earl?"

"Apart from knocking my brains out, yes! God, it's black down here."

"I have a cigarette lighter, if it would help," Etienne offered.

"Yes," Earl said. "Let me have it. No one's going to see that down here. You did shut the door after you, didn't you, Etienne?"

"*Mais oui.*"

Earl lit the lighter and held it high. He saw that he had walked into a metal column supporting the ground floor of the house. A number of them were visible in the gloom. Turning slowly he saw a passageway leading off to the left.

"This way."

At the end was a large, heavy, wooden door.

"I believe this is it," Etienne said.

The latch and hinges of the door looked old and rusty but, on examining them, Earl found they had been well greased. He lifted the latch and tugged on the door. It swung open silently and they went in.

"Ye Gods!" Earl exclaimed.

"Voudoun this certainly is not!" said Guillemette.

They found themselves on the threshold of a large ritual area. Three concentric circles were marked on the floor in lines that seemed to glow phophorescently. In the center of the circles was a tall altar covered with a black cloth. On it stood an ornate gold chalice and a gold candelabra holding six black candles and one red.

In front of the candelabra lay a black-handled knife with a wavy, Kris-like blade. On the rear wall of the room, just visible in the faint light, hung the head of a huge black goat with four horns. A black candle was attached to each of the horns.

"Four horns?" Earl said. "I've never heard of a four-horned goat."

"Technically I believe it's a sheep," Guillemette said. "They're called Jacobs sheep and, yes, they have four horns rather than two."

"Wow! Very impressive," Earl said.

"Well, thank you. I'm glad you like it!"

All three spun around at the sound of the voice. Light flooded the room as Robert Vital flipped a recessed switch in the wall.

"Welcome to my ritual room," he said. "I'm sorry, Guillemette, but this is not a room for welcoming the loa."

55

"It's not just millions, or even billions," Patricia Jackson said. "It's in the multi-trillions! It's unbelievable."

The little group sat in the Oval Office of the White House. Senator Highland shuffled his papers and looked anxiously around at the others. The Budget Director continued.

"We have to provide food and shelter to all who were made homeless; we have to rebuild homes, hospitals, offices and factories, roads and bridges. And as fast as we start to rebuild another calamity destroys. The crops situation—especially in the South—is also a huge concern."

"Health issues are major." The Surgeon General, Christine Miffett-Webster, caught the president's eye. "We are trucking in water to hundreds of sites, but we can't keep up, especially with the growing sanitation problems. Virtually every state has called out its National Guard. As I've said before: we have to mobilize the army, Mr. President."

"You're right, Christine. Let's see to it. I was hoping it would all go away before it came to that, but I can see that it's not going to. Bill?" He looked at Bill Highland. "What's the latest word from your people?"

The senator swallowed. His normally cheery face was serious.

"Dunk—Duncan Webster—has reported that they're close to a confrontation. As you know, sir, they're leaving for Rome, which is where the enemy is situated. This is going to be the big one, he says. The 'do or die'."

"I still have great difficulty swallowing this!" Dick Dibell, the National Security Advisor, burst out, shaking his head in despair. "I'm sorry, sir, but really— magical warfare? I mean … "

Bill was pleased to see that the president didn't back down.

"I know, Dick," he said. "We've all had to revise our belief systems here. But we all heard what Bill had to say in his briefing a moment ago and, I have to admit, it does seem to make a certain amount of sense out of what, until now, seemed nonsense. I'm not saying I understand any of it, mind you. But then there's a hell of a lot about nuclear warfare I don't understand. But I'm willing to keep an open mind. And I expect you to do the same. All right, Dick?"

The National Security Advisor looked extremely uncomfortable, but slowly nodded his head.

"If you say so, sir."

"I do say so." The president looked around the room. "And understand that anything we have discussed in here, regarding this, is to be treated in the strictest confidence. I don't want to tune in tomorrow and see "Hard Copy," or "Current Affair," or anyone, highlighting a piece on the president of these United States turning to magic!"

There was uneasy laughter.

"Now," he continued. "To get serious. What Pat said a moment ago is only too true. The multi-trillion dollar drain is forcing us toward bankruptcy. I can't begin to tell you what that would mean to this country. Not to mention all those emerging countries who rely on us and look to us for just about everything. If what Bill tells us is true—and we have to go along with it as our only working hypothesis—then we must pray that this Committee of his has that special strength that our army, navy, air force, and marines combined do not have. But we shall soon know. The deadline, Bill, is… ?"

"October thirty-first, Mr. President."

"Hallowe'en, would you believe!" Dick Dibell shook his head in disbelief.

56

Earl, Guillemette, and Etienne were together back in Guillemette's room. Vital had taken them there, at gunpoint, and locked them in.

"You shall stay here until I decide what to do with you," he said. "It is unfortunate you were so curious. I cannot afford for you, or anyone, to besmirch my image here, you see. I have business in Port-au-Prince this evening. When I return later tonight we will sit down together and have a conference."

"How nice!" Earl sneered. "All very civilized."

"Yes," Vital said, looking hard at Earl. "I *am* civilized. And I shall find a civilized way to dispose of you!"

He left, locking them together in the room.

"So much for your mother's old buddy," Earl said, studying the window. They were on the third floor of the house.

"He's changed," the black woman said. "I would guess he got over-ambitious. He always was pretentious and trying to climb the social ladder. I remember he once said that one day he would own the largest rum factory in the Caribbean. Now he does."

"By selling his soul," Etienne muttered.

"Well, we've got to get out of here," Earl said. "The others are expecting our input for the big fight, and the clock's ticking. We can't let them down."

"Do you think our friend Monsieur Vital is part of that same group, the ones in Rome?" Etienne asked.

Guillemette shook her head.

"I don't think so. There are Satanists all over the world, but they're not all affiliated with one another. There's not a Satanic Pope or anything, so far as I know. And I think Robert Vital is more of a *Boko* than a true Satanist."

"What's a Boko?"

"He—or she; a Boko can be female—is a sort of black magician of Voudoun," she replied. "There are many of them scattered across Haiti. The Boko puts curses on people—for a price, of course. He'll charge you to put a curse on your enemy and then go to that enemy, tell him he's been cursed, and charge him a higher fee to remove the curse."

"Charming!" said Earl. "I guess you can amass quite a lot of money that way, with superstitious people."

"They are also said to be capable of making zombies," Guillemette added, with a slight smile. "Not that any of us believe in those, right?"

"Right," Earl said, hesitantly. "But at the same time I don't want him experimenting with us!"

"All right," Etienne said. "Somehow we have to get out of here."

"We're too high up to get out of the window and jump down," Earl said. "And it's getting darker all the time—though that might be in our favor." He leaned out of the window as far as he dared. "There's not even a drainpipe we can shimmy down or a lower balcony or awning we can drop onto."

"What about up?" Guillemette asked.

"What?"

"Up, my man! How close are we to the roof?"

Earl carefully twisted around and looked up.

"You know, you're right! We could, possibly, climb out and up onto the roof. It all rather depends on the strength of that rain gutter above; whether it'll take our weight as we grab hold."

"Let me give it a try," Etienne said, going to the window. "I am much smaller and lighter than either one of you two. I might be able to do it."

"And then what?"

"I will take a sheet from the bed up with me so that, when you climb up, you will have something else on which to rely beside the gutter."

Guillemette turned to the Frenchman. "Go for it, Etienne."

He draped a bedsheet around his shoulders and climbed out of the window, carefully standing up on the window ledge. Earl held onto his legs to steady him. Etienne reached up and was just able to grasp the edge of the gutter above. Carefully he tested it, pulling down on it and slowly adding his whole weight. It held.

"All right, *mes amis*, I am going for it," he said.

With Earl pushing up on his feet, the little Frenchman was able to haul himself up to the roof. At one point the gutter gave a loud crack, as a fastener somewhere along its length gave way, but it held and Etienne scrambled onto the flat roof.

Earl turned to Guillemette.

"You're next, my love," he said.

"Why, Earl!" she said.

She kissed him on the cheek and climbed up onto the window ledge. Etienne had ripped the sheet in half, lengthwise, and knotted it together. It was now longer, but still strong. He looped his end around his waist and lowered the rest of it down toward the window. Guillemette grasped it. With the help of both men— one pushing up from below and the other pulling from above—she was soon on the roof beside Etienne.

With the two helping from above it didn't take long for Earl to be up and joining them also. He gave a sigh of relief and hugged them both.

"So far so good," he said.

"Yes," Guillemette said. "But now what?"

They inspected the roof, walking slowly all around the perimeter, looking down.

"Out of the frying pan … " muttered Earl.

"We could, perhaps, lower ourselves down again into another one of the rooms that is not locked," Etienne suggested.

"First we'd need to find one with the window open," Earl responded, "and trust the gutter is as good and strong there as where we climbed up. Then we'd have to hope that the room we got into wasn't locked. Let's think a bit more before we try that."

They walked around the roof edge again.

"*Ici!* Here," Etienne said. He stood at a rear corner of the building. "You see, the house is on the hill so at the back here it is only two storeys high, while at the front it is three. So, we must concentrate our efforts at the rear."

"Very good, Etienne," Earl said.

"But that's still a long way down." Guillemette peered over the edge. "And it's so dark now I can barely see the ground."

"I would like to try something," Etienne still had the length of sheet and now held it out to Earl. "Here, Earl. Do you think that, holding one end of this, you could support my weight hanging on the other end?"

Earl moved forward, grasped the Frenchman around the waist and hoisted him up in the air.

"God! You don't weigh much at all!" he said setting him down again. "Yes. Sure I could. Why?"

The Frenchman chuckled. "See," he said, pointing. "There is that large satinwood tree close to the house. Not close enough, it would seem. But," he tugged gently on the sheet Earl held. "If you were to lower me down at the corner of the house, here, Earl, and then start to swing me like a pendulum ... "

"You know, we might be able to do it!" Earl cried excitedly. "Yes, if I can swing you far enough you could grab hold of one of those two branches. I think it's worth a try."

"And then what?"

They both turned to look at Guillemette.

"So you get into the tree," she said. "Then how can we get down? You sure aren't going to swing me on any bedsheet, Earl, my man!"

"Non, non!" Etienne waved his hands in the air. "I will climb down from the tree and go looking for a ladder. If I cannot find one, then I will come back through the house and open up a window in an unlocked room, as we suggested."

"I think it's worth a try," Earl said.

The Haitian woman looked from one to the other of them and then shrugged her shoulders. "What have we got to lose?"

With the end of the sheet tied securely around his waist, Etienne allowed Earl to slowly lower him over the side of the building. Guillmette bit her lip as she watched.

"Okay," Earl grunted, when the length of linen was at its limit. "Give a push off from the wall if you can, to get it started swinging."

The little Frenchman dutifully kicked out and caught the corner of the building with his foot. Gritting his teeth, Earl began to swing the laden sheet. Agonizingly slowly it began to swing back and forth across the corner of the house. As the distance to the tree branches decreased, Etienne stretched out his hands. Breathlessly Guillemette watched him.

"Can't keep this up much longer," Earl grunted as he swung. "He seems to be getting heavier by the second!"

"For goodness sake, don't drop him!" Guillemette murmured.

"Don't drop me, *mon ami*," Etienne echoed, as he swung toward the tree and away again. "Nearly there."

His fingers brushed the tips of the branches then, with two more swings, his arms were going in among the leaves. Suddenly he grabbed hold of a branch and the swinging stopped, almost causing Earl to topple off the roof. Guillemette grabbed him around the waist.

"Whoa! You there, Etienne?"

"*Oui*. You can let go of the sheet."

Earl did so and they watched their friend swing downward as the branch he had grasped took the full weight. But he held on. The branch settled and Etienne crawled further onto it. He looked back at his friends on the roof. They could only just make out his grinning face in the gathering dusk. Then he was gone, climbing down the tree like a monkey.

It was ten minutes before Etienne reappeared, lugging an old ladder with several rungs missing. It was just too short to reach the roof, so he had to find some boxes on which to stand it. Finally, with fingers crossed for luck and a few prayers to the gods, Guillemette and Earl climbed down and stood on the ground beside the Frenchman.

"Fantastic!" Earl cried. "Well done, Etienne! Now, let's get the hell out of here. Where to, Guillemette?"

They took a circuitous route around the town and finally emerged on a dirt trail leading north, towards Port-au-Prince.

"We'll follow this for a while," Guillemette said. "It should branch off in a mile or two and we can swing out towards Kenscoff and then Pétionville."

"Where are we aiming for?"

She smiled. "Earl, you remember Mambo Jannica?"

He nodded. Jannica was the Voudoun Mambo who had helped them over a year ago, when the Comittee had had to work against a group of Russian and Cuban psychometry experts. She had a hounfor on the northern coast of Haiti.

"But isn't that a long way off?" Earl asked.

"Not if we do it in easy stages," Guillemette replied. "We do need to speak with a lot of other hounfors along the way, anyway. But our final destination will be Môle St. Nicholas and the hounfor of my sister mambo, Jannica."

57

"Don't be more than a couple of hours," Dunk said, looking at his watch. "It's quarter of three now. Be back here, at the hotel, by five at the latest. Okay?"

"You worry too much," Beth said. She gave him a quick peck on the cheek and she and Tanya headed for the big revolving door leading out to the main street, Via Vittorio Veneto. She looked back over her shoulder. "I know that, starting tomorrow, we're going to be far too busy for shopping, Dunk. Don't worry, we won't be long." She blew him a kiss and the two women disappeared through the doors onto the streets of Rome.

With a sigh of despair Dunk turned to the right and headed for the hotel's coffee shop, where he'd left Rudy.

The Ambasciatori Palace was one of the best hotels in the Ludovisi Quarter, regarded as the Mayfair of Rome. It was situated on the main thoroughfare of that area which climbed, in a Z-shape, from the Piazza Barberini to the Porta Pinciana. Even on short notice Bill Highland had managed to arrange rooms for them there.

"Let them relax for a couple of hours, *mein Freund,*" Rudy said, with a smile, as Dunk plopped down in the seat beside him. "We have matters of such supreme importance ahead of us, let them recover from the flight over here and relax for the short while they are able." He bent over a large bowl of *caffe latte.*

Dunk sighed. "I guess you're right, Rudy. I'm just a little worried, that's all. Partly that they're out in a strange city, but mostly because of who we know is here." He signaled the waiter. *"Un capuccino, per favore."*

"Ach! They will be all right. You will see. Let them enjoy themselves for a moment. Tomorrow is another day."

"I suppose so."

Beth and Tanya had every intention of relaxing for awhile, of shifting the focus of their minds after what had seemed such a long time of intense concentration. The psychic and the Witch hurried along Via Veneto, passing sidewalk tables set out beneath a blue-and-white awning, intent on covering as much ground as possible in the scant two hours they had available.

"Believe me, we'll make time later for some more serious shopping," Beth said. "You can't be in Rome and not do that. But for now we'll just have a quick browse around."

Tanya nodded. "I agree! Where are we going first?"

"Well, we'll just have a quick run down here. I understand there are some fantastic bookstores on this street. Dunk wants to get to them if we have time. And then I suggest we take a cab across to Via Condotti and Via Frattina. They're supposed to be the shopping streets. They're only just a half dozen blocks west of here. Just off the Spanish Steps. Oh, God!" She clutched Tanya's arm. "Look at that sweater!"

"Yes," Tanya said dryly. "Only 30,000 lire!"

"They are here."

Gualtiero della Rovere looked up to see the portly shape of Patrizio Ganganelli filling the doorway.

"They are staying in the Ludovisi Quarter," continued the cardinal. "Ambasciatori Palace."

"Expensive," della Rovere murmured.

Ganganelli shrugged. "It is the American taxpayers' money! They are all the same. They all try to live off each other!"

Della Rovere was tempted to remark about the cardinal's own lifestyle, but refrained. "So what do we do now?" he asked.

Ganganelli came into the room and sat down. It was a small, dark office della Rovere used in the upper north wing of the Vatican. Small and cramped. He didn't understand how Ganganelli had been able to obtain his large, plush office. It didn't seem fair.

"The two women have left the men and gone out. Shopping!" Ganganelli spat out the word distastefully. "It will be the last shopping they do."

Della Rovere didn't ask how his cohort knew all this. He was aware that Ganganelli spent a lot of time skrying, with an ancient crystal ball said to have once belonged to Pope Gelasius III. He presumed that was how he'd obtained the information.

⚡

"My God! Look at the time!"

Beth hugged the packages to herself and tried to stretch her arm to look at her watch. It was almost five o'clock.

"Shoot!" she said. "Dunk is going to be mad. We'd better get out of here and grab a cab."

The two women hurried through the store to the exit and burst out onto the sidewalk. As they stood looking up and down for one of the yellow taxis a large limousine with dark-tinted windows drew up in front of them.

"Oh, great!" Beth muttered. "Block our way now so I can't even see a taxi!"

The chauffeur got out and came around to the sidewalk.

"*Buon giorno! Signorinas* Martin and Demidas?" he asked.

Beth's mouth dropped open.

"Yes," Tanya said. "That's us. Why?"

The chauffeur opened the rear door of the vehicle.

"Courtesy of the hotel," he said. "I was sent to get you."

"That Dunk thinks of everything," Tanya said, as they sat back and relaxed in the spacious rear of the limousine. "But I wonder how he knew which store we'd be at."

Beth sat forward. "God! What fools we've been!"

"W-what do you mean?"

"Stop!" Beth called to the driver. "Damn! What's the Italian for 'stop'?"

There was a glass partition between the passenger compartment and the driver. Beth banged on it. The driver took no notice.

Tanya tried to open the door.

"It's locked. Probably controlled from up front," she said.

"Damn! I can't believe we let ourselves be taken so easily!"

Beth stared out at the passing scene, trying to memorize the route they were taking.

"We're heading south," Tanya said.

"How do you know?"

"The sun. See? It's over there. It sets in the west, of course."

"Good," Beth said. "At least that's something. Now help me try to remember some of these street names as we pass them. It might help."

The two women realized that, with the dark tinted windows of the limousine, no one outside could see them if they tried to attract attention. But when the car stopped briefly at an intersection Beth was delighted to see one of the *polizia municipale*—the city police, as opposed to the *caribinieri*, or military-type police—standing right by the car, directing traffic. She banged on the glass of the window and shouted.

The policeman glanced back at the limousine. The chauffeur smiled and waved to him, as though it was he who had banged on the glass. The traffic policeman smiled back, nodded, and waved on the vehicle.

They rounded the Colosseum and headed south again on Via Claudia and then Via Navicella. At the Porta Metronia the driver turned right on Via Druso, then left onto Via di Porta San Sebastiano.

"Here's the Arco di Druso," Beth said. "I got a postcard of that at the hotel. It's the arch that carried the aqueduct for the baths on the Appian Way. That gives us a clue as to where we are. And here's the Porta San Sebastiano: the gate through the old Aurelian Wall. I bet we're going down the old Appian Way."

"Via Appia Antica," Tanya sang out. "That's the old Appian Way, isn't it?"

"Right."

The road dropped down and Beth spotted a milestone.

"Start counting milestones!" she cried.

The road passed under a railway and then went by a small church. Further on they saw the second milestone just after the road started to ascend again. The driver suddenly turned left.

"Via Appia Pignatelli," Beth read.

Almost immediately the limousine turned into the entrance to THE CATACOMBS OF PRAETEXTATUS, according to the small sign Beth saw.

"Oh, great!" she said. "It says, 'Admission only with special permission'. In other words, we're not going to see any tourists here!"

The chauffeur came around to the door and opened it.

"*Va via!* Get out!"

They got out hesitantly and stood looking about them. The chauffeur got back in the car and started to drive away.

"Hey! Wait!" Beth shouted. She ran a few steps after the vehicle but then stopped as it picked up speed, turned back onto the road and disappeared.

"Welcome to Rome!"

They both turned to find a short, stocky man, wearing gold-rimmed spectacles and the robes of a cardinal, standing studying them.

"Ganganelli!" Beth said.

He bristled, and pulled himself up as much as was possible. His face reddened.

"*Cardinal* Ganganelli!" he hissed.

"Yes," Beth replied. "We saw you at Washington International Airport, when you zapped poor old Rudolf."

A smile broke out on the cardinal's face.

"And how is our dear German friend?" he asked. "Not yet fully recovered, I trust?"

"He's doing just fine," Beth replied.

Another figure appeared beside Ganganelli, holding open the door leading down to the catacombs.

"Come," Ganganelli said. "Allow me to give you a tour of these ancient ruins."

58

"We must take this one step at a time," Rudolf said. "It is of no use to get emotional, Dunk, *mein jung Freund.*"

"I know, Rudy. I'm sorry." Dunk shook his head to clear it and stopped pacing the room. He sat down opposite the German and looked out of the window at the brightly lit streets of Rome. From its position on the hill the Ambasciatori Palace hotel gave a commanding view of the city.

"This is a big city," Dunk continued. "They could be holding them anywhere."

"But we have certain means at our disposal," Rudy said. "Our young Elizabeth, she is the ESP specialist, *nein?* Then you will try to lock minds with your beautiful lady. You can be sure she will be sending out thoughts if she is at all able."

"That's for sure," Dunk agreed. "You're right, Rudy. We do have the means. Let's give it a try."

He made himself comfortable in the chair and closed his eyes, breathing deeply and filling his body with light. The German settled quietly and left him to it.

Duncan's breathing slowed and he grew calmer and more in control of his thoughts and feelings. When he had completed building his ball of protection he tentatively opened his mind to Beth, sending out a mind probe over the ancient city. His mind searched the area, sweeping from side to side like a searchlight. For a moment he thought he'd made contact, but found it to be a stranger. He had a brief vision of a young man sitting on a bed in a dark apartment, holding a stick of incense in each hand and humming "aum" as he sent out his thoughts. When the young man came in contact with Dunk, he recoiled. Dunk had a brief flash of the young man's eyes jerking wide open and him dropping one of the incense sticks. Recognizing a student starting on the path, Dunk smiled and moved on.

As his mind-probe penetrated Rome, Dunk felt suddenly excited. There came a sudden warmth, and a feeling of recognition. Then, with a flash of white light, there she was! Beth stood in his mind, smiling.

"I knew you'd come," she said.

"Where are you?" he asked.

"It's one of the old pagan catacombs."

A map, as though drawn quickly on a piece of paper, appeared in Duncan's mind but, just as suddenly, it was torn away again. Lightning seemed to flash, thunder crashed, and the worst headache he had ever known suddenly throbbed in his skull. Everything went black for a moment. When he came to, he found himself stretched on the floor beside the chair, Rudolf bathing his temples with a cold, damp cloth.

"What happened?"

"I was hoping you would be able to tell me," the German said. He helped the younger man back up onto the chair. "Take your time, Duncan. Breathe deeply and ground yourself first. Then tell me what you saw."

Dunk told the older man of seeing Beth and about the map, which he presumed was of the catacombs.

"I guess the people who took Beth and Tanya realized she was sending thoughts out to me and stepped in to zap us." He took a few deep breaths. "It was all so quick," he said. "I just didn't get a good look at the map, but she definitely said the catacombs."

Rudolf nodded. *"Gut! Das ist gut."*

He had a city map spread out on the coffee table and now pulled it over and pointed.

"Here, Duncan, *mein Freund,* is the catacomb where Tanya saw the Satanists, when she released the power of her coven. You remember? The old home of Mussolini. It is the Villa Torlonia, and it is not far from this hotel."

"Of course!" Dunk was excited. "Yes! Tanya said there were catacombs underneath it. That must be where they're holding them. And what better place to keep them?" He was starting to feel better. He got to his feet, swayed for a moment then steadied himself. "But I'm okay now. Come on, Rudy. Let's go get 'em!"

"Nein!"

"What?"

"No, *mein Freund.* Firstly, they will be expecting us to go chasing after them now. They will be waiting. Secondly, the hours of darkness are the hours of the evil ones. Daylight is far better for the powers of light and goodness. And thirdly, we will need to prepare and arm ourselves if we are to go and challenge these fiends. We must protect ourselves if we are to protect those we love."

In his heart Duncan knew that his friend was right. It would have been madness to go chasing off after such powerful Satanists in the middle of the night. Far better to do it in daylight and with as much magical protection as Rudolf could come up with. Dunk watched as the old German went to the closet and pulled out the ancient leather bag that he'd come to regard as a treasure chest of magical paraphernalia. It was going to be a long night.

After a hasty breakfast Duncan and Rudolf took a taxi east from the hotel to the Villa Torlonia. The taxi turned along Via Campania, down to Piazza Porta Pia and then onto the wide Via Nomentana. It didn't take long to reach the main gates of the villa at the corner of Via Alesandro Torlonia, but for Duncan anything was too long. The gates were closed.

Rudy consulted his watch.

"They should be opening at any moment," he said, paying the driver.

Twenty minutes later they were entering the main building itself. It sat in the middle of a large gravel driveway which surrounded the house and also branched off onto small, private roads that led about the estate. They paid their admission fees and took a brochure. Eagerly Duncan scanned it for details of the catacombs.

"They were created in the second and third centuries," said Rudy. "And some sections of them are closed off from tourists because of rock falls."

"You can bet our Satanists are somewhere in the sections that tourists are denied access to," Duncan muttered. "Where do we begin, Rudy?"

"I think in the office of the administrator," the tall German said.

It was another hour and a half before their search began in earnest. Signor Donatello Aldobrandini took very seriously his position with the Commune of Rome and was not easily persuaded of the necessity for the Archivist of Frankfurt University and his assistant to have access to the closed areas of the Villa Torlonia's catacombs. But eventually he succumbed to the flattery—and bribery—put on him by the charming German professor. Dunk and Rudy set off on their exploration of the underground warren.

"The brochure says nearly five and a half miles of passages." Dunk sounded glum.

"But more than half are closed," Rudy said. "We will not bother with the two miles that are open to the public. Another mile and a half, possibly two, are under collapsed rock. So that leaves us with only one and a half to two miles to investigate, does it not?"

Duncan smiled. "The way you put it, it doesn't sound too bad," he said.

But it was late afternoon before they had finished. Their search had afforded them nothing. Even with access to the closed areas they had found no sign of the Satanists' temple, and certainly no trace of Beth and Tanya.

"I do not think we have managed to find all the subterranean passages," Rudy said, sitting on a stone step and filling his pipe. "But my feeling is that we would not find the ladies even if we did. I do not believe they are here."

Duncan plunked down beside him, his face glum.

"I agree, Rudy. It's as much a feeling—an intuition, if you like—that they're not here. But, damn it! Beth said they were in the catacombs!"

"*Ja.* And I am sure she is right. But, *Bruder* Duncan, the city of Rome is full of catacombs. So the question is, which ones?" He puffed on his pipe for awhile. "*Mein Freund*, we will return to the hotel and we will use other methods."

"We, of all people, should be in a position to find them," Rudolf said as he studied the street map of Rome on the top of the coffee table. He dug into the pocket of his jacket and produced what looked like a small, brass plumb-bob. Dunk recognized it at once as a pendulum used for radiesthesia, or dowsing.

"You think you can find them that way?" he asked.

His friend nodded. "It is one way, *ja*. And I have found it effective in the past. I shall do this, then we will study the results."

Dunk settled quietly and watched. Rudolf sat with his left hand on the map, holding the pendulum suspended from his right hand. It hung on its fine chain with the point of the weight less than an inch off the table's surface. The chain he held lightly between his thumb and first finger.

In his mind Rudolf saw Beth and Tanya. He focused on them and then, speaking softly in German, asked, "Are they in the north quadrant of the city?"

Although he had been holding the pendulum still, it gradually started to swing from side to side, growing stronger and stronger in its movement.

"Ah! No."

The swinging subsided and the pendulum came to rest again.

"Are they in the east quadrant of the city?"

Again the pendulum swung from side to side. So the old German worked at locating the two women. He found that the pendulum swung toward and away from him when he asked about the southern section, indicating a "yes." Then he started to narrow down the area.

"Are they on the west bank of the river? ... The east bank? ... Are they south of the Colosseum?"

With his left finger tracing the map, he went on to ask, "Are they in this section? ... This? ... This? ... Is this the location?"

Finally he sat back.

"See? They are indeed in the catacombs, but the more familiar ones that are south of the city. You leave the city by the Porta San Sebastiano, travel down the old Appian Way to the second milestone, and then turn left onto this small road. There is a catacomb on the left. 'Praetextatus', it says on the map. And it also says that it is not open to the public."

59

Beth and Tanya lay on the rough red-earth floor against the wall of the underground chamber. Both were bound around the wrists and ankles, with their hands behind their backs.

They had not slept at all through the night and only fitfully through most of the day. Shortly after being left alone Beth had tried to contact Dunk by E.S.P. and felt she had succeeded in getting through to him. Then she was hit by a tremendous psychic force which had left her in agony on the floor, her head splitting. She had slept for awhile after that.

"So what *is* this place, Beth?" Tanya asked.

They had no idea what time it was. The place where they lay was pitch dark, damp, and cold. They had managed to roll together, side by side, for warmth and comfort.

"We're in one of the chambers where the passageways meet. I think they used to use them for feasts to honor the dead. It's all carved out of this soft tufa rock."

"I'd heard of the catacombs, but wasn't exactly sure what they were. They were used for burials, weren't they?"

"By the pagans and then the early Christians," Beth said. "Yes. I was reading a guidebook, flying over from the States. The Romans went in for cremation, so that's why the early Christians had to bury their dead outside the walls of the city. They dug down and made these long passageways with tombs built into the sides. They're called *loculi,* the niches."

"H-how deep underground are we?"

"We're on the fifth level—I counted as they brought us down. It's probably the deepest. The guidebook said these things go down to about twenty meters. That's what, about sixty feet?" Beth suddenly became concerned. "Tanya! You're not claustrophobic, are you?"

"I didn't think I was. But then I've never been in a situation like this before. I really don't like this; I keep thinking of the roof falling in!"

"Well, if it's any comfort, these catacombs have been here for nearly two thousand years," Beth said, trying to sound cheerier than she felt. "So I don't think they're likely to cave in right now."

"Any luck with your ropes?" the Wiccan priestess asked. She had been trying, off and on through most of the night and day, to loosen her own bindings.

"No," Beth replied. "The more I pull at them the tighter they seem to become. I've lost all feeling in my hands."

They lay in silence for awhile.

"Beth?"

"Yes."

"What do you think they intend to do with us?"

Beth had been involved in the search for, and fight against, the Satanists for much longer than Tanya. She knew how ruthless they could be. But there was no point in alarming the other woman unnecessarily.

"They're probably going to use us as bargaining tools," she said. "You know, they'll get in touch with Dunk and Rudy and say they'll only return us if they back off and go home."

It sounded possible, and for a brief moment Beth herself felt comforted.

"But they're Satanists," Tanya said. "Don't you think they might be planning to kill us?"

The redhead sighed a long sigh.

"Let's hope not, Tanya. Let's hope not."

The hard ground was most uncomfortable, and they wriggled into positions where they were sitting up and leaning against the rough wall. Then they settled down to meditate and send their thoughts out to Dunk and Rudolf. Beth thought about astrally projecting, but the pain from the ropes wouldn't allow her to relax enough to concentrate. She settled for what E.S.P. projection she could manage, hoping that whoever had caught her at it the previous night wouldn't do so again.

"Two sleeping beauties!"

The low, oily voice woke both women out of their reveries. Beth turned her head to see the tall, angular cardinal standing at the entrance to the cavern. He held a bright oil lantern, its wick turned up high, and leered down at them.

"Where's Ganganelli?" she asked.

"Don't you bother your pretty little head about him," della Rovere replied. "He'll be along all in good time. I just came on ahead to … to see what I could see, shall we say?"

Beth didn't like the sound of that. She exchanged glances with Tanya.

"Does he know you're here?" Tanya asked.

The bony figure didn't reply. He set down the lamp and came over to stand near them. His eyes ran over their bodies. Suddenly he knelt down and reached out a hand to touch Tanya's long, black hair.

"Mmm! Beautiful," he murmured, more to himself than to them. "Soft and silky." He held it to his nose and sniffed it. "Mmm! Wonderful."

"Ganganelli isn't going to like it if you start fooling around," Beth said urgently.

Della Rovere suddenly leaned toward her and gave her a sharp slap on the cheek.

"Shut up! It's not a matter of what Cardinal Ganganelli wants or doesn't want. Right now it's a question of what I want."

He returned his attention to Tanya. He reached out and fondled her breasts.

Tanya had been sitting with her legs drawn up slightly. Suddenly she kicked out with them, hitting the licentious cardinal solidly in the crotch. With a howl of pain he fell back, letting go of Tanya and clutching himself between the legs.

"Owow! Oh, my God! Ow!"

"That'll teach you to keep your slimy hands to yourself!" Tanya cried. "Bastard!"

Groggily della Rovere got to his feet.

"You'll pay for that," he snarled. "Both of you! You'll pay for that."

"Are you going to kill us?" Beth asked.

He laughed humorlessly. "Kill you? You'll soon be asking—no, praying—for death! But death is not going to come easily, believe me. I shall see to that!"

There was a noise in the passageway and all three turned as Cardinal Ganganelli came into the cavern. He looked hard at each of them. He said nothing, but Beth sensed that he had accurately assessed the situation.

"Are they still tied?" he asked.

The taller cardinal nodded.

"All right! Remember—" he spoke sharply to the other man, "we have a special use for these two. They need to be left untouched till then. Do I make myself clear, your Eminence?" He spoke the title sarcastically.

Beth watched as della Rovere first stood and looked the other man in the eye and then, slowly, lowered his own eyes and backed away.

"Yes. I understand," he muttered.

"Good! See that you remember it."

Dunk turned off Via Appia Antica onto the left fork, marked Via Appia Pignatelli. He drove rapidly past the entrance to the Catacombs of Praetextatus, on the left, and continued on toward Via Attica Nuova. The next turn to the left, Vicolo S. Urbano, was a small private road leading to a villa gate. Dunk turned up that road and pulled off short of the gate. Parking the rented Fiat under an umbrella pine, he and Rudy got out.

"Damn! It's going to be sunset soon," Dunk said. "So much for trying to get to them in daylight hours, with the powers of the light. But I didn't see any vehicles at the catacombs, did you?"

"Nein!" Rudy responded. "Though they may have been dropped off there. Just because there were no cars in evidence does not mean they are not all there."

"Agreed," Dunk said. "Come on. We'll cut straight down from here and approach from the back."

A small stone building stood at the entrance to the catacombs. It housed a gift shop, a small office, and the pay booth and turnstile at the head of the steps down to the lower levels. From a distance Dunk studied the building.

"Looks as though the iron gates are locked," he said.

"If so, we must wait," Rudy replied.

Dunk slipped quietly across and tried the gates. To his surprise, they opened. He turned and beckoned the German to join him.

"D'you think they're here?"

The older man shrugged.

"Okay," Dunk continued. "Let's go for it. We'll either find Beth and Tanya or we'll come face-to-face with the enemy."

Quietly they opened the wrought-iron gates and went inside. They stood at the top of the steps for a long time listening. No sound came from below. Dunk picked up a leaflet from the counter beside the pay booth. A fine layer of dust covered everything. He blew some off the brochure.

"Oh, great!" he said, looking at it. "There are five levels of passageways for a total of nine and one-half miles! They could be anywhere in there, Rudy!"

"Let me see." The German took the leaflet and consulted it. "More than half of it is closed up because of roof collapses. Nearly all of the lowest level is closed, as are half of the fourth and third levels. No wonder this is only open by appointment. They do not want to lose tourists." He smiled grimly.

"So where shall we start?" Dunk asked.

"At the lowest level, and work our way up."

Flashlights were for sale at the counter. They helped themselves to two, fitted them with new batteries, and descended the stone stairs. With the brochure, which included a map of each level, they quickly found the steps down to the next level and, from there, a smaller flight that went directly to the bottom, or fifth, level. When they arrived they stopped once again and listened.

"It's like a damn maze!" Dunk said, studying the layout over Rudolf's shoulder.

It was then they heard the scream.

60

The two cardinals carried Tanya along a passageway and into another chamber, where they dropped her on the floor. She looked around to see that it had been furnished, after a fashion, with seats of red tufa, carved out of the living rock and scattered around the perimeter. A large marble table, dressed as an altar, stood in the center. Covered with a black silk cloth, it held various gold and silver ritual tools, which glinted in the light of the many candles burning within the chamber.

The candles burning on the altar were black, as were those placed around a large circle marked on the floor. A thurible sat in the center of the altar, yellowish sulphurous smoke rising from it. Tanya wrinkled her nose at the smell. Beside the thurible were a gold goblet and various rods and other implements. Across the front of the altar lay a gleaming, silver sword.

"Go and get the other one," Ganganelli said to della Rovere. "I have things to attend to here."

"I don't know that I can manage her by myself," said the tall, thin cardinal.

"Just drag her by her feet! Don't bother trying to lift her." The portly figure in scarlet dismissed his cohort and headed toward the rear of the cavern, where two large trunks stood against the wall. He opened the lid of one and busied himself sorting through the contents.

With a shrug, della Rovere retraced his steps to the outer cavern. He found Beth still slumped against the wall. Thoughtfully he approached her.

"So, you are the one with the extra sensory perception," he said.

Beth was surprised he knew about it.

"I have some, yes," she admitted.

He smiled a cruel smile.

"No, not just 'some', my dear. As we understand it you are very gifted in that direction."

"So?"

"So, I wonder if your super-senses can tell you what I plan to do now?" he said, slowly moving toward her.

Beth's second sight focused on the man and she stiffened as she saw a dull red aura suddenly emanating from him. It pulsated, growing larger and becoming tinged with deep purples and blacks. Within it were flashes of orange and bright crimson. Suddenly, as though she were watching a movie, she saw him leap upon her and roll her over onto her knees. Her face was in the dirt of the floor. He ripped the clothes from her, pushed himself on her, and violated her.

Beth screamed.

Della Rovere had not yet reached her, but he pulled back as she screamed. Then he moved swiftly forward again and slapped her viciously across the face. Beth felt blood in her mouth as her teeth dug into her cheek. He slapped her again and she screamed again, trying unsuccessfully to kick out at him. He grabbed her arms, and she felt his long bony fingers digging into her muscles as he tried to force her over, face down.

Then, suddenly, there was a shout and she felt his hands snatched from her. She fell on her side and saw a figure in the dim light, fighting with the cardinal. For a moment she thought it was Ganganelli but then she saw that there were actually two new arrivals. Joyously she recognized them as Dunk and Rudy.

The two men dragged the tall priest backward away from Beth. Dunk let go of him to swing his fist, connecting with della Rovere on the side of the head. Dunk felt the pain in his hand as he connected, but was delighted to see the other man's head snap sideways and his body fall to the floor. Dunk leapt in and straddled the fallen man, beating at him unmercifully.

"Dunk! Dunk! Stop! Enough, *mein Freund!*"

Somehow the old German pulled the younger man off the now-inert figure and held him tight. Dunk's mind cleared and he saw the fallen priest would be unable to get up for some time. Quickly he thanked Rudy then turned to Beth.

"I'm okay, thanks Rudy. Beth! Beth, my love! Are you all right?"

Quickly they unbound her and Dunk knelt, holding her in his arms. She clung to him, sobbing.

"There, there! It's all right, my love," he whispered in her ear.

"Ad majorem Satanus gloriam!"

A powerful, resonating voice echoed about the chamber. The three of them swung around to see the figure of Ganganelli standing at the end of the far passageway. His face was twisted in fury and his arms were raised high. He screamed a number of words sounding like names, which Dunk didn't understand, and then swung both hands down to point at the trio.

"Ad extremum!" he cried.

The ground beneath them started to tremble. There was a distant rumble, which grew and seemed to sweep toward them. Rocks started to fall from the roof of the chamber.

"Schnell! Schnell!" Rudy cried. He tried to grab them both up. Dunk helped Beth to her feet and together the three of them made a move, stumbling toward the passage by which they had entered.

Behind them Ganganelli's voice rose in pitch. He screamed out commands. The ground shook as though from a tremendous earthquake, and rocks and dirt came crashing down on them.

As the dust settled and slowly started to clear, the three friends unsteadily got to their feet. Behind them was a mound of fallen red rock, completely blocking where the entrance to the cavern had been. They examined it and listened for sounds from the other side. There was nothing but silence.

"What do you think happened?" Beth asked, still clinging to Dunk.

"Ganganelli obviously called upon the forces of evil," he replied. "He caused the roof to fall in. And obviously he didn't care that his fellow Satanist was lying there on the ground."

"I am afraid that he was crushed by the falling rocks," Rudy said. "He had no chance. No chance at all."

"But what about Ganganelli himself?" Beth asked.

"Oh, you can be sure *he's* okay," Dunk said. "He was back inside the other passageway, wherever that leads."

"Do you think he's trapped in there then?"

Rudy shook his head.

"Nein. I wish it were so but, from what I recall of the map of this catacomb, there are other ways in and out."

Dunk had a sudden thought.

"Beth! Where's Tanya?"

"Oh my God!" She clung to him even tighter. "They've still got her! They'd taken her off to some inner place where they said they were going to do their ritual. They were about to take me there too. Dunk! We've got to get her out!"

"Of course we have, Beth! We won't leave her here, I promise you. Let's get back up to the top, take a breather and plan our next step. We can study the map and see how to get back in, around this rock fall."

Slowly they made their way back to the stairs descending from the outside. Dunk's flashlight had been lost in the excitement; Rudy's single, feeble beam lit their way back through the blackness. Wearily they climbed up the long stretch toward the upper levels.

As they neared the top of the first long stairway, they clearly heard the sound of footsteps above.

Rudolf put his finger to his lips and they stood stock-still on the stone steps. He flicked off the light and they were in pitch darkness. Above they heard the continuing sound of footsteps and occasional muttered conversations. It sounded as though a large number of people were descending into the lower chambers.

"What are we going to do?" Beth whispered.

"I honestly don't know," Dunk said.

The footsteps came down the first set of stairs and then turned off along the passageway, heading for a different set. The trio breathed a collective sigh of relief.

"Who do you think they were?" Beth asked, as they cautiously emerged into the upper passage. "It's far too late in the day for tourists, I would think."

"Definitely not tourists," Dunk said. "No, that must be the rest of the Satanists, arriving for the ritual." He turned to the German. "Rudy, we're coming up to the big one. This is the most important fight of our lives. Our country's at stake. What are we going to do?"

61

The rickety old 1935 Ford pickup truck wheezed its way up the last hill before coasting down into the village of Môle St. Nicholas, on the northwest coast of Haiti. Its hood had long since been lost, along with the right front fender, and the driver's door was tied permanently shut with a rough piece of rope. A steady plume of white steam had been issuing from the side of the radiator for the last five miles.

Guillemette sat up front with the driver while Earl and Etienne shared the bed of the truck with two goats and a wooden crate filled with chickens. As the truck came to a halt Earl and Etienne climbed over the tailgate and down onto the dirt road. They all thanked the driver for the lift and started walking along the same road. It wound through the village and once again climbed into the hills. Half an hour later they turned off the dusty path, broke through the trees, and came into sight of the village *hounfor*, the Voudoun church buildings.

"Guillemette! *Vous êtes arrivé! Bienvenue!*"

A tall, portly Haitian woman dressed in white came toward them. She wore a white turban about her head and had strings of brightly colored beads draped across her body, forming a cross, running from each shoulder to the opposite hip. Earl recognized her as the mambo Jannica, whom he had met on their trip to the Republic the previous year.

Guillemette greeted her effusively and then introduced Etienne.

"Enchanté, madame," said the Frenchman.

"Earl you remember, I know, Jannica."

"Ah, yes! Your Earl," said the mambo, looking kindly at him. "You danced well for the loa last time we met, as I recall."

"Well, thank you," Earl said, not sure whether to be pleased or not.

Jannica ushered them up to the large hut where she and the houngan, Malagigi, lived. He was a small, wiry man with wrinkled skin as black as pitch. Again there were introductions.

"We will eat after you have rested," Jannica said. "I've got everything ready for the ritual, so don't worry about that."

"You know why we are here?" Etienne asked. "I am surprised!"

"Nothing surprises me anymore, about this whole country!" Earl said. "Everybody knows everything, even before I do." He turned to Guillemette. "I'd lost track of time. Is it tonight, then? The big ritual?"

She nodded, her face serious. "Yes it is, Earl. I just hope everyone's all right in Rome. Perhaps after we've eaten I'll take a few minutes to try to check on them."

"That's a good idea."

Two hours later, after a delicious meal of goat-meat stew followed by fresh papaya and prickly pear, Guillemette retired with her obsidian crystal ball to try to contact Dunk, Rudy, Beth, and Tanya. Earl and Etienne opted to take a nap so they'd be fresh for the evening's work.

"When I saw them, Rudy, Dunk and Beth were setting up their circle for the ritual," Guillemette said. "We should be starting ours about the same time that they do. And hounfors all across Haiti will be doing the same, all in tune with us."

"I cannot believe that Tanya was taken," Etienne said, shaking his head. "You are sure about that, of course, *ma chère?*"

"Oh, yes. I'm afraid so, my man. I didn't make direct contact—they were all too busy—so I just had to get what I could through the scrying scenes. I don't know how it happened, but Tanya was being held by the Satanists as they started their preparations."

"We must send her energy," Earl said.

The Haitian woman nodded. "That's what I thought. Perhaps right now, before we start the ritual, we should all send her white light, for strength and protection."

A little later the three of them went into the peri-style, where Jannica and Malagigi had taken their places before the central altar. This was built about the *poteaumitan,* or central post, holding up the thatched roof of the peristyle. White candles covered the altar and were standing on the ground in a large, rough circle which extended to the rows of empty seats around the outer section of the temple, where the villagers normally sat on Friday nights. The drummers were in their places off to one side, within easy sight of the priestess. They had already struck up a steady, throbbing beat which reverberated through the peristyle. Earl was aware of the rhythmic pounding coming up from the dirt floor to his bare feet. All three of them were now dressed, as were the houngan and mambo, in white.

As the drummers picked up the beat, at a sign from Jannica, the processional started. La Place, an old man carrying an even older cavalry sabre, led the way into the peristyle. He was followed by the two standard-bearers, carrying the colorful flags of the hounfor. After them came the hounsi, the initiated ones.

When everyone was in place, the ceremony started. Jannica knelt and sang a litany that was responded to by the hounsi. While this was going on, Malagigi went around the circle consecrating it—he would take a mouthful of rum from the bottle he carried and then spray it out of his mouth onto the floor. Then he would mutter words in a language known only to the priest and priestess and continue this process around the whole area.

Guillemette, Earl, and Etienne stood with the hounsi. When the houngan had finished, the mambo got to her feet and danced an intricate step about the altar. At that point she approached Guillemette and offered her the *asson,* the ritual rattle which she carried.

Guillemette curtsied and accepted it, becoming the leading priestess for the rite. Jannica dropped into place with the hounsi and Guillemette moved to the front of the altar.

She nodded to the drummers, who changed the beat to a faster one. Earl became very much aware of the loud, rhythmic "chinking" of the ogan, which added an unusual depth to the drumbeats.

Guillemette started what looked to Earl to be the same intricate dance Jannica had been doing, but Guillemette danced faster and faster. As she danced, she sang. Earl heard the name of the loa Legba repeated time and again in the song. Suddenly Guillemette stopped, at exactly the same second that the drums became still. There was absolute silence. Earl felt the sweat start all over his body. He glanced at Etienne, but the little Frenchman had his eyes glued to the beautiful Haitian woman.

Malagigi now approached Guillemette and handed her a bowl of white meal. She took it and, in complete silence, dipped her hand into it. She then allowed it to trickle out of her fingers onto the floor. Swiftly she drew a *vévé*, its swirling, intricate design filling the area directly in front of the altar. Earl thought he recognized what looked like a stylized tombstone and two coffins. It was a design he'd seen drawn before; the vévé of Gédé, god of the dead. But Guillemette did not stop there. She moved around and started a second figure, and then a third. They were the designs for Ogoun, the warrior god, and for Damballah-Wédo, the Father of the Loa. The latter was a stylized drum with a snake on either side.

Earl was startled when Guillemette straightened up and let out a high-pitched cry. It echoed around the peristyle and across the hounfor. Guillemette grabbed a long-bladed knife from the altar and started spinning around and around, dancing about the altar, though not once stepping on the newly created vévés. She waved the knife so wildly about her Earl was concerned she'd cut herself. The drummers went wild, pounding their instruments in what to Earl sounded like a cacophony: a riotous sound that throbbed through his head and body. Gradually the noise seemed to take form and he found himself first tapping his feet, and then moving them—dancing. He noticed that Etienne was also dancing, as were all the hounsi. Everyone moved in a vibrant rhythm about the circle, pounding their feet into the earth and clapping their hands. Some had their eyes tightly closed, while others' were wide with ecstasy.

Then the rhythms slowed. Gradually the dancers cooled and came to a halt. Guillemette knelt down in the center of the three vévés, still holding the knife. She started to sing a litany to which everyone responded. Even Earl, who had no idea what the words were, found himself mouthing the right sounds in concert with the others. Then that, too, came to an end.

La Place, who at some point had left the circle area, walked in leading a long-haired, pure-white goat with large, curving horns. Its horns and four hooves had been painted and polished gold, and its bright eyes sparkled in the light of the burning candles.

La Place led him in to stand beside Guillemette. Earl's eyes were locked onto the animal.

"Father Damballah!" The black woman's voice filled the peristyle. "Lord Gédé! Mighty Ogoun! Hear me and be with us now!"

Earl tried to catch Etienne's eye, but the Frenchman looked as though he were in a trance. He did not acknowledge his friend, but gazed unseeing about the ritual area.

"Here is your sacrifice," Guillemette continued. "This we bring to you. Do you approve?"

Malagigi came forward with his bottle of rum. He stuck the end into the goat's mouth and tipped it up. The goat swallowed the liquid. Malagigi bowed low and backed away again.

"Most dear of all the loas," Guillemette cried again. "We are glad that you accept our sacrifice. We ask of you a gift. We ask that you should join with us, with all the Forces of the Light, in repelling that great Force of Darkness that tonight tries to overthrow a mighty country. Here, beloved loas, is our gift to you. Now let us receive your gift to us!"

She turned and, to Earl's surprise and horror, slit the throat of the goat so that its blood flowed across the dirt floor, touching and blending with the lines of the three vévés. There came a tremendous crash from the drummers as they dove into a frenetic beat that far outdid anything previous. Immediately everyone became animated and Earl was swept up once again in the wild dancing. This time everyone danced all over the ritual area, trampling the blood and the vévés themselves into the dirt floor. La Place, meanwhile, had dragged the goat's carcass out of the peristyle and busied himself skinning it and cutting it up, to roast the meat over a great fire pit he had built. Later the meat would be shared among the celebrants, the best pieces going onto the altar for the gods themselves … when they appeared.

62

Ganganelli was angry. The Americans had traced him to the catacombs; they'd had the nerve to enter his domain! He dearly hoped the collapsing roof had crushed them, but he had his doubts. It was too bad about della Rovere, he thought, but that was the price one had to pay. He'd been a worthy servant in the service of the Lord Belial, true, but Ganganelli had noticed that there had certainly been times, recently, when della Rovere had seemed to balk at his leadership. No, there would be no mourning.

The cardinal made his way back to the main cavern, where the circle was set out for the coming ritual. He glanced to the side and was gratified to see the Wiccan priestess still lying there. At least *she* had not been lost. She was an important cog in the machinery of that night's magical workings.

As he busied himself topping up the incense in the thurible on the altar, Ganganelli heard the sound of approaching footsteps. One by one, black-robed figures entered the temple. Greetings were exchanged and everyone fell into his or her place. The three female members of the order were present, again dressed in their gray robes.

"You and you!" Ganganelli snapped at two of the larger male Satanists. "Get the woman and bring her to the altar." To the trio of females he said, "You three prepare her."

The men moved across, picked up Tanya, and carried her to the center of the circle, where they laid her on the ground before the altar. Agara Brachi went to the trunks at the back of the cavern and returned with a small glass vial. She knelt beside Tanya and raised the Wiccan's head.

"Here," she said. "Drink this. It will make you feel better. It will help you get through this."

Tanya's mouth was parched. She had eaten and drunk nothing in many hours. As Agara held the flask to her lips, she drank. The liquid was sweet and surprisingly relaxing. She suddenly felt very sleepy.

"Get on with it," Ganganelli snapped, as he moved around the circle checking the positions of the candles and the placing of censers about the periphery.

Agara and the other two women untied Tanya and then removed her clothes. As she lay there naked, Agara pointed to something around Tanya's neck. It was a small silver talisman hanging on a length of red silk between her breasts, just over her heart. Agara moved forward to take it. As her fingers touched the metal there was a crackle and flash, like the discharge of static electricity. Agara leapt back.

"Shit! What the hell's that?" She sucked at her fingers where they had been burned.

The other women gasped and stood up, calling Ganganelli to come. He hurried over to them.

"What is it?" he snorted impatiently.

"Look!"

"So! The fools have some knowledge, I see," he said, studying the engraving on the medal. "It's a typical Wiccan talisman of protection. No problem." He drew an ornate dagger from his belt and, being careful not to touch the metal, inserted it under the red silk. With a quick upward pull he cut through the ribbon. Gingerly taking it by the ends, Ganganelli lifted it away from Tanya and carried the talisman out of the circle, where he threw it down in a corner.

"Get on with it!" he said to the women. "We're losing precious time."

The two big men lifted Tanya and laid her on the altar itself. The women moved around, stretching her arms to the sides and spreading her legs.

The twelve Templars of the Sacred Heart of Belial moved into the circle and stood, heads bowed. Ganganelli stood at the head of the altar, the gleaming sword in his hands. Opposite him stood Agara, with the gold dish of sacred water and the aspergillum, carrying out the duties hitherto performed by the Satanic Lord's faithful servant, and now missing Templar, Gualtiero della Rovere. One of the other women stood at Tanya's head, gently swinging the gold thurible. The other was at her feet, holding a crystal vial of oil.

"*Ad majorem Satanus gloriam,*" Ganganelli sang out.

"*Ad majorem Satanus gloriam,*" responded the rest of the congregation.

Ganganelli raised the sword high, then lowered it and kissed the blade. He turned and slowly walked, counterclockwise, about the altar to its southern point.

The cowled figures parted to let him through. He walked to the outer edge of the circle and lowered the sword blade, pointing it at the drawn line.

"Ab ovo usque ad mala," he murmured, and started to trace the line of the circle, again moving in a counter-clockwise direction, enclosing the people inside. As he reached each of the four cardinal points—east, north, west, and south again—he paused to raise the sword, kiss its blade, and lower it again.

He returned to the altar and lay the sword down along the naked body of Tanya so that its handle rested between her breasts. Her eyes were closed and her breathing was deep and regular.

Ganganelli took the Priapic Wand from the altar and dipped the tip into the red wine of the gold chalice at Tanya's head.

"Oh Lord Belial, Who hast formed us in Thine image and in Thine likeness, deign to bless and consecrate this Sacred Circle and this Living Altar erected as a dwelling place for Thee."

He shook the wine from the end of the wand onto Tanya's breasts and pubic area.

"Mighty and Omnipotent Lord Belial," he continued. "Grant us that which we wish for this night. Let the destruction we have envisioned for the United States of America be devastating and complete. On this most auspicious of nights, when all the mighty forces of the universe conjoin to bring You energies unlike any for a thousand years, come to us! Join with us, in this our worthy undertaking."

Surreptiously, Ganganelli glanced at his wrist-watch, visible below the golden sleeve of his robe. It was essential to lead through this ritual with accurate timing, he knew. The climax, the moment of supreme sacrifice, was to take place at midnight precisely. One minute either side would be catastrophic. The Lord Belial was a hard taskmaster. He demanded exactness of his worshippers.

Ganganelli spread his arms wide. The three women, led by Agara, turned and moved around the circle, sprinkling and censing the male members of the order, then consecrating them with the oil. That done, they returned to the altar. Ganganelli himself then moved around to consecrate the women, each of whom opened the front of her robe and then left it open.

"Conjuro et confirmo super vos Angeli fortes Satanus, et sancti in nominae ... "

Ganganelli continued with the liturgy, naming demonic servants of the Black Lord and calling upon them for their support.

" ... Lucifugé, Rofocale, Ashtoreth, Belial, qui creavit mundum, quod pro me labores et adimpleas omnem meum petitonem, juxta meum vella et votum meum, in negotio et causa mea."

"Domine dirige nos!" sang out the congregation.

"Domine dirige nos," said Ganganelli.

With another glance at his watch, he opened a box to reveal the black hosts of the Satanic Eucharist.

Rudolf Küstermeyer moved around in a clockwise direction, pointing his right index finger at the circle he had scratched in the red earth of the cavern's floor.

"O Mighty Gods, Lords of Being; Goddesses of Life and Fertility, we invite and request that you be with us here tonight in this our humble Circle."

Duncan and Elizabeth stood in the center, before a packing crate they were using as an altar. All three were naked. On the altar burned a single white candle. In a broken shard of pottery sat a burning cone of incense. An ashtray engraved with the words "Souvenir of Rome: the Catacombs" held a mixture of water and salt.

Dunk caught Beth's eye and smiled. She returned the smile, then focused her attention on Rudolf again. The old German seemed to have attained a special dignity since entering the circle area, she thought. He was standing straighter, somehow—taller. He held his head high and spoke with great authority, his voice strong and firm.

Reluctantly they had decided that there wasn't time to rescue Tanya immediately. They knew the Satanists were about to start their ritual, one that could mean the death of the country they loved and the slaughter of thousands of innocent people. Earlier they had sat in the dusty entrance office of the catacombs and joined hands, sending their thoughts and protective light to the Wiccan priestess, to give her the energy to endure the ordeal they knew she was facing. Dunk had then gone to the car and returned with Rudy's black leather bag of paraphernalia. They descended as far as the third level and found a large cavern to use as their own temple. They had found a packing case in one of the otherwise empty loculi and had commandeered it to serve as an altar.

"This is not what I had in mind," Rudy said. "For such an important rite we should have everything possible on our side. We had no ritual bath. We do not have all the proper tools. We have no robes."

"We can make do, Rudy," Dunk responded. "We've done it before."

"We don't need robes," Beth added. "When we made the talismans we just went skyclad—"

"Ja. Ja. You are right, *meine Freunde.* It is just that we should have everything exactly right, if possible. These are not amateurs we are dealing with. Ganganelli is a Satanist of the first order, as I have told you. I would dearly wish to go into this battle with all of my armor on, as it were."

"I don't know too much about ceremonial magic yet," Dunk said thoughtfully, "but I do know quite a bit about Witchcraft. That is the simplest, the most plain magic. Witches don't go in for all the elaborate trappings of the ceremonialists, yet their magic is just as potent."

"That is true," Rudy agreed. "Now if we were concerned with conjuration—making entities appear to do our bidding—we would stand no chance." His bright eyes peered out from under his bushy eyebrows. "But you have made an excellent point, *Bruder* Duncan. We are here concerned with calling upon the gods for protection, to help in our fight against the forces of evil. It is not like making talismans, where everything used must be so accurate. *Ja!* We will do all right, *meine Freunde!"*

So they stood wearing nothing but their talismans of protection and watched as the old German cast and consecrated the circle. He came back to the altar and

they consecrated one another. In addition to the salt,
water, and incense, Rudy insisted that they also consecrate each other with the holy oil he kept in his bag.
With it they each sealed the openings of their bodies.
They then marked an equal-armed cross on the position
of the third eye, and a pentagram over their hearts.

"*Gut!* It is done. Now we may begin."

63

In the darkness of the cavern a gray-clad figure struck a small gong. Its low tones reverberated around the meeting place. Agara threw more incense onto the brazier and bowed low before the Satanic altar.

Ganganelli took up the chalice of wine, raised it toward the ceiling, and cried: "Belial!"

"Belial!" came the response.

Ad majorem Satanus gloriam!

Ad majorem Satanus gloriam!

The answering cries thundered back from the celebrants.

Ganganelli drank deeply of the wine. He handed it to Agara, who also drank. In turn, the other two women swallowed wine. Agara refilled the chalice from a bottle on the floor beside the altar. The golden goblet was sent around the circle of men. Several times it was refilled as it traveled around. Eventually it was returned to the altar, at the head of the recumbent, drugged Wiccan priestess.

The gong echoed again.

"Gaudeamus igitur," said Ganganelli. "Let us therefore rejoice!"

Slowly the ring of cowled figures started to move, stamping their feet as they ponderously wound their way counterclockwise about the central altar in the perversion of a dance. Low gutteral sounds came from some of them; others slapped their hands together or beat their thighs to generate a crude rhythm by which they moved. Ganganelli stood still and silent, watching them, a half-smile on his face.

They circled faster. The three women moved in amongst them, divesting themselves of their robes as they went. There were cries and shouts, like the caws of feasting crows and the braying of asses. Black robes fell to the ground and were trampled underfoot. Even as they danced the figures made crude, intermittent connections, male to female and male to male. At one point one of the women fell to the floor with three men on top of her. The others danced on, leaping over them. One man tripped and fell and was kicked by passing feet.

As the noise increased—the shouts and yells, gasps and cries—Ganganelli glanced yet again at his watch. He allowed the stumbling, staggering, scabrous processional to continue for a few moments longer, then he raised his hands high.

"Belial!" he cried.

The figures came to a reluctant halt. Bodies separated from bodies. The smell of sweat hung in the air.

"Belial!" came the faltering response.

"Prepare now to meet Our Lord," Ganganelli continued. He lowered his arms and turned to the living altar.

"Behold! Thou art He Who is at the beginning and the end of time!"

Rudolf's voice rang out loud and strong.

"Thou art in the heat of the sun and the coolness of the breeze. The spark of Life is within Thee, as is the darkness of Death. For Thou art the cause of existence and the Gatekeeper at the end of time."

Beth reached out her hand and Duncan took it. He gave it a reassuring squeeze.

Rudolf continued.

"Lord-dweller in the sea, we hear the thunder of Thy hooves upon the shore and see the fleck of foam as You pass by. Your strength is such that You might lift the world to touch the stars. Yet gentle, ever, art Thou, as a lover. Thou art He Whom all must face at the appointed hour, yet are You not to be feared. For Thou art Brother, Lover, Son. Death is but the beginning of Life, and Thou art He who turns the key."

Rudolf moved across to the altar and sprinkled some dried, crushed wolf-claw and common nettle onto the glowing charcoal. Then he took up the salted water and went to the east and sprinkled it. He repeated this at the south, west, and north, then returned to the altar. His eyes met those of Beth and he gave an almost imperceptible nod.

Beth let go of Duncan's hand and took a deep breath. She hoped and prayed she would remember the words she had so recently memorized. Standing with her legs wide and bringing her arms up to shoulder height, she said:

"Thou art the Warrior Queen! The defender of Your people. With strong arms do you bend the bow and wield the Moon-Axe. Thou art She who tamed the Heavenly Mare and rides the Winds of Time. Thou art Guardian of the Sacred Flame, the fire of all beginnings. Thou art the Sea-Mare, the firstborn of the Sea Mother, who commands the waters of the Earth. Thou art Sister to the Stars and Mother to the Moon. Within Thy womb lies the destiny of Your people. For Thou art the Creatrix. Thou art daughter to the Lady with ten thousand names; Thou art Epona, the White Mare."

The three of them joined hands across the altar. Slowly they moved, with a sideways slipping step, three times, clockwise, about the altar. Then they dropped hands again.

"Gracious Lord and Beauteous Lady," said Rudolf. "We invite you to enter this our humble Circle, a place hallowed to Thee. In the names of all the mighty Powers of Light we entreat Thee to come to our aid on this night of all nights. Now is the time when the Powers of Darkness would cross swords with the Angels of Light for the purse which is the freedom of the world. Tonight, at the conjugation of certain fixed stars in malefic degrees, the Templars of the Sacred Heart of Belial collude for the destruction of the United States of America. Join with us; send us your love and your power, your strength; allow us to face these followers of the Left Hand Path and to thwart their designs. Let the Powers of the Light be forever triumphant! So mote it be!"

"So mote it be!" echoed Dunk and Beth.

As they stood there, a bright light started to grow at the side of the altar. At first Beth thought it was a reflection of the candle, but it grew brighter and brighter. Soon she couldn't ignore it. With the others she turned to look directly at it.

"Mein Gott!" muttered Rudolf.

64

Tanya heard a low, sonorous chanting. Her head ached. She had no idea where she was. Slowly she eased her eyes half-open.

It came flooding back to her. She was lying on the altar in the middle of the underground Satanic temple. The sounds she heard were those of the Satanists themselves, as they stood in a circle about where she lay. She glimpsed several of them and was surprised to see they were naked. Of those in her range of vision, most were old and disfigured. One man had a hunched back and his body was almost completely covered with coarse black hair. Standing next to him was a tall, skeletally-thin figure with sunken cheeks and dark-rimmed eyes. His head was bald and his stomach protruded like pictures she'd seen of starving children in foreign lands. Another figure she made out was obese, his body dripping with sweat. His tiny eyes were sunk into his fat face and he huffed and puffed as though he'd been over-exerting himself.

Tanya became aware of a weight on her body. She glanced down to see that it was the sword she'd noticed when she'd first been brought into this cavern, what seemed like such a long time ago. The pommel was toward her, the crosshilt just below her breasts, and the blade stretched down, resting on her pubic area. With a start she heard a voice above her and recognized it as the Satanic Cardinal Ganganelli's.

"Prepare to meet our Lord," he said. Then he picked up the sword and held it high. Tanya tried not to flinch as he lifted it from her body.

"Mighty Belial," he cried, in stentorian tones. "Here lies that which we promised Thee. Here, for Thine amusement, is the waiting body of a White Witch; a High Priestess of that Old Religion. Take her! Enjoy her! Then, may it please Thee, we shall sacrifice her to You and drink of her blood in Your name! All that we ask in return is that You send out Your fury and ferocity to smash and destroy the land that calls itself the United States of America. Send out Your storms and hurricanes, tornadoes and whirlwinds. Let there be floods and earthquakes, fires and volcanoes. Let Your force be known and let all see that the Forces of Darkness are those that shall rule the world! At midnight will the planets and stars at last align in that configuration which is most opportune for what we desire. We call upon Thee to strike then, at the very moment we strike the blade into this Wiccan; to draw upon all the ancient powers that are at play on this auspicious night. Come, Lord! Come, Belial! Show yourself to your servants and accept this our sacrifice!"

He lay down the sword again, this time beside Tanya's body, on the outer edge of the altar. She looked at it and weighed her chances of fighting her way out of there with it. Suddenly she grew cold. It was as though the temperature had plummeted. She shivered uncontrollably. She heard Ganganelli's sharp intake of breath and then saw a sight she could not believe.

Looking down the length of her body, she saw a swirling grey mist between her outspread feet. Like a whirling dust-devil it swayed from side to side, then grew and took solid form. It gradually materialized, solidifying into the most abhorrent creature she had ever seen. It was larger than a human in size, though more or less of human shape. Its face was mottled red and purple, and its crimson eyes glowed as though fires burned deep within its skull. Needle-sharp, blackened teeth stuck out at different angles from its mouth as it licked thin, red lips—as though savoring a meal to come. The creature was naked and its skin was a dark reddish-brown tufted with coarse black clumps of hair. From its loins a fearsome blackened organ thrust out at her, its root buried beneath the overhanging folds of a filthy, obese belly. The stench from the creature was terrible; even Ganganelli was having difficulty controlling his reaction to it.

Tanya looked upon the diabolical beast and knew she was doomed. If she did not die from the demonic thrusting that was sure to come from such a creature she knew her throat would subsequently be cut and her life blood drunk by these maniacs. If she had to die she wanted it to be a clean death. One of her own doing. In an instant her mind was made up; she knew what she had to do.

"Mighty Lord," Ganganelli cried. "Take your pleasure and let us all rejoice!"

The lascivious creature made a move toward the recumbent Witch.

In an instant Tanya rolled to her side. She pushed the handle of the sword off the altar while grasping the tip of the blade and swinging it toward herself. She gave a loud cry: "The Powers of Light! Long live the Goddess and the God!" In one movement, she rolled off the altar and onto the upturned sword blade. Rather than pain, she felt a sudden burst of joy and ecstacy, as though a long-awaited pleasure had suddenly burst upon her. She saw a glowing, loving figure before her, streching out arms to catch her as she fell. As the blade pierced her body, Tanya smiled, and died.

Ganganelli stood speechless, his staring eyes fixed on the bloody blade sticking out from the back of the black-haired Witch, lying still on the ground beside the altar. He had been robbed of his sacrifice, of his victory! A demented, maniacal snarl brought him back to his senses. The grotesque creature swelled up, suddenly increasing in size until it towered above the altar. A deep-throated roar came from its mouth, filling the room with the gagging stench of sulphur. It flung out an arm, its claw-like fingers pointing at the fallen female figure. Another, louder roar issued from its throat and part of the roof of the cavern gave way, showering many of the Satanists with rocks. Two men fell to the ground.

"Quick!" Ganganelli yelled to the stupefied onlookers. "Agara! Get onto the altar. He has to have someone now! Move!"

The face of the newest female Satanist turned white as the blood drained from it. There was no way she would give herself to this Dread Creature of Darkness. She would do many things for the cause she espoused—sex in all perverted forms was even pleasurable to her—but she could not bring herself to do this.

At a signal from Ganganelli, two Satanist men grabbed hold of Agara and dragged her, kicking and screaming, to the altar. Others ran to help them. One of the other women helped to hold her down. The Lord Belial had to be appeased, they all realized. They held onto the wildly struggling young woman.

"Here, my Lord," cried Ganganelli. "You shall not be without pleasure or sacrifice."

The beast focused its attention on the living altar and moved toward it.

"Noooo!" Agara screamed.

She kicked and punched, scratching and biting those who held her, desperate to get away from the repulsion whose burning eyes now concentrated on her.

Suddenly a blinding flash of brilliant yellow light caused all to stop and stare. Three dark, indistinct forms, like solidifying shadows, loomed up outside the circle of worshippers. A gleaming silver sword, over six feet in length, flashed across the tops of the Satanists' heads and prodded the beast in the back. With a deafening roar the creature turned around to face its tormentor. It found a materialized figure in ancient armor, taunting it. Ogoun, the warrior god of Voudoun, was ready to do battle.

The Satanists broke from the circle and ran for the opening to the passage leading out. One of the materialized shapes turned into a monstrous snake, coiled and hissing, which blocked their way. Damballah-

Wédo, serpent deity and Voudoun's "ancient and venerable father," had come to face the forces of darkness. The Satanists cowered and turned to the other exit from the cavern, but a second mighty, shadowy figure obstructed the way: Gédé, chthonic god of death. In his hands he wielded a sharp-pointed pick-axe, one of his symbols. This trio of Voudoun loa, called upon by worshippers across North America and throughout the islands of the Caribbean, had materialized to do battle. The panicking Satanists tumbled into each other in confusion.

Ganganelli turned quickly and moved toward the two trunks at the back of the cave. A smiling black man in top hat and mourning coat moved to block his way with the pick-axe. Ganganelli raised his hand and directed energy at the man to move him from his path. The energy was diverted so that it hit a wall and bounced back. Ganganelli himself was thrown backward and sat down hard on the rock floor.

The Creature of Darkness again swelled in size—it was now twice that of a normal human being. It swung its arms and spat fire at the figure in armor, Ogoun, who again swung the sword at him. The fire bounced off the armor.

The creature flung out its arms and bolts of lightning flashed from them, crashing against the walls and roof of the cavern and causing great chunks of rock to come crashing down. The Satanists screamed and fought with each other to get out of the way. Some fell and were buried beneath the debris. Agara stayed prone on the altar, all sense and feeling gone from her, paralyzed with fear.

As Ogoun, the figure in armor, prodded at the beast it bellowed and turned from side to side, thrashing out with its arms and bringing down more and more rocks. Both exits from the cavern were quickly blocked. There was bedlam among the terror-stricken Satanists.

Then a sudden quiet fell on the scene. All became still and the fighting, scrambling figures stopped their struggles and looked toward the altar area. A blue light had started to fill the room. Even the creature became still and looked all around in bewilderment. The three shadow figures of the Voudoun loa—Ogoun, Gédé and Damballah—slowly dissipated.

At the altar, one on either side of Tanya's fallen figure, there appeared two figures, male and female. Both were dazzling in appearance and incredibly beautiful. The woman wore a blue-white, full-length gown. Her hair was waist-length, and her eyes sparkled like diamonds. The man was muscular and dressed in a short, white tunic. His hair fell to his shoulders and he had a moustache and beard.

Agara gazed at the couple in amazement. She felt a deep and forgiving love emanating from them. She watched as they gently and lovingly gathered up the body of the fallen Wiccan priestess and removed the sword, which they tossed on the floor. The female figure then advanced on the still-quaking and bemused beast.

"Begone, evil being!" The words sounded in the chamber like the soft sounds of a wind-chime half-heard from a distance. "Begone, back to your dwelling. Do not return to this plane again."

The Lord Belial seemed to recover himself enough to draw away from the Creatures of Light, and looked quickly about the temple. He hissed, a long sibilant sound, as he searched unsuccessfully for sight of Ganganelli. Then he gradually faded once more into grey smoke and disappeared.

Agara lay still and watched as the Lord and the Lady of the Light smiled warm and tender smiles at one another and then, too, faded away, taking the dead Witch with them.

Despite the basic nature of their circle and their tools, Rudolf, Dunk, and Beth had been successful in joining with the mighty power sent out from innumerable Light groups across the nation, and had brought the God and Goddess of Life and of Light to the aid of the threatened country, once again bringing victory to Good over Evil.

As she stood staring at the light emanating from the altar, Beth swore she could see the God and the Goddess, or some similar Creatures of Light, standing there. The light was brilliant, and she was almost certain there were figures within it. Slowly the light faded and there, lying on the floor, was the body of Tanya.

65

 Traffic on the MacDonald Cartier Freeway, outside Toronto, was backed up all the way to Cambridge. A short but intense rain shower had made the surface of the road just slick enough that one car had lost control and smashed into a bridge abutment. The drivers of following cars were pulled over waiting for the ambulance to arrive.

"Well, at least it was quick for the poor bastard," one man said.

"Yeh. He probably never knew what happened," said another.

"Yankee plates," commented a third. "District of Columbia."

"I thought they all drove Cadillacs down there," said the first man. "This one sure looks like an old heap. What's left of it."

"Probably his brakes failed. He shouldn't have got hisself killed through a little bit of bad weather like this."

"Yeh!"

They stood quietly studying the crumpled old green Cougar with the one brown door.

66

"This is becoming a habit," Dunk said sitting back, smiling at Beth, and sipping a cup of coffee. "I remember after our last adventure—the one that started it all—we all got together here at your place, too, Bill."

"That's right. So you did." Bill Highland smiled around at his six friends. Mrs. Webster, the senator's housekeeper, set down a fresh pot of coffee, refilled the plate of cookies, and left the room. Earl leaned forward and helped himself to a cookie.

"So you were telling me," Bill continued. "You were the only one there with a vehicle?"

"That's right," Dunk said. "I'd parked it up the road where it wouldn't be spotted. It seemed all the Satanists had been dropped off so there wouldn't be any tell-tale cars parked outside the catacombs when they were supposed to be closed down for the night. Their cars weren't due to pick them up again till some time later."

"I sent young Duncan off for the police," Rudy said, puffing happily on his old briar pipe. "We found that the Satanists could not get out of their cavern because of the rock falls, and we had to report the death of Tanya, of course."

"It was an *agente* of the Commissario di Pubblico Sicurezza who came out," Dunk continued. "What a mouthful, eh? It seems every district of Rome has its own local subdivision."

"They were very suspicious about Tanya's death," Beth added. "I thought we were all going to end up in an Italian jail!"

"So you say there was a confession?" Etienne perched on the edge of his chair and reached for more coffee.

"Not exactly," Dunk said. "More of an accusation."

"But you had to dig into the fifth level cavern?" Guillemette asked quietly. "Through the rock fall?"

Beth nodded.

"Dunk had alerted the police, so they brought shovels," Rudy said. "We helped them dig. When we got inside there were still a few of them alive."

"And the woman—what was her name?" Dunk turned to Beth.

"Agara Brachi."

"Oh, yes. Well, she was hysterical. When she quieted down, she told the police that it was Ganganelli who had killed Tanya."

"Certainly only his and Tanya's fingerprints were on the sword," Rudy added.

"But what's this about her talking to you on the side?" Bill asked, ladling sugar into his cup.

"That's it," Dunk said earnestly. "She pulled me to one side and told me that Tanya was responsible for the whole break-up of the group. She said that Tanya fell on the sword herself." He looked around at the serious faces. "She took her own life. I think this Agara had a score to settle with Ganganelli, which is why she told the police he did it."

"But there was no Ganganelli, *mes amis,*" Etienne reminded them.

"Nein!"

"No," Duncan said. "One of the Satanists said he'd seen the cardinal duck inside one of the big trunks by the wall when the roof started falling in. But they were sure empty when the police broke in. There was no sign of him anywhere."

Rudy clicked his tongue and shook his head.

"Perhaps he's buried under some of the rocks," Guillemette said hopefully.

"Possible. But somehow I doubt it," Earl said, tugging at his beard. "The man's too slippery for that."

"Well, to use an old cliché, 'all's well that ends well'," said the senator. "There's no way he can go back to the church with a murder charge over his head. And you've broken up the anti-American group. The Committee has very definitely established itself as a force to be reckoned with, by any who would use the powers of evil. There was no bad weather over the U.S. at all! No lives lost and no destruction of property! I can't tell you how pleased the old man is. Now we can get serious about the clean-up from the previous disasters."

"But not everything *did* end well, Bill," Duncan said, his face serious. "Let's not forget our Wiccan High Priestess."

"Ja!"

"Mais oui."

Dunk turned to the senator. "When Tanya saw that she was to be given to the beast, and then to be sacrificed, she determined to throw a wrench in the works. By having the courage to kill herself, she not only left the beast without a sexual sacrifice—though another could be found, and Agara Brachi was forced into that role—but more importantly, Tanya deprived them of the very special sacrifice of a Wiccan High Priestess. That was something that would have given a real fillip of power to their side of the battle, it seems. Something that would have been a real titillation to the beast Belial."

"I would like to propose a séance," Guillemette said. "I think it important that we let Tanya know how much we appreciate the sacrifice she made."

"What a wonderful idea," Dunk said. "Etienne, what do you say? Are you up to it?"

They sat around Bill Highland's wide oak dining table. Heavy drapes had been drawn across the windows, and Mr. and Mrs. Webster relegated to the kitchen. The senator had been reluctant to join in, but was finally persuaded and now sat between Beth and Guillemette. Everyone had their hands flat on the table top, fingers spread wide, little fingers touching their neighbors' little fingers. Etienne sat at the head of the table with his eyes closed. He breathed deeply. The room's lights, operated by a dimmer switch, were turned down to their lowest.

Beth leaned across to Bill and whispered, "Barrister will come through first."

"Who?"

"Sssh!" Everyone hushed them.

"Barrister! Barrister is the name, Senator." A loud English voice issued from the little Frenchman. It was the voice of his Doorkeeper, which Beth, Dunk, and Rudy recognized from their visit to Paris.

"Greetings, Barrister," Rudy said. Once again he had been elected spokesman.

"And how may I help you?"

"We would like to make contact with someone newly crossed-over," the German said. "Our dearly beloved friend Tanya Demidas. May we speak with her, or is it too soon?"

"Ah, the delightful Tanya" responded the British voice. "Yes, indeed. She has settled in very well and very quickly. Let me see if she is available."

"Good God!" Bill muttered. "It's like placing a phone call!"

"Ssh!" Guillemette hushed him.

"My friends! My dear, dear friends!" It was Tanya's soft, gentle voice. They all recognized it.

"Tanya!" Rudy's voice had a catch in it. He coughed, quickly, to clear it.

Dunk felt a lump in his throat and Beth wished she could let go of her hands to wipe the tears from her eyes.

"Tanya," Rudy continued. "We wanted to make contact. We wanted to … just to let you know, that we know … "

"Ah, Rudy! Thank you. Thank you all. I love you and I'd do it all over again. It was just something that had to be done."

"It did work," Dunk burst out. "Oh, sorry, Rudy."

"*Ja!* It worked very well, my lady." He used the formal Wiccan mode of address. "What you did started the chain of events that led to the defeat of the Forces of Evil. The Voudoun followers in their respective hounfors, all working together, called upon their loa to come to our aid. Then, in harmony with them, the many and various groups of positive workers across North America drew upon their powers to bring the very divinities of fruitfulness to our aid. All working together, and blending with the ages-old power generated by such people over millenia, the deities who materialized were able to fling down into the abyss the demonic apparition Belial. What you did, my Lady, which took so much courage, started the chain of events that broke the Satanists' backs. Our friends in Haiti … " he smiled round at Guillemette and Earl, and glanced at their medium, Etienne, " … they sent tremendous forces. And then Dunk, Beth, and I did what little we could."

"It was as it should be," Tanya said. "This was the purpose of my latest life. I shall return to the earth plane again, when the time is right. But this was what I had to do this time. I'm so happy that it all worked out. And I'm so happy to have known each one of you. Blessed Be, my dear brothers and sisters."

"Blessed be," they all responded.

ABOUT THE AUTHOR

RAYMOND BUCKLAND has been interested in the occult and matters metaphysical for fifty years; has been actively involved in various aspects of the subject for forty years; and has been writing about it for nearly thirty years. He has written more than twenty-five books, has lectured and presented workshops across the United States, and has appeared on major television and radio shows nationally and internationally. He has also written screenplays, been a technical advisor for films, and appeared in films and videos.

In recent years Ray has focused his attention on fiction. The two "Committee" novels are the first of his book-length fiction to be published.

Ray comes from an English Romany (Gypsy) family and presently resides, with his wife Tara, on a small farm in central Ohio. After writing, his other passion is homebuilt airplanes.

TO GET A FREE CATALOG

To obtain our full catalog, you are invited to write (see address below) for our bi-monthly news magazine/catalog, *Llewellyn's New Worlds of Mind and Spirit*. A sample copy is free, and it will continue coming to you at no cost as long as you are an active mail customer. Or you may subscribe for just $10 in the United States and Canada ($20 overseas, first class mail). Many bookstores also have *New Worlds* available to their customers. Ask for it.

TO ORDER BOOKS AND TAPES

If your book store does not carry the titles described on the following pages, you may order them directly from Llewellyn by sending the full price in U.S. funds, plus postage and handling (see below).

Credit card orders: VISA, MasterCard, American Express are accepted. Call us toll-free within the United States and Canada at 1-800-THE-MOON.

Postage and Handling: Include $4 postage and handling for orders $15 and under; $5 for orders *over* $15. There are no postage and handling charges for orders over $100. Postage and handling rates are subject to change. We ship UPS whenever possible within the continental United States; delivery is guaranteed. Please provide your street address as UPS does not deliver to P.O. boxes. Orders shipped to Alaska, Hawaii, Canada, Mexico and Puerto Rico will be sent via first class mail. Allow 4-6 weeks for delivery. **International orders:** Airmail – add retail price of each book and $5 for each non-book item (audiotapes, etc.); Surface mail – add $1 per item.

Minnesota residents add 7% sales tax.

Llewellyn Worldwide
P.O. Box 64383-102, St. Paul, MN 55164-0383, U.S.A.

For customer service, call (612) 291-1970.

THE COMMITTEE
by Raymond Buckland

"Duncan's eyes were glued to the destruct button. He saw that the colonel's hand never did get to it. Yet, even as he watched, he saw the red button move downwards, apparently of its own volition. The rocket blew into a million pieces, and the button came back up. No one, Duncan would swear, had physically touched the button, yet it had been depressed."

The Cold War is back in this psi-techno suspense thriller where international aggressors use psychokinesis, astral projection and other psychic means to circumvent the U.S. intelligence network. When two routine communications satellite launches are inexplicably aborted at Vandenberg Air Force Base in California, one senator suspects paranormal influences. He calls in a writer, two parapsychologists and a psychic housewife—and The Committee is formed. Together, they piece together a sinister occult plot against the United States. The Committee then embarks on a supernatural adventure of a lifetime as they attempt to beat the enemy at its own game.

Llewellyn Psi-Fi Fiction Series
1-56718-100-7, 240 pgs., mass market

$4.99

THE MESSENGER
by Donald Tyson

"She went to the doorway and took Eliza by her shoulders. 'But you mind what I tell you. Something in this house is watching us, and its thoughts are not kindly. It's all twisted up and bitter inside. It means to make us suffer. Then it means to kill us, one by one.'"

Sealed inside a secret room of an old mansion in Nova Scotia is a cruel and uncontrollable entity, created years earlier by an evil magician. When the new owner of the mansion unknowingly releases the entity, it renews its malicious and murderous rampage. Called on to investigate the strange phenomena are three women and four men—each with their own occult talents. As their investigation proceeds, the group members enter into a world of mystery and horror as they encounter astral battles, spirit possession—even death. In their efforts to battle the evil spirit, they use seance, hypnotic trance and magical rituals, the details of which are presented in fascinating and accurate detail.

Llewellyn Psi-Fi Fiction Series
0-87542-836-3, 240 pgs., mass market

$4.99

THE CELTIC HEART
Kathryn Marie Cocquyt

T*he Celtic Heart* tells the adventurous, epic tale of spirit, love, loss, and the difficult choices made by three generations of the Celtic Brigantes tribe, who once lived off the coast of North Wales on an island they named *Mona mam Cymru* ("Mother of Wales," or Anglesey).

Follow the passionate lives of the Brigantes clan and the tumultuous events during the years leading up to the Roman Invasion in A.D. 61, when Anglesey was a refuge for Celts struggling to preserve their inner truths and goddess-based culture against the encroachment of the Roman Empire and Christianity. As their tribal way of life is threatened, the courageous natures of the Chieftain Solomon, the Druidess Saturnalia, and the young warriors Kordelina and Aonghus are tested by the same questions of good and evil that face us today.

Filled with ritual, dream images, romance, and intrigue, *The Celtic Heart* will take you on an authentic and absorbing journey into the history, lives, and hearts of the legendary Celts.

1-56718-156-2, 6 x 9, 624 pp., softbound

$14.95

THE RAG BONE MAN
A Chilling Mystery of Self-Discovery
Charlotte Lawrence

This occult fiction, mystery and fantasy is a tale of the subtle ways psychic phenomena can intrude into anyone's life—and influence the even the most rational of people!

The Rag Bone Man mixes together a melange of magickal ingredients—from amulets, crystals, the tarot, past lives and elemental beings to near death experiences, shapeshifting and modern magickal ritual—to create a simmering blend of occult mystery and suspense.

Rian McGuire is a seemingly ordinary young woman who owns a New Age book and herb shop in a small Maryland town. When a disturbing man leaves a mysterious old book in Rian's shop and begins to invade her dreams, she is launched into a bizarre, often terrifying journey into the arcane. Why is this book worth committing murder to recover? As Rian's family and friends gather psychic forces to penetrate the mysteries that surround her, Rian finally learns the Rag Bone Man's true identity—but will she be able to harness the undreamt-of power of her own magickal birthright before the final terrifying confrontation?

ISBN: 1-56718-412-X, mass market, 336 pp.
$4.99